Elephant And Frog

-

Folklore, Fairy Tales and Legends from Central Africa

Compiled & Edited by Clive Gilson

Tales from the World's Firesides

Book 5 in Part 3 of the series: Africa

Elephant And Frog,

edited by Clive Gilson, Solitude, Bath, UK

www.clivegilson.com

First published as an eBook in 2022

2nd edition © 2022 Clive Gilson

3rd edition © 2023 Clive Gilson

Printed by IngramSpark

ISBN: 978-1-915081-04-9

I have edited Clive Gilson's books for over a decade now – he's prolific and can turn his hand to many genres - poetry, short fiction, contemporary novels, folklore and science fiction – and the common theme is that none of them ever fails to take my breath away. There's something in each story that is either memorably poignant, hauntingly unnerving or sidesplittingly funny.

Lorna Howarth, *The Write Factor*

Tales From The World's Firesides is a grand project. I've collected thousands of traditional texts as part of other projects, and while many of the original texts are available through channels like Project Gutenberg, some of the narratives can be hard to read for modern audiences, and so the Fireside project was born. Put simply, I collect, collate and adapt traditional tales from around the world and publish them as a modern archive.

This is the fifth book in *Part 3 – Africa*, following on from the titles in *Parts 1* and *2* covering a host of nations and regions across Europe and North America.

I'm not laying any claim to insight or specialist knowledge, but these collections are born out of my love of story-telling and I hope that you'll share my affection for traditional tales, myths and legends.

Images by Open Clipart Vectors and DIY Team from Pixabay

Contents

ORIGINAL FICTION BY CLIVE GILSON

- Songs of Bliss
- Out of the Walled Garden
- The Mechanic's Curse
- The Insomniac Booth
- A Solitude of Stars

AS EDITOR – *FIRESIDE TALES – Part 1, Europe*

- Tales From the Land of Dragons
- Tales From the Land of The Brave
- Tales From the Land of Saints And Scholars
- Tales From the Land of Hope And Glory
- Tales From Lands of Snow and Ice
- Tales From the Viking Isles
- Tales From the Forest Lands
- Tales From the Old Norse
- More Tales About Saints and Scholars
- More Tales About Hope and Glory
- More Tales About Snow and Ice
- Tales From the Land of Rabbits
- Tales Told by Bulls and Wolves
- Tales of Fire and Bronze
- Tales From the Land of the Strigoi
- Tales Told by the Wind Mother
- Tales from Gallia
- Tales from Germania

EDITOR – *FIRESIDE TALES – Part 2, North America*

- Okaraxta - Tales from The Great Plains
- Tibik-Kìzis – Tales from The Great Lakes & Canada
- Jóhonaa'éí –Tales from America's Southwest
- Qugaaĝix̂ - First Nation Tales from Alaska & The Arctic
- Karahkwa - First Nation Tales from America's Eastern States
- Pot-Likker - Folklore, Fairy Tales, and Settler Stories from America

EDITOR – *FIRESIDE TALES – Part 3, Africa*

- Arokin Tales – Folklore & Fairy Tales from West Africa
- Hadithi Tales – Folklore & Fairy Tales from East Africa
- Inkathaso Tales – Folklore & Fairy Tales from Southern Africa
- Tarubadur Tales – Folklore & Fairy Tales from North Africa
- Elephant And Frog – Folklore from Central Africa

Preface

I've been collecting and telling stories for a couple of decades now, having had several of my own works published in recent years. My particular focus is on short story writing in the realms of magical realities and science fiction fantasies.

I've always drawn heavily on traditional folk and fairy tales, and in so doing have amassed a collection of many thousands of these tales from around the world. It has been one of my long-standing ambitions to gather these stories together and to create a library of tales that tell the stories of places and peoples from the four corners of our world.

One of the main motivations for me in undertaking the project is to collect and tell stories that otherwise might be lost or, at best forgotten. Given that a lot of my sources are from early collectors, particularly covering works produced in the late eighteenth century, throughout the nineteenth century, and in the early years of the twentieth century, I do make every effort to adapt stories for a modern reader. Early collectors had a different world view to many of us today, and often expressed views about race and gender, for example, that we find difficult to reconcile in the early years of the twenty-first century. I try, although with varying degrees of success, to update these stories with sensitivity while trying to stay as true to the original spirit of each story as I can.

I also want to assure readers that I try hard not to comment on or appropriate originating cultures. It is almost certainly true that the early collectors of these tales, with their then prevalent world views, have made assumptions about the originating cultures that have given us these tales. I hope that you'll accept my mission to preserve these tales, however and wherever I find them, as just that. I have, therefore, made sure that every story has a full attribution, covering both the original collector / writer and the collection title that this version has been adapted from, as well as having notes about publishers and other relevant and, I hope, interesting source data. Wherever possible I have added a cultural or indigenous attribution as well, although for some of the tiles, the country-based theme is obvious.

Elephant And Frog tells tales and stories that originate in Central Africa. Like all human cultures, African folklore and religion represents a variety of social facets of the various cultures in Africa. These particular folktales are from Central African regions such as Uganda and the Congo, and they play an important role in many of these Central African cultures. Stories reflect a group's cultural identity, and preserving the stories of Africa helps to preserve many aspects of diverse and intriguing cultural groupings. Storytelling affirms pride and identity.

In Africa, stories are created by and for the ethnic group telling them. Different ethnic groups in Africa have different rituals or ceremonies for storytelling, which creates a sense of belonging to a cultural group. To outsiders hearing an ethnic group's stories, it provides an insight into the community's beliefs, views, and customs. For people within the community, it allows them to encompass their group's uniqueness. They show the human desires and fears of a group, such as love, marriage, and death.

Folktales are also seen as a tool for education and entertainment. They provide a way for children to understand the material and social environment. Every story has a moral to teach people, such as goodwill prevailing over evil. For entertainment, stories are set in fantastic, non-human worlds. Often, the main character of the story would be a talking animal, or something unnatural would happen to a human character. Even though folktales are for entertainment, they bring a sense of belonging and pride to communities in Africa.

There are different types of African stories: animal tales and day-to-day tales. Animal tales are more oriented towards entertainment but still have morals and lessons to them. Animal tales are normally divided into trickster tales and ogre tales. In animal tales, a certain animal would always have the same character or role, so the audience does not have to worry about characterisation. The Hare was always the trickster, while the Hyena was always tricked by the Hare. Ogres are always cruel, greedy monsters. The messengers in all the stories were the Birds. Day-to-Day tales are the most serious tales, never including humour, that explained the everyday life and struggles of an African community. These tales take on famine, escape from death, courtship, and family matters, using a song form when the climax of the story was being told.

African stories have certain common structural devices associated with them. Villagers would gather around a common meeting place at the end of the day to listen and tell their stories. Storytellers had certain commands to start and end the stories, "Ugai Itha" to get the audience's attention and begin the story, and "Rukirika" to signal the end of a tale. Each scene of a story is depicted with two characters at a time, so the audience does not get overwhelmed. In each story, victims can overcome their predators and take justice out on the culprit. Certain tools were used in African folktales. For example, idiophones, such as drums, were used to make the sounds of different animals. Repetition and call-back techniques in prose or poem were also used to get the audience involved in the stories.

One feature in this collection is a preponderance of tales from the region around the great central lakes. In particular, the culture of Uganda is made up of diverse ethnic groups. Lake Kyoga forms the northern boundary for the Bantu-speaking people, who dominate much of East, Central, and Southern Africa. In Uganda, they include the Baganda, mentioned in several of these tales.

The Baganda are the largest single ethnic group in Uganda. They occupy the central part of Uganda which was formerly the Buganda Province. They are a Bantu-speaking people and their language is called Luganda.

In the north, the Lango and the Acholi peoples predominate, who speak Nilotic languages. To the east are the Iteso and Karamojong, who also speak a Nilotic language, whereas the Gishu are part of the Bantu and live mainly on the slopes of Mt. Elgon. They speak Lumasaba, which is closely related to the Luhya of Kenya.

As ever with these fascinating collections, it has been a real journey of discovery working through tales and adapting them for today's early twenty-first century audience. The journey is utterly rewarding, with so many delightfully entertaining, poignant and instructional facets to take into account. I do hope you enjoy these tales as much as I do.

Clive, Bath, 2023

The Creation Of Man

This tale has been edited and adapted from Henry Morton Stanley's book, My Dark Companions, published in 1893 by Sampson, Lowe, Marston and Company, London.

In the old, old time, all this land, and indeed all the whole earth was covered with sweet water. But the water dried up or disappeared somewhere, and the grasses, herbs, and plants began to spring up above the ground, and some grew, in the course of many moons, into trees, great and small, and the water was confined into streams and rivers, pools and lakes, and as the rain fell it kept the streams and rivers running, and the pools and lakes always fresh.

There was no living thing moving upon the earth, until one day there sat by one of the pools a large Toad. How long he had lived, or how he came to exist, is not known. It is suspected, however, that the water brought him forth out of some virtue that was in it.

In the sky there was only the Moon glowing and shining, and on the earth there was but this one Toad. It is said that they met and conversed together, and that one day the Moon said to him, "I have an idea. I propose to make a man and a woman to live on the fruits of the earth, for I believe that there is rich abundance of food on it fit for such creatures."

"Nay," said the Toad, "let me make them, for I can make them fitter for the use of the earth than you can, for I belong to the earth, while you belong to the sky."

"Truly," replied the Moon, "you have the power to create creatures which shall have but a brief existence, but if I make them, they will have something of my own nature, and it is a pity that the creatures of one's own making should suffer and die. Therefore, O Toad, I propose to reserve the power of creation for myself, that the creatures may be endowed with perfection and enduring life."

"Ah, Moon, be not envious of the power which I share with you, but let me have my way. I will give them forms such as I have often dreamed of. The thought is big within me, and I insist upon realising my ideas."

"And you be so resolved, observe my words, both you and they shall die. You I shall slay myself and end utterly, and your creatures can but follow you, being of such frail material as you can give them."

"Ah, you are angry now, but I heed you not. I am resolved that the creatures to inhabit this earth shall be of my own creating. Attend to your own empire in the sky."

Then the Moon rose and soared upward, where with his big, shining face he shone upon all the world.

The Toad grew great with his conception, until it ripened and issued out in the shape of twin beings, full-grown male and female. These were the first like our kind that ever trod the earth.

The Moon beheld the event with rage, and left his place in the sky to punish the Toad, who had infringed the privilege that he had thought to reserve for himself. He came directly to Toad's pool, and stood blazingly bright over it.

"Miserable," he cried, "what have you done?"

"Patience, Moon, I but exercised my right and power. It was within me to do it, and the deed is done."

"You have exalted yourself to be my equal in your own esteem. Your conceit has clouded your wit, and obscured the memory of the warning I gave you. Even had you obtained a charter from me to attempt the task, you could have done no better than you have done. As much as you are inferior to me, so these will be inferior to those I could have endowed this earth with. Your creatures are pitiful things, mere animals without sense, without the gift of perception or self-protection. They see, they breathe, they exist. Their lives can be measured by one round journey of mine. Were it not out of pity for them, I would even let them die.

"Therefore for pity's sake I propose to improve somewhat on what you have done. Their lives shall be lengthened, and such intelligence as malformed beings as these can contain will I endow them with, that they may have guidance through a life which, with all my power, must be troubled and sore. But as for you, whilst you exist my rage is perilous to them, therefore to save your kin I end you."

Saying which the Moon advanced upon Toad, and the fierce sparks from his burning face were shot forth, and fell upon the Toad until he was consumed.

The Moon then bathed in the pool, that the heat of his anger might be moderated, and the water became so heated that it was like that which is in a pot over a fire, and he stayed in it until the hissing and bubbling had subsided.

Then the Moon rose out of the pool, and sought the creatures of Toad, and when he had found them, he called them to him, but they were afraid and hid themselves.

At this sight the Moon smiled, as you sometimes see him on fine nights, when he is a clear white, and free from stain or blur, and he was pleased that Toad's creatures were afraid of him. "Poor things," said he, "Toad has left me much to do yet before I can make them fit to be the first of earthly creatures."

He took hold of them, and bore them to the pool wherein he had bathed, and which had been the home of Toad. He held them in the water for some time, tenderly bathing them, and stroking them here and there as a potter does to his earthenware, until he had moulded them into something similar to the shape we men and women possess now. The male became distinguished by breadth of shoulder, depth of chest, larger bones, and more substantial form. The female was slighter in chest, slimmer of waist, and the breadth and fulness of the woman was midmost of the body at the hips.

Then the Moon gave them names. The man he called Bateta, the woman Hanna, and he addressed them and said, "Bateta, see this earth and the trees, and herbs and plants and grasses. The whole is for you and your wife Hanna, and for your children whom Hanna your wife shall bear to you. I have re-made you greatly, that you and yours may enjoy such things as you may find needful and fit. In order that you may discover what things are not noxious but beneficial for you, I have placed the faculty of discernment within your head, which you must exercise before you can become wise. The more you prove this, the more will you be able to perceive the abundance of good things the earth possesses for the creatures which are to inhabit it.

"I have made you and your wife as perfect as is necessary for the preservation and enjoyment of the term of life, which by nature of the materials the Toad made you of must needs be short. It is in your power to prolong or shorten it. Some things I must teach you. I give you first an axe. I make a fire for you, which you must feed from time to time with wood, and the first and most necessary utensil for daily use. Observe me while I make it for you."

The Moon took some dark clay by the pool and mixed it with water, then kneaded it, and twisted it around until its shape was round and hollowed within, and he covered it with the embers of the fire, and baked it, and when it was ready he handed it to them.

"This vessel," continued the Moon, "is for the cooking of food. You will put water into it, and place whatsoever edible you desire to eat in the water. You will then place the vessel on the fire, which in time will boil the water and cook the food. All vegetables, such as roots and bulbs, are improved in flavour and give superior nourishment by being thus cooked. It will become a serious matter for you to know which of all the things pleasant in appearance are also pleasant for the palate. But should you be long in doubt and fearful of harm, ask and I will answer you."

Having given the man and woman their first lesson, the Moon ascended to the sky, and from his lofty place shone upon them, and upon all the earth with a pleased expression, which comforted greatly the lonely pair.

Having watched the ascending Moon until he had reached his place in the sky, Bateta and Hanna rose and travelled on by the beautiful light which he gave them, until they came to a very large tree that had fallen. The thickness of the prostrate trunk was about twice their height. At the greater end of it there was a hole, into which they could walk without bending. Feeling a desire for sleep, Bateta laid his fire down outside near the hollowed entrance, cut up dry fuel, and his wife piled it on the fire, while the flames grew brighter and lit the interior. Bateta took Hanna by the hand and entered within the tree, and the two lay down together. But presently both complained of the hardness of their bed, and Bateta, after pondering awhile, rose, and going out, plucked some fresh large leaves of a plant that grew near the fallen tree, and returned laden with it. He spread it about thickly, and Hanna rolled herself on it, and laughed gleefully as she said to Bateta that it was soft and smooth and nice, and opening her arms, she cried, "Come, Bateta, and rest by my side."

Though this was the first day of their lives, the Moon had so perfected the unfinished and poor work of the Toad that they were both mature man and woman. Within a month Hanna bore twins, of whom one was male and the other female, and they were tiny doubles of Bateta and Hanna, which so pleased Bateta that he ministered kindly to his wife who, through her double charge, was prevented from doing anything else.

Thus it was that Bateta, anxious for the comfort of his wife, and for the nourishment of his children, sought to find choice things, but could find little to please the dainty taste which his wife had contracted. Whereupon, looking up to Moon with his hands uplifted, he cried out, "O Moon, list to your creature Bateta! My wife lies languishing, and she has a taste strange to me which I cannot satisfy, and the children that have been born to us feed upon her body, and her strength decreases fast. Come down, O Moon, and show me what fruit or herbs will cure her longing."

The Moon heard Bateta's voice, and coming out from behind the cloud with a white, smiling face, said, "It is well, Bateta. I come to help you."

When the Moon had approached Bateta, he showed the golden fruit of the banana, which was the same plant whose leaves had formed the first bed for himself and his wife.

"O Bateta, smell this fruit. How do you like its fragrance?"

"It is beautiful and sweet. O Moon, if it be as wholesome for the body as it is sweet to smell, my wife will rejoice in it."

Then the Moon peeled the banana and offered it to Bateta, upon which he boldly ate it, and the flavour was so pleasant that he sought permission to take one to his wife. When Hanna had tasted it she also appeared to enjoy it, but she said, "Tell Moon that I need something else, for I have no strength, and I am thinking that this fruit will not give to me what I lose by these children."

Bateta went out and prayed to Moon to listen to Hanna's words, to which when he had heard them , he said, "It was known to me that this should be, so look round, Bateta, and tell me what you see moving yonder."

"Why, that is a buffalo."

"Rightly named," replied Moon. "And what follows it?"

"A goat."

"Good again. And what next?"

"An antelope."

"Excellent, O Bateta, and what may the next be?"

"A sheep."

"Sheep it is, truly. Now look up above the trees, and tell me what you see soaring over them."

"I see fowls and pigeons."

"Very well called, indeed," said Moon. "These I give to you for meat. The buffalo is strong and fierce, leave him for your leisure, but the goat, sheep, and fowls, shall live near you, and shall partake of your bounty. There are numbers in the woods which will come to you when they are filled with their grazing and their pecking. Take any of them, either goat, sheep, or fowl, bind it, and chop its head off with your hatchet. The blood will sink into the soil. The meat underneath the outer skin is good for food, after being boiled or roasted over the fire. Haste now, Bateta. It is meat your wife craves, and she needs naught else to restore her strength. So prepare instantly and eat."

The Moon floated upward, smiling and benign, and Bateta hastened to bind a goat, and made it ready as the Moon had advised. Hanna, after eating of the meat which was prepared by boiling, soon recovered her strength, and the children throve, and grew marvellously.

One morning Bateta walked out of his hollowed house, and a change had come over the earth. Right over the tops of the trees a great globe of shining, dazzling light looked out from the sky, and blazed white and bright over all. Things that he had seen dimly before were now more clearly revealed. By the means of the strange light hung up in the sky he saw the difference between that which the Moon gave and that new brightness which now shone out. The trees and their leaves seemed clad in a luminous coat of light, while underneath it was but a dim reflection or shadow, and to the sight it seemed like the colder light of the Moon.

And in the cooler light that prevailed below the foliage of the trees there were gathered hosts of new and strange creatures. Some were large, others of medium size, and others of small size. Astonished at these changes, he cried, "Come out, O Hanna, and see the strange sights, for truly I am amazed, and know not what has happened."

Obedient, Hanna came out with the children and stood by his side, and was equally astonished at the brightness of the light and at the numbers of creatures which in all manner of sizes and forms stood in the shade ranged around them, with their faces towards the place where they stood.

"What may this change portend, O Bateta?" asked his wife.

"Nay, Hanna, I know not. All this has happened since the Moon departed from me."

"You must call him again, Bateta, and demand the meaning of it, else I shall fear harm to you, and to these children."

"You are right, my wife, for to discover the meaning of all this without other aid than my own wits would keep us here until we perished."

Then he lifted his voice, and cried out aloud, and at the sound of his voice all the creatures gathered in the shades looked upward, and cried with their voices, but the meaning of their cry, though there was an infinite variety of sound, from the round, bellowing voice of the lion to the shrill squeak of the mouse, was, "Come down to us, O Moon, and explain the meaning of this great change to us. For you only who made us can guide our sense to the right understanding of it."

When they had ended their entreaty to the Moon, there came a voice from above, which sounded like distant thunder, saying, "Rest where you stand, until the brightness of this new light shall have faded, and you distinguish my milder light and that of the many children which have been born to me, when I shall come to you and explain."

Thereupon they rested each creature in its own place, until the great brightness, and the warmth which the strange light gave faded and lessened, and it was observed that it disappeared from view on the opposite side to that where it had first been seen, and also immediately after at the place of its disappearance the Moon was seen, and all over the sky were visible the countless little lights which the children of the Moon gave.

Presently, after Bateta had pointed these out to Hanna and the children, the Moon shone out bland, and its face was covered with gladness, and he left the sky smiling, and floated down to the earth, and stood not far off from Bateta, in view of him and his family, and of all the creatures under the shade.

"Listen, O Bateta, and you creatures of prey and pasture. A little while ago, you have seen the beginning of the measurement of time, which shall be divided hereafter into day and night. The time that lapses between the Sun's rising and its setting shall be called day, that which shall lapse between its setting and re-rising shall be called night. The light of the day proceeds from the Sun, but the light of the night proceeds from me and from my children the stars, and as you are all my creatures, I have chosen that my softer light shall shine during the restful time wherein you sleep, to recover the strength lost in the waking time, and that you shall be daily waked for the working time by the stronger light of the Sun. This rule never-ending shall remain.

"And whereas Bateta and his wife are the first of creatures, to them, their families, and kind that shall be born to them, shall be given pre-eminence over all creatures made, not that they are stronger, or swifter, but because to them only have I given understanding and a gift of speech to transmit it. Perfection and everlasting life had also been given, but the taint of the Toad remains in the system, and the result will be death,, death to all living things, Bateta and Hanna excepted.

"In the fulness of time, when their limbs refuse to bear the burden of their bodies and their marrow has become dry, my first-born shall return to me, and I shall absorb them. Children shall be born innumerable to them, until families shall expand into tribes, and from here, as from a spring, mankind will outflow and overspread all lands, which are now but wild and wold, aye, even to the farthest edge of the earth.

"And listen, O Bateta, the beasts which you see, have sprung from the ashes of the Toad. On the day that he measured his power against mine, and he was consumed by my fire, there was one drop of juice left in his head. It was a life-germ which soon grew into another toad. Though not equal in power to the parent toad, you see what he has done. Yonder beasts of prey and pasture and fowls are his work. As fast as they were conceived by him, and uncouth and ungainly they were, I dipped them into Toad's Pool, and perfected them outwardly, according to their uses, and, as you see, each specimen has its mate.

"Whereas, both you and they alike have the acrid poison of the toad, you from the parent, they in a greater measure from the child toad, the mortal taint when ripe will end both man and beast. No understanding nor gift of speech has been given to them, and they are as inferior to you as the child toad was to the parent toad.

"Those qualities that you discover in them, you may employ in your services. Meantime, let them go out each to its own feeding-ground, lair, or covert, and grow and multiply, until the generations descending from you shall have need for them. Enough for you with the bounties of the forest, jungle, and plain, are the goats, sheep, and fowls. At your leisure, Bateta, you may strike and eat such beasts as you see akin in custom to these that will feed from your hand. The waters abound in fish that are yours at your need, and the air swarms with birds which are also yours, as your understanding will direct you.

"You will be wise to plant all such edibles as you may discover pleasing to the palate and agreeable to your body, but be not rash in assuming that all things pleasant to the eye are grateful to your inwards.

"So long as you and Hanna are on the earth, I promise you my aid and counsel, and what I tell you and your wife you will do well to teach your children, that the memory of useful things be not forgotten, for after I take you to myself, I come no more to visit man.

"Enter your house now, for it is a time, as I have told you, for rest and sleep. At the shining of the greater light, you will waken for active life and work, and family care and joys. The beasts shall also wander each to his home in the earth, on the tops of the trees, in the bush, or in the cavern. Fare you well, Bateta, and have kindly care for your wife Hanna and the children."

The Moon ended his speech, and floated upward, radiant and gracious, until he rested in his place in the sky, and all the children of the Moon twinkled for joy and gladness so brightly, as the parent of the world entered his house, that all the heavens for a short time seemed burning. Then the Moon drew over him his cloudy cloak, and the little children of the Moon seemed to get drowsy, for they twinkled dimly, and then a darkness fell over all the earth, and in the darkness man and beast retired, each to his own place, as the Moon had directed.

A second time Bateta waked from sleep, and walked out to wonder at the intense brightness of the burning light that made the day. Then he looked around him, and his eyes rested upon a noble flock of goats and sheep, all of whom bleated their morning welcome, while the younglings pranced about in delight, and after curvetting around, expressed in little bleats the joy they felt at seeing their chief, Bateta.

His attention was also called to the domestic fowls. There were red and white and spotted cocks, and as many coloured hens, each with its own brood of chicks. The hens trotted up to their master, cluck, cluck, clucking, the tiny chicks, following each its own mother, cheep, cheep, cheeping, while the cocks threw out their breasts and strutted grandly behind, and crowed with their trumpet throats, "All hail, master."

Then the morning wind rose and swayed the trees, plants, and grasses, and their tops bending before it bowed their salutes to the new king of the earth, and thus it was that man knew that his reign over all was acknowledged.

After the Moon had given goats and sheep and fowls for his companions, his own lively intelligence was sufficient to teach Bateta many things. The goats became great pets, and used to follow him about. He observed that there was a certain plant to which the goats flocked with great greed, to feed upon the tops until their bellies became round and large with it. One day the idea came to him that if the goats could feed so freely upon it without harm, it might be also harmless to him. Whereupon he pulled the plant up and carried it home. While he was chopping up the tops for the pot his pet goats tried to eat the tuber which was the root, and he tried that also. He cut up both leaves and root and cooked them, and after tasting them he found them exceedingly good and palatable, and from then onwards manioc became a daily food to him and his family, and from them to his children's children.

A few months afterwards, another double birth occurred, and a few months later there was still another, and Bateta remembered the number of months that intervened between each event, and knew that it would be a regular custom for all time. At the end of the eighteenth year, he permitted his first-born to choose a wife, and when his other children grew up he likewise allowed them to select their wives. At the end of ninety years, Hanna had born to Bateta two hundred and forty-two children, and there were grandchildren, and great-grandchildren, and countless great-great-grandchildren, and they lived to an age many times the length of the greatest age amongst us now-a-days.

Later, Bateta coaxed a dog to live with him because he found that the dog preferred to sit on his haunches and wait for the bones that his family threw aside after the meal was over, rather than hunt for himself like other flesh-eating beasts. One day Bateta walked out into the woods, and his dog followed him. After a long walk Bateta rested at the foot of the straight tall tree called the palm, and there were a great many nuts lying on the ground, which perhaps the monkeys or the wind had thrown down.

The dog after smelling them lay down and began to eat them, and though Bateta was afraid he would hurt himself, he allowed him to have his own way, and he did not see that they harmed him at all, but that he seemed as fond as ever of them. By thinking of this he conceived that they would be no harm to him, and after cooking them, he found that their fat improved the flavour of his vegetables, hence the custom came down to us. Indeed, the knowledge of most things that we know today as edibles came down to us through the observation of animals by our earliest fathers. What those of old knew not was found out later through stress of hunger, while men were lost in the bushy wilds."

When they were so old that it became a trouble to them to live, the Moon came down to the earth as he had promised, and bore Bateta and Hanna to himself, and soon after the first-born twins died and were buried in the earth, and after that the deaths were many and more frequent. People ceased to live as long as their parents had done, for sickness, dissensions, wars, famines, and accidents ended them and cut their days short, until they at last forgot how to live long, and cared not to think how their days might be prolonged. And it has happened after this manner down to us who now live. The whole earth has become filled with mankind, but the dead that are gone and forgotten are far greater in number than those now alive upon the earth.

You see now, my friends, what mischief the Toad did to all mankind. Had his conceit been less, and had he waited a little, the good Moon would have conceived us of a nobler kind than we now are, and the taint of the Toad had not cursed man. So, abandon headstrong ways, and do not be rash, but pay good heed to the wise and old, lest you taint in like manner the people, and cause the innocent, the young, and the weak to suffer. I have spoken my say. If you have heard anything displeasing, remember I but tell the tale as it was told to me.

The Mwindo Epic

The Mwindo epic is an oral tale from the Congo told by the Nyanga people. The origins and creation of the Mwindo epic are mostly unknown since the story is only passed down orally.

The Mwindo Epic, like many oral myths, is spoken as well as performed. The myth is performed mostly by a single storyteller wielding a calabash, various bells and other forms of noisemakers. The narrator is usually accompanied by four younger men who play on a percussion stick. Audience participation is important. The audience will often sing along with the narrator and the percussionists during the songs, and repeat certain lines of the story while the narrator pauses between sections.

This version of the tale has been edited and adapted from various sources and is my own retelling based on those sources.

The village of Tubondo was ruled by the evil chief Shemwindo. He decreed upon his seven wives that they must only produce him daughters. If a son was to be born, the baby and his mother would be executed. Shemwindo had calculated that he would become very rich in his later years as each daughter would fetch a very pretty dowry.

Shemwindo lay with each of his wives and they all became pregnant very quickly. When their term was due, the first six wives each gave birth to a healthy daughter. The seventh wife, Nyamwindo, however, suffered an unduly long pregnancy, meaning that she was unable to contribute to household duties as expected. This should have caused much strife, but mysteriously, when she awoke each day, her chores had been done for her by some unknown agent.

The mysterious helper was none other than her unborn son. Then, when her son was ready, he climbed from her womb and emerged into the world through Nyamwindo's middle finger. Nyamwindo named her son Mwindo, and he was born already wielding a flyswatter made from a buffalo tail, an adze-axe, and a long rope in a bag of good fortune from the goddess Kahonbo.

Shemwindo was furious and he determined to kill the boy immediately. He threw seven spears at the boy, but each spear was swatted away by Mwindo with his buffalo tail fly swatter. Then he caught Mwindo and buried him alive in a sandpit, but Mwindo simply climbed out during the night.

Finally Shemwindo sealed Mwindo in a drum case and threw him into the river. To Shemwindo's horror the drum case floated, and Mwindo sat in the drum looking at the riverbank for a moment. He shrugged his shoulders and decided to sail away and find his aunt, Shemwindo's sister, Iyangura.

On his journey Mwindo encountered many aquatic animals, such as crocodiles, hippos and water snakes. He boasted to each one of them about his skills and his prowess. This annoyed the river deity, Mukiti, who sent Musoka, the sister-in-law of Iyangura, to block his passage down the river. Mukiti, it must be said, was Musoka's husband. At first the blockade worked well, but then Mwindo started to dig into the sandy riverbed, and he passed right underneath Musoka.

Mukiti was a serpent spirit and he then decided to stop the boy himself. Just he was about to strike, a small group of Iyangura's handmaidens caught sight of him and ran to tell their mistress about the trap that Mwindo was floating towards. Iyangura sprang into the river, slashed open the drum, and pulled Mwindo to safety, telling him to run to her house immediately.

Mukiti, meanwhile, thwarted for just a moment, held council with his followers and planned his next attempt to kill the boy. He was overheard by Katee, the hedgehog god, who made his way to warn Mwindo of the dangers ahead if he continued on to his aunt's house. Mwindo was unmoved by Katee's warning, and he continued on his way regardless. Katee decided to help Mwindo and he dug a tunnel directly to Iyangura's house.

While they were digging, however, Mukiti had already instructed his ally, Kasiyembe, to set multiple pit traps in the floors at Iyangura's house. Once Mwindo emerged from his tunnel at Iyangura's house, Kasiyembe challenged him to a dancing contest, with the aim of having the boy fall into one of the traps. Each trap contained razor-sharp spikes, and the boy was sure to die.

Once again an ally came to Mwindo's aid. Mwindo danced across each trap in turn but did not fall because Master Spider built bridges of invisible silk over each trap, and so Mwindo was saved yet again.

Kasiyembe was not done yet. He summoned Nkuba, the lightning god, to hurl lightning at Mwindo. Nkuba fired seven bolts of lightning at Mwindo but he just missed him every time. Mwindo summoned his own powers of magic and he, in turn, set fire to Kasiyembe's hair, so that his head blazed with flames and spitting sparks. Mwindo also caused all of the local rivers, lakes and seas to dry up so that there was no hope of putting out the fire. Even Kasiyembe could not survive such a battle and he died there and then in great agony.

Iyangura felt deeply sorry for Kasiyembe, and she implored Mwindo to show mercy and to bring Kasiyembe back to life. Her tears moved Mwindo to compassion and he waved his buffalo tail fly swatter over Kasiyembe's face. Kasiyembe miraculously returned to the living world, unharmed and unblemished, and the rivers, lakes and seas all flowed with water again. On his waking, Kasiyembe repented of his former allegiances, and he gladly accepted Mwindo as is lord and master.

Mwindo was now determined to return home and face his father. He spoke at length with Iyangura, and she promised that she would return with him, bringing a company of warriors along with her for Mwindo's aid. Iyangura also took Mwindo to meet with the Baniyana, the bat gods, who were also Mwindo's maternal uncles, so that they could forge his body with iron and so make him stronger than any man alive in the world. When this was done the Baniyana joined the procession heading back to Tubondo.

When the party camped near to Tubondo, Mwindo used his magic to provide meats and drinks and good food for everyone. Once they were rested and fed, Mwindo sent his uncles and his warriors out to fight Shemwindo and his village soldiers. The battle did not go well. All of Mwindo's warriors were wiped out by Shemwindo's men, and only one of his uncles, one of the bat gods, made it back to their camp alive. Mwindo had to act quickly. He went to the heart of the village and summoned Nkuba, the lightning god. Seven lightning bolts immediately smashed into the village, destroying every building and burning every villager to ash. As a final act, Mwindo used his magic to restore his dead uncles to life.

In the middle of this uproar, Shemwindo managed to escape. He went to a kikota plant, dug it up, opened a trap door and descended into the Underworld, the realm of the Nyanga Pantheon. Mwindo, however, would not be denied his revenge.

When Mwindo learned of this, he went down to the underworld the same way as his father, Shemwindo, had done. Mwindo fell in darkness until he landed in the great cavernous jungles of the Underworld. He followed a path until he came to the hut of Kahindo, daughter of Muisa, the God of the Dead. Kahindo should have been a beautiful young maiden, but she was infected with yaws, which left pus-filled sores all over her body, but she nevertheless fell in love with Mwindo and agreed to help him beat her father. She warned Mwindo that when they met, Mwindo must not accept a seat, food, or drink from Muisa, or Mwindo will be forced to remain in the land of the dead forever. In gratitude, Mwindo washed Kahindo's sores, and in the morning she looked a little better.

Mwindo met with Muisa, who admitted that he was sheltering Shemwindo, but stated that he would not give the chieftain to Mwindo unless Mwindo proved his worth by doing a "little task." He must grow a banana forest and harvest the fruit, all in one day. Mwindo agreed.

That night, Mwindo stayed again in Kahindo's house and washed her wounds. In the morning, she looked much better. Mwindo then used his powers to make the banana forest grow. One of Muisa's servants saw this and told his master.

Muisa was angry and he sent his cowry shell belt to kill Mwindo. The belt began strangling Mwindo, but at the last minute he managed to knock it away with his sceptre. Mwindo then sent the sceptre to punish Muisa, and the sceptre battered the god's head into the ground.

Later Mwindo returned with the harvested bananas, but Muisa said that he must still do one more task. In the morning, he must harvest a bucket of honey from the god's honey tree. Mwindo was frustrated, but he agreed.

That night, Mwindo stayed again in Kahindo's house and washed her wounds once more. In the morning, she looked completely normal. Then Mwindo used smoke to drive the killer bees away from the tree, but he found the trunk to be petrified and impossible to break. He called on Nkuba, who blew up the tree by hurling a thunderbolt into the Underworld.

Once again, one of Muisa's servants saw this, and warned his master. Muisa again sent his cowry shell belt to kill Mwindo, and once again the belt began strangling Mwindo, but at the last minute he knocked it away with his sceptre. Once again, Mwindo sent the sceptre to punish Muisa, and the sceptre battered the god's head into the ground.

After that Mwindo returned with the honey, but Muisa said he could not give him Shemwindo because the chieftain had already escaped back to the upper world by another tunnel. Outraged, Mwindo beat the god flat with his sceptre and promised to leave him that way until he found Shemwindo. Mwindo then said goodbye to Kahindo and followed his father back out of the Underworld.

Mwindo followed his father's trail to a cave which was blocked by the huge aardvark spirit, Ntumba. Mwindo warned Ntumba to step aside, but Ntumba refused. Mwindo called on Nkuba to blow up the cave, and found that Shemwindo was hiding behind the aardvark. Shemwindo got away again, and Mwindo punished the aardvark by inflicting him with elephantiasis, a painful swelling disease.

Mwindo returned to the world and pursued his father all the way to the Great Rift Valley, where the trail was lost. Mwindo realised that his father had escaped into the clouds, but he did not know how to follow him. Then he saw the giant children of the Sky God playing nearby and asked for their help. They said they would help if Mwindo made them a snack, so he brought them twelve enormous bowls, cut from tree trunks, full of good things to eat.

As the children finished their snack, they turned the bowls upside down and stacked them, making a stairway into the clouds. Mwindo climbed the bowls and came to the village of the Sky God, Sheburungu. Sheburungu now refused to give up Shemwindo unless Mwindo gambled for him. Mwindo wagered all his cattle from Tubondo and he lost the first wager. Then he bet all his houses and again he lost them all. After that he then wagered all his people, even his mother and his aunt, but yet again he lost. Finally he bet his conga sceptre and then he began to win everything back, until he owned all of the Sky God's town and his father's life.

Shemwindo was finally brought forth in chains. Mwindo gave the Sky God back his town and then retraced his steps. He cured Ntumba of elephantiasis. He healed Muisa's wounds, but when Muisa offered his daughter Kahindo to him in marriage, Mwindo refused for he knew that he must return to the world and marry a human maiden.

Mwindo returned to Tubondo, helped to rebuild the city, and ruled as a wise and powerful king. He had three brass thrones made, which floated ten feet off the ground. Mwindo sat in the middle, his aunt on the right, and his imprisoned father on the left. Shemwindo's punishment was to live the rest of his life watching his son be a better ruler than he was.

The Goat, The Lion, And The Serpent

This tale has been edited and adapted from Henry Morton Stanley's book, My Dark Companions, published in 1893 by Sampson, Lowe, Marston and Company, London.

A Goat and a Lion were travelling together one day on the outskirts of a forest, at the end of which there was a community of mankind comfortably hutted within a village, which was fenced round with tall and pointed stakes.

The Goat said to the Lion, "Well, now, my friend, where do you come from this day?"

"I have come from a feast that I have given many friends of mine, to the leopard, hyena, wolf, jackal, wild cat, buffalo, zebra, and many more. The long-necked giraffe and dew-lapped eland were also there, as well as the springing antelope."

"That is grand company you keep, indeed," said the Goat, with a sigh. "As for poor me, I am alone. No one cares for me very much, but I find abundance of grass and sweet leafage, and when I am full, I seek a soft spot under a tree, and chew my cud, dreamily and contentedly. And of other sorrows, save an occasional pang of hunger, in my wanderings I know of none."

"Do you mean to say that you do not envy me my regal dignity and strength?"

"I do not indeed, because as yet I have been ignorant of them."

"What? Don't you know that I am the strongest of all who dwell in the forest or wilderness? Don't you know that when I roar all who hear me bow down their heads, and shrink in fear?"

"Indeed, I do not know all this, nor am I very sure that you are not deceiving yourself, because I know many whose offensive powers are much more dangerous, my friend, than yours. True, your teeth are large, and your claws are sharp, and your roar is loud enough, and your appearance is imposing, but still, I know a tiny thing in these woods that is much more to be dreaded than you are, and I think if you matched yourself against it in a contest, that same tiny thing would become victor."

"Bah!" said the Lion, impatiently. "You anger me. Why, even today all who were at the feast acknowledged that they were but feeble creatures compared with me, and you know that if I but clawed you once there would be no life left in you."

"What you say in regard to me is true enough, and, as I said before, I do not pretend to the possession of strength. But this tiny thing that I know of is not likely to have been at your feast."

"What may this tiny thing be that is so dreadful?" asked the Lion, sneeringly.

"The Serpent," answered the Goat, chewing his cud with an indifferent air.

"The Serpent!" said the Lion, astounded. "What, that crawling reptile, which feeds on mice and sleeping birds, that soft, vine-like, creeping thing that coils itself in tufts of grass, and branches of bush?"

"Yes, that is its name and character clearly."

"Why, my weight alone would tread it until it became flat like a smashed egg."

"I would not try to do so if I were you. Its fangs are sharper than your great corner teeth or claws."

"Will you match it against my strength?"

"Yes."

"And if you lose, what will be the forfeit?"

"If you survive the fight, I will be your slave, and you may command me for any purpose you please. But what will you give me if you lose?"

"What you please."

"Well, then, I will take one hundred bunches of bananas, and you had better bring them here alongside of me, before you begin."

"Where is this Serpent that will fight with me?"

"Close by. When you have brought the bananas he will be here, waiting for you."

The Lion stalked proudly away to procure the bananas, and the Goat proceeded into the bush, where he saw Serpent drowsily coiled on a slender branch.

"Serpent," said the Goat, "wake up. Lion is raging for a fight with you. He has made a bet of a hundred bunches of bananas that he will be the victor, and I have pledged my life that you will be the strong one. And, hark you, obey my hints, and my life is safe, and I shall be provided with food for at least three moons."

"Well," said Serpent, languidly, "what is it that you wish me to do?"

"Take position on a bush about three cubits high, that stands near the scene where the fight is to take place, and when Lion is ready, raise your crest high and boldly, and ask him to advance near you that you may see him well, because you are short-sighted, you know. And he, full of his conceit and despising your slight form, will advance towards you, unwitting of your mode of attack. Then fasten your fangs in his eyebrows, and coil yourself round his neck. If there is any virtue left in your venom, poor Lion will lie stark before long."

"And if I do this, what will you do for me?"

"I am your servant and friend for all time."

"It is good," answered the Serpent. "Lead the way."

Accordingly Goat led Serpent to the scene of the combat, and the latter coiled itself in position, as Goat had advised, on the leafy top of a young bush.

Presently Lion came, with a long line of servile animals, bearing one hundred bunches of bananas. And, after dismissing them, he turned to the Goat, and said, "Well, Goatee, where is your friend who is stronger than I am? I feel curious to see him."

"Are you Lion?" asked a sibilant voice from the top of a bush.

"Yes, I am, and who are you that do not know me?"

"I am Serpent, friend Lion, and short of sight and slow of movement. Advance nearer to me, for I see you not."

Lion uttered a loud roaring laugh, and went confidently near the Serpent, who had raised his crest and arched his neck. Lion went so near that his breath seemed to blow the slender form to a tremulous movement.

"You shake already," said Lion, mockingly.

"Yes, I shake but to strike the better, my friend," said Serpent, as he darted forward and fixed his fangs in the right eyebrow of Lion, and at the same moment its body glided round the neck of Lion, and became buried out of sight in the copious mane.

Like the pain of fire the deadly venom was felt quickly in Lion's head and body. When it reached the heart, Lion fell down and lay still and dead.

"Well done," cried Goat, as he danced around the pile of bananas. "Provisions for three moons have I, and this doughty roarer is of no more value than a dead goat."

Goat and Serpent then vowed friendship for one another, after which Serpent said, "Now follow me, and obey. I have a little work for you."

"Work! What work, O Serpent?"

"It is light and agreeable. If you follow that path, you will find a village of mankind. There you will proclaim to the people what I have done, and show this carcase to them. In return for this they will make much of you, and you will find abundance of food in their gardens, tender leaves of manioc and peanut, mellow bananas, and plenty of rich greens daily. True, when you are fat and a feast is to be made, they will kill you and eat you. But, for all your kind, comfort, plenty, and warm, dry housing is more agreeable than the cold damp jungle, and destruction by the feral beasts."

"Nay, neither the work nor the fate is grievous, and I thank you, O Serpent, but for you there can be no other home than the bush and the tuft of grass, and you will always be a dreaded enemy of all who come near your resting-place."

Then they parted. The Goat went along the path, and came to the gardens of a village, where a woman was chopping fuel. Looking up she saw a creature with grand horns coming near to her, bleating. Her first impulse was to run away, but seeing, as it bleated, that it was a fodder-eating animal, with no means of offence, she plucked some manioc greens and coaxed it to her, upon which the Goat came and spoke to her, saying, "Follow me, for I have a strange thing to show you a little distance off."

The woman, wondering that a four-footed animal could address her in intelligible speech, followed, and the Goat trotted gently before her to where Lion lay dead. The woman upon seeing the body, stopped and asked, "What is the meaning of this?"

The Goat answered, "This was once the king of beasts. The fear of him was upon all that lived in the woods and in the wilderness. But he too often boasted of his might, and became too proud. I therefore dared him to fight a tiny creature of the bush, and the boaster was slain."

"And how do you name the victor?"

"The Serpent."

"Ah! You say truth. Serpent is king over all, except man," answered the woman.

"You are of a wise woman," answered the Goat. "Serpent confessed to me that man was his superior, and sent me to you that I might become man's creature. Henceforth man shall feed me with greens, tender tops of plants, and house and protect me, but when the feast-day comes, man shall kill me, and eat my flesh. These are the words of Serpent."

The woman listened to all Goat's words, and retained them in her memory. Then she unrobed the Lion of his furry spoil, and conveyed it to the village, where she astonished her folk with all that had happened to her. From that day to this the goat kind has remained with the families of man, and people are grateful to the Serpent for his gift to them. For had not the Serpent commanded it to seek their presence, the Goat would have remained forever wild like the antelope, its brother.

The Story Of Kintu And Nambi

This tale is known as The Buganda Legend, and has been edited and adapted from various sources.

In the distant past, Kintu was the only person on earth, living alone with his cow, and that made Kintu feel quite lonely. Ggulu, the creator of all things, lived up in heaven with his many children, who occasionally came down to earth to play by riding on a rainbow all the way to the ground. Since rainbows do not last for very long, they had to make sure they left to go back home before the rainbow disappeared.

On one such occasion, Ggulu's daughter Nambi and some of her brothers encountered Kintu and his cow in Buganda. This was the first time they had ever seen a man, and they were afraid. But they soon made friends with Kintu, and they stayed a long time talking with him. He told them how lonely he was and Nambi, who had a soft heart, felt sorry for Kintu. In fact, Nambi instantly took a liking to Kintu and decided to stay and marry him.

"Why did you say that? You know our father Ggulu will never allow you to go away and marry Kintu," they told her.

Nambi replied, "I will go. I promised Kintu, and father would never wish for me to break a promise. I will go home now and tell father, and then pack up all my things and go to the Earth to live there forever."

Her brothers pleaded with her, eventually convincing her to return to heaven with Kintu, to ask for her father's permission for the marriage.

Ggulu was not pleased and only blessed the marriage after Nambi had pleaded so much. Before he would finally consent, however, he set Kintu some tasks to complete. Accordingly, Kintu was given a small house to live in where Ggulu's servants could keep a close watch. On the first day, Kintu had to eat all of the food that was given to him. He was able to eat it all at first, but then as he was about to give up, he thought, 'No, this is my destiny, and I cannot be given a task I cannot handle because of my strong faith.' Because of this, Kintu was able to work magic of his own, and he noticed a hole had suddenly appeared in the floor. He dumped the rest of the food into the hole, and Ggulu was impressed to see that Kintu had completed the first task. But he was not done testing Kintu.

On the second day, Kintu woke up to find Ggulu's servants handing him a basket. His task was to fetch water from a well far away and fill up an empty tank next to his house. Kintu set off for the well, but did not know how he was going to retrieve the water from that deep in the ground. A spider crawled over to him and spun a strong web around the basket, letting Kintu lower the basket into the well and get the water. By sunset, he had filled the empty tank. Again, Ggulu was pleased, but was not ready to let him take his daughter.

On the third day, Kintu was asked to use Ggulu's axe to chop pieces of rock, which Ggulu used as firewood, and not chip the axe. He was told to then bundle the rock pieces and carry them to Ggulu. Kintu used his magic for this task, and he soon came running up to Ggulu with bundles of chopped rocks under his arms. Ggulu was very pleased, and he told Kintu to meet him the next morning for breakfast.

Kintu said yes and ate with Ggulu on the morning of the fourth day after a good night's rest. "I have one more task for you," said Ggulu. "You have to find your cow among my herd of cows in the field. If you can do this, then you can marry Nambi."

As soon as Ggulu finished these words, a wasp, only visible to Kintu, took him straight to his cow in the middle of the field. Ggulu gave him permission to marry his daughter, and he allowed Kintu to go back home to prepare and called for Nambi to tell her of his decision.

"I must warn you, if you want to be happy on the Earth you must go secretly and never return to Cloud Land. Pack your things very carefully, and the two brothers who know Kintu will go with you and see that you arrive safely. No matter what, it is very important that you do not tell any of the others that you are going. If your brother Death, Walumbe, hears of it, he will want to go with you. This would ruin beautiful Earth."

Nambi agreed, and she and the two brothers packed all her things in bundles. She said good-bye to her father, and they waited for a rainbow to slide back down to Earth. When they arrived the brothers talked for a little bit with Kintu, told him of their father's warning, and then went back to Cloud Land. Nambi and Kintu began to make their new life together, and they got along and loved each other very much. Then, one day, Nambi realized that she did not have millet for her chicken.

"I have forgotten the millet seed!" she shouted. "I have to go back and get some bags of millet seed so my chickens will not starve to death."

Kintu tried to hold her back, but could not. Nambi went back quickly and found some bags of seed. Just as she has found a rainbow to return to Earth, she saw her brother Walumbe.

"Where are you going?" he asked. Nambi was very frightened, and though she tried to hide what she was doing, Walumbe knew she was hiding something from him. "I know you are not telling me something," he said.

"You cannot come with me," cried Nambi. "I am going to the Earth, and our father said you were not to go with me."

"So you were trying to keep a secret from me! Go ahead and leave, but I shall come and visit the two of you very shortly," said Walumbe.

Nambi began to cry as she slid down the rainbow with her bags of millet seed, but her fears quickly left her as she saw Kintu again.

As Nimbi began to forget about what had happened, Walumbe came down to see them. She told Kintu all about her brother and said, "We must get rid of him! Whatever it takes…we just have to get rid of him. My father told me he would ruin Earth."

All of their ways to get rid of Walumbe weren't working, so Kintu made a deal with Walumbe. He offered their first child to Walumbe if only he would leave them alone on Earth. Walumbe agreed, and left.

Kintu and Nambi lived happily for a long time and had many children. As they were about to completely forget their deal,

Walumbe came back to take their first child. Kintu was very angry and tried to get rid of him, but this time Walumbe would not leave.

Walumbe said angrily, "Since you did not keep your promise and give me your first child, now I will stay on the Earth always, and I will take what I want"

Kintu and Nambi had so many children that Uganda was full of people, but still every now and then bad Walumbe comes to take one away, sometimes an old man, sometimes a young one, and sometimes even a little baby. Despite Walumbe's wanderings, though, Uganda still has people who have beautiful banana gardens, many cows and chickens. Even the rainbows still come down from the Cloud Land and touch the Earth, as they did in the days when Nambi played with her brothers.

The Queen Of The Pool

This tale has been edited and adapted from Henry Morton Stanley's book, My Dark Companions, published in 1893 by Sampson, Lowe, Marston and Company, London.

Izoka was a woman originally of Umane, the big town above Basoko, and she was known as the Queen of the Pool. Should you ever pass by Umane, you may ask any of the people if these words are true, and you will find that they will certify to what I shall now tell you.

Izoka was the daughter of a chief of Umane whose name was Uyimba, and her mother was called Twekay. One of the young warriors called Koku lifted his eyes towards her, and as he had a house of his own which was empty, he thought Izoka ought to be the one to keep his hearth warm, and be his companion while he went fishing. The idea became fixed in his mind, and he applied to her father, and the dowry was demanded. And, though it was heavy, it was paid, to ease his longing for her.

Now, Izoka was in every way fit to be a chief's wife. She was tall, slender, and comely of person. Her skin was like down to the touch, her kindly eyes brimmed over with pleasantness, her teeth were like white beads, and her ready laugh was such that all who heard it compared it to the sweet sounds of a flute which the perfect player loves to make before he begins a tune, and men's moods became merry when she passed them in the village. Well, she became Koku's wife, and she left her father's house to live with her husband.

At first it seemed that they were born for one another. Though Koku was no mean fisherman, his wife excelled him in every way. Where one fish came into his net, ten entered into that of Izoka, and this great success brought him abundance. His canoe returned daily loaded with fish, and on reaching home they had as much work to clean and cure the fish as they could manage. Their daily catch would have supported quite a village of people from starving. They therefore disposed of their surplus stock by bartering it for slaves, and goats, and fowls, hoes, carved paddles, and swords, and in a short time Koku became the wealthiest among the chiefs of Umane, through the good fortune that attended Izoka in whatever she did.

Most men would have considered themselves highly favoured in having such fortunate wives, but it was not so with Koku. He became a changed man. Prosperity proved his bane. He went no more with Izoka to fish. He seldom visited the market in her company, nor the fields where the slaves were at work, planting manioc, or weeding the plantain rows, or clearing the jungle, as he used to do. He was now always seen with his long pipe, and boozing with wretched idlers on the plantain wine purchased with his wife's industry, and when he came home it was to storm at his wife in such a manner that she could only bow to it in silence.

When Koku was most filled with malice, he had an irritating way of disguising his spitefulness with a wicked smile, while his tongue expressed all sorts of contrary fancies. He would take delight in saying that her smooth skin was as rough as the leaf with which we polish our spear-shafts, that she was dumpy and dwarfish, that her mouth reminded him of a crocodile's, and her ears of an ape's. Her legs were crooked, and her feet were like hippopotamus hoofs, and she was scorned for even her nails, which were worn to the quick with household toil, and he continued in this style to vex her, until, at last, he became persuaded that it was she who tormented him.

Then he accused her of witchcraft. He said that it was by her witch's medicines that she caught so many fish, and he knew that someday she would poison him. Now, in our country this is a very serious accusation. However, she never crossed her husband's humour, but received the bitterness with closed lips. This silent habit of hers made matters worse. For, the more patience she showed, the louder his accusations became, and the worse she appeared in his eyes. And indeed it is no wonder. If you make up your mind that you will see naught in a wife but faults, you become blind to everything else.

Her cooking also according to him was vile, there was either too much palm-oil or too little in the herb-mess, there was sand in the meat of the fish, the fowls were nothing but bones, she was said to empty the chilli-pot into the stew, the house was not clean, there were snakes in his bed, and so on and so on. Then she threatened, when her tough patience quite broke down, that she would tell her father if he did not desist, which so enraged him that he took a thick stick, and beat her so cruelly that she was nearly dead. This was too much to bear from one so ungrateful, and she resolved to elope into the woods, and live apart from all mankind.

She had travelled a good two days' journey when she came in sight of a lengthy and wide pool which was fed by many springs, and bordered by tall, bending reeds, and the view of this body of water, backed by deep woods all round, appeared to her so pleasing that she chose a level place near its edge for a resting-place. Then she unstrapped her hamper, and sitting down turned out the things she had brought, and began to think of what could be done with them. There was a wedge-like axe which might also be used as an adze, there were two hoes, a handy Basoko bill-hook, a couple of small nets, a ladle, half-a-dozen small gourds full of grains, a cooking-pot, some small fish-knives, a bunch of tinder, a couple of fire-sticks, a short stick of sugar-cane, two banana bulbs, a few beads, iron bangles, and tiny copper balls. As she looked over all these things, she smiled with satisfaction and thought she would manage well enough. She then went into the pool a little way and looked searchingly in for a time, and she smiled again, as if to say, "better and better."

Now with her axe she cut a hoe-handle, and in a short time it was ready for use. Going to the pool-side, she commenced to make quite a large round hole. She laboured at this until the hole was as deep and wide as her own height. Then she plastered the bottom evenly with the mud from the pool-bank, and after that she made a great fire at the bottom of the pit, and throughout the night that followed, after a few winks of sleep, she would rise and throw on more fuel. When the next day dawned, after breaking her fast with a few grains baked in her pot, she swept out all the fire from the well, and wherever a crack appeared in the baked bottom she filled it up carefully, and she also plastered the sides all round smoothly, and again she made a great fire in the pit, and left it to burn all that day.

While the fire was baking the bottom and walls of the well, she hid her hamper among a clump of reeds, and explored her neighbourhood. During her wanderings she found a path leading northward, and she noted it. She also discovered many nuts, sweet red berries, some round, others oval and the fruit, which is a delight to the elephants, and loading herself with as many of these articles as she could carry, she returned, and sat down by the mouth of the well, and refreshed herself. The last work of the day was to take out the fire, plaster up the cracks in the bottom and sides, and re-make the fire as great as ever. Her bed she made not far from it, with her axe by her side.

On the next morning she determined to follow the path she had discovered the day before, and when the sun was well-nigh at the middle of the sky, she came suddenly in view of a banana-grove, whereupon she instantly retreated a little and hid herself. When darkness had well set, she rose, and penetrating the grove, cut down a large blanch of bananas, with which she hurried back along the road. When she came to a stick she had laid across the path, she knew she was not far from the pool, and she remained there until it was sufficiently light to find her way to the well.

By the time she arrived at her well it was in a perfect state, the walls being as sound and well-baked as her cooking-pot. After half-filling it with water, she roasted a few bananas, and made a contented meal from them. Then taking her pot she boiled some bananas, and with these she made a batter. She now emptied the pot, smeared the bottom and sides of it thickly with this sticky batter, and then tying a vine round the pot she let it down into the pond. As soon as it touched the ground, the minnows flocked greedily into the vessel to feed on the batter. And on Izoka suddenly drawing it up she brought out several score of minnows, the spawn of catfish, and some of the young of the bearded fish which grow to such an immense size in our waters. The minnows she took out and dried to serve as food, but the young of the cat and bearded fish she dropped into her well. She next dug a little ditch from the well to the pool, and after making a strong and close netting of cane splinters across the mouth of the ditch, she made another narrow ditch to let a thin rillet of spring water supply the well with fresh water.

Every day she spent a little time in building a hut, in a cosy place surrounded by bush, which had only one opening. Then she would go and work a little at a garden wherein she had planted the sugar-cane, which had been cut into three parts, and the two banana bulbs, and had sowed her millet, and her sesamum, and yellow corn which she had brought in the gourds, and every day she carefully fed her fish in the well. But there were three things she missed most in her loneliness, and these were the cries of an infant, the proud cluck of the hen after she lays an egg, and the bleating of a kid at her threshold. This made her think that she might replace them by something else, and she meditated long upon what it might be.

Observing that there were a number of ground-squirrels about, she thought of snares to catch them. She accordingly made loops of slender but strong vines near the roots of the trees, and across their narrow tracks in the woods. And she succeeded at last in catching a pair. With other vines rubbed over with bird-lime she caught some young parrots and wagtails, whose wing feathers she chopped off with her bill-hook. And one day, while out gathering nuts and berries for her birds, she came across a nest of the pelican, wherein were some eggs, and these she resolved to watch until they were hatched, when she would take and rear them. She had found full occupation for her mind, in making cages for her squirrels and birds, and providing them with food, and had no time at all for grief.

Izoka, however, being very partial to the fish in her well, devoted most of her leisure to feeding them, and they became so tame, and intelligent that they understood the cooing notes of a strange song which she taught them, as though they were human beings. She fed them plentifully with banana-batter, so that in a few months they had grown into a goodly size. By-and-by, they became too large for the well, and as they were perfectly tame, she took them out, and allowed them to go at large in the pool, but punctually in the early morning, and at noon and sunset, she called them to her, and gave them their daily portion of food, for by this time she had a goodly store of bananas and grain from her plantation and garden. One of the largest fish she called Munu, and he was so intelligent and trustful in his mistress's hands that he disliked going very far from the neighbourhood, and if she laid her two hands in the water, he would rest contentedly in the hollow thus formed. She had also strung her stock of shells and beads into necklaces, and had fastened them round the tails of her favourite fish.

Her other friends grew quite as tame as the fish, for all kinds of animals learn to cast off their fears of mankind in return for true kindness, and when no disturbing shocks alarm them. And in this lonely place, so sheltered by protecting woods, where the wind had scarce power to rustle the bending reed and hanging leaves, there was no noise to inspire the most timid with fright.

If you try, you can fancy this young woman Izoka sitting on the ground by the pool-side, surrounded by her friends, like a mother by her offspring. In her arms a young pelican, on one shoulder a chattering parrot, on the other a sharp-eyed squirrel, sitting on his haunches, licking his fore-feet. In her lap another playing with his bushy tail, and at her feet the wagtails, wagging friskily their hind parts and kicking up little showers of dusty soil. Between her and the pool a long-legged heron, who has long ago been snared, and has submitted to his mistress's kindness, and now stands on one leg, as though he were watching for her safety. Not far behind her is her woodland home, well stored with food and comforts, which are the products of her skill and care. Swifts and sand-martins are flying about, chasing one another merrily, and making the place ring with their pipings. The water of the pool lies level and unwrinkled, save in front of her, where the fish sometimes flop about, impatient for their mistress's visit.

This was how she appeared one day to the cruel eyes of Koku her husband, who had seen the smoke of her fire as he was going by the path which led to the north. Being a woodman as well as a fisher, he had the craft of the hunt, and he stealthily approached from tree to tree until he was so near that he could see the beady eyes of the squirrel on her shoulder, who startled her by his sudden movements.

It was strange how quickly the alarm was communicated from one to another. His brother squirrel peeped from one side with his tail over his back like a crest, the parrot turned one eye towards the tree behind which Koku stood, and appeared transfixed, the heron dropped his other leg to the ground, tittered his melancholy cry, *Kwa-le*, and dropped his tail as though he would surge upward. The wagtails stopped their curtseying, the pelicans turned their long bills and laid them lazily along their backs, looking fixedly at the tree, and at last Izoka, warned by all these signs, also turned her head in the same direction, but she saw no one, and as it was sunset she took her friends indoors.

Presently she came out again, and went to the pool-side with fish-food, and cooed softly to her friends in the water, and the fish rushed to her call, and crowded around her. After giving them their food, she addressed Munu, the largest fish, and said, "I am going out tonight to see if I cannot find a discarded cooking-vessel, for mine is broken. Beware of making friends with any man or woman who cannot repeat the song I taught you," and the fish replied by sweeping his tail to right and left, according to his way.

Izoka, who now knew the woods by night as well as by day, proceeded on her journey, little suspecting that Koku had discovered her, and her manner of life and woodland secrets. He waited a little time, then crept to the pool-side, and repeated the song which she had sung, and immediately there was a great rush of fish towards him, at the number and size of which he was amazed. By this he perceived what chance of booty there was here for him, and he sped away to the place where he had left his men, and he cried out to them, "Come, hurry with me to the woods by a great pool, where I have discovered loads of fish."

His men were only too glad to obey him, and by midnight they had all arrived at the pool. After stationing them near him in a line, with their spears poised to strike, Koku sang the song of Izoka in a soft voice, and the great and small fish leapt joyfully from the depths where they were sleeping, and they thronged towards the shore, flinging themselves over each other, and they stood for a while gazing doubtfully up at the line of men. But soon the cruel spears flew from their hands, and Munu, the pride of Izoka, was pierced by several, and was killed and dragged on land by the shafts of the weapons which had slain him. Munu was soon cut up, he and some others of his fellows, and the men, loading themselves with the meat, hastily departed.

Near morning Izoka returned to her home with a load of bananas and a cooking-vessel, and after a short rest and refreshment, she fed her friends, the ground-squirrels, the young pelicans, the parrots and herons, and scattered a generous supply for the wagtails, and martins, and swifts. Then she hurried with her bounties to the pool-side. But near the water's edge there was a sight which almost caused her to faint. There were tracks of many feet, bruised reeds, blood, scales, and the refuse of slaughtered fish. She cooed softly to her friends. They heard her cry, but approached slowly and doubtingly. She called out to Munu, "Munu-nunu, oh, Munu, Munu, Munu," but Munu did not come, and the others stood well away from the shore, gazing at her reproachfully, and they would not advance any nearer. Perceiving that they distrusted her, she threw herself on the ground and wept hot tears, and wailing, "Oh! Munu, Munu, Munu, why do you doubt me?"

When Izoka's grief had somewhat subsided she followed the tracks through the woods until she came to the path, where they were much clearer, and there she discovered that those who had violated her peaceful home, had travelled towards Umane. A suspicion that her husband must have been of the number served to anger her still more, and she resolved to follow the plunderers, and endeavour to obtain justice. Swiftly she sped on the trail, and after many hours' quick travel she reached Umane after darkness had fallen. This favoured her purpose, and she was able to steal, unperceived, near to the open place in front of her husband's house, where she saw Koku and his friends feasting on fish, and heard him boast of his discovery of the fine fish in a forest pool. In her fury at his daring villainy she was nearly tempted to rush upon him and cleave his head with her bill-hook, but she controlled herself, and sat down to think. Then she made the resolution that she would go to her father and claim his protection, a privilege she might long ago have used had not her pride been wounded by the brutal treatment her person had received at Koku's hands.

Her father's village was but a little distance away from Umane, and in a short time all the people in it were startled by hearing the shrill voice of one who was believed to be long ago dead, crying out in the darkness the names of Uyimba and Twekay. On hearing the names of their chief and his wife repeatedly called, the men seized their spears and sallied out, and discovered, to their astonishment, that the long-lost Izoka was amongst them once again, and that she was suffering from great and overpowering grief. They led her to her father's door, and called out to Uyimba and his wife Twekay to come out, and receive her, saying that it was a shame that the pride of Umane should be suffering like a slave in her father's own village. The old man and his wife hurried out, torches were lit, and Twekay soon received her weeping daughter in her arms.

Everybody wanted to know Izoka's story, so she was made to sit down on a shield and tell all her adventures since she had eloped from Umane. The people listened in wonder to all the strange things that were told, but when she related the cruelty of Koku, the men rose to their feet all together, and beat their shields with their spears, and demanded punishment of Koku, and that Uyimba should lead them there and then to Umane.

They accordingly proceeded in a body to the town, to Koku's house, and as he came out in answer to the call of one of them, to ascertain what the matter was, they fell upon him, and bound him hand and foot, and carrying him to their superior chief's house they put him to his trial. Many witnesses came forward to testify against his cruel treatment of Izoka, and of the robbery of the fish and of the manner of it, and the great chief placed Koku's life in the power of Uyimba, whose daughter he had wronged, who at once ordered Koku to be beheaded, and his body to be thrown into the river. The sentence was executed at the river-side without loss of time.

The people of Uman and Uyimba's village then demanded that, as Izoka had shown herself so clever and good as to make birds, animals, and fish obey her voice, some mark of popular favour should be given to her, whereupon the principal chief of Umane, in the name of the tribe, ceded to her all rights to the Forest Pool, and the wood and all things in it round about as far as she could travel in half a day, and also all the property of which Koku stood possessed.

Izoka, by the favour of her tribe, thus became owner of a large district, and mistress of many slaves, and flocks, goats, and fowls, and all manner of useful things for making a settlement by the Pool. There is now a large village there, and Izoka's legend is well known in many lands near Umane and Basoko as the Queen of the Pool, and at last accounts she was still living, prosperous and happy, but she has never been known to try marriage again.

The Builder Of Ability And The Builder Of Haste

This tale has been edited and adapted from Kate Douglas Wiggin and Nora Archibald Smith's collection, The Talking Beasts, A Book of Fable and Wisdom, and illustrated by Harold Nelson. The book was published in 1922.

Two men called themselves one name.

One of them said, "I am Ndala, the builder of ability."

The other one said, "I am Ndala, the builder of haste."

They said, "We will go to trade."

They started out and eventually they arrived in the middle of road when a storm came.

They stopped, saying, "Let us build grass-huts!"

Ndala, the builder of haste, built in haste. He entered into his hut.

Ndala, the builder of ability built his hut with care.

The storm came. The howling winds, the lashing rain and the daggers of lightening killed Ndala, the builder of ability, for he was still finishing his hut.

Ndala, the builder of haste escaped, because his hut was finished. It sheltered him when the storm came on.

The Elephant And The Lion.

This tale has been edited and adapted from Henry Morton Stanley's book, My Dark Companions, published in 1893 by Sampson, Lowe, Marston and Company, London.

A huge and sour-tempered elephant went and wandered in the forest. His inside was slack for want of juicy roots and succulent reeds, but his head was as full of dark thoughts as a gadfly is full of blood. As he looked this way and that, he observed a young lion asleep at the foot of a tree. He regarded him for a while, then, as he was in a wicked mood, it came to him that he might as well kill the lion, and he accordingly rushed forward and impaled him with his tusks. He then lifted the body with his trunk, swung it about, and dashed it against the tree, and afterwards kneeled on it until it became as shapeless as a crushed banana pulp.

He then laughed and said, "Ha! ha! This is a proof that I am strong. I have killed a lion, and people will say proud things of me, and will wonder at my strength."

Presently a brother elephant came up and greeted him.

"See," said the first elephant, "what I have done. It was I that killed him. I lifted him on high, and now he lies like a rotten banana. Do you not think that I am very strong? Come, be frank now, and give me some credit for what I have done."

The second elephant replied, "It is true that you are strong, but that was only a young lion. There are others of his kind, and I have seen some of them, who would give you considerable trouble."

"Ho, ho!" laughed the first elephant. "Get out, stupid. You may bring his whole tribe here, and I will show you what I can do. Aye, and to your dam to boot."

"What? My own mother, too?"

"Yes. Go and fetch her if you like."

"Well, well," said the second elephant, "you are far gone, there is no doubt. Fare you well." He then proceeded on his wanderings, resolved in his own mind that if he had an opportunity he would send someone to test the boaster's strength.

The first elephant called out to him as he moved off, "Away you go. Goodbye to you."

In a little while the second elephant met a lion and lioness, full-grown, and splendid creatures, who turned out to be the parents of the youngster which had been slain. After a sociable chat with them, he said, "If you go further on along the path you will meet a kind of game which requires killing badly. He has just mangled your cub."

Meantime the first elephant, after chuckling to himself very conceitedly, proceeded to the pool nearby to bathe and cool himself. At every step he went you could hear his "Ha, ha, ha! I have killed a lion!"

While he was in the pool, spurting the water in a shower over his back, he suddenly looked up, and at the water's edge beheld a lion and lioness who were regarding him sternly.

"Well! What do you want?" he asked. "Why are you standing there looking at me in that way?"

"Are you the rogue who killed our child?" they asked.

"Perhaps I am," he answered. "Why do you want to know?"

"Because we are in search of him. If it be you that did it, you will have to do the same to us before you leave this ground."

"Ho, ho!" laughed the elephant loudly. "Well, listen. It was I who killed your cub. Come now, it was I. Do you hear? And if you do not leave here mighty quick, I shall have to serve you both in the same way as I served him."

The lions roared aloud in their fury, and switched their tails violently.

"Ho, ho!" laughed the elephant gaily. "This is grand. There is no doubt I shall run soon, they make me so skeery," and he danced round the pool and jeered at them, then drank a great quantity of water and blew it in a shower over them.

The lions stirred not, but kept steadfastly gazing at him, planning how to make their attack.

Perceiving that they were obstinate, he threw another stream of water over the lions and then backed into the deepest part of the pool, until there was nothing seen of him but the tip of his trunk. When he rose again the lions were still watching him, and had not moved.

"Ho, ho!" he trumpeted, "still there! Wait a little, I am coming to you."

He advanced towards the shore, but when he was close enough the lion sire sprang into the air, and alighted on the elephant's back, and furiously tore at the muscles of the neck, and bit deep into the shoulder. The elephant retreated quickly into the deepest part of the pool, and submerged himself and his enemy, until the lion was compelled to abandon his back and begin to swim ashore. No sooner did the elephant feel himself relieved than he rose to the surface, and hastily followed and seized the lion with his trunk. Despite his struggles the lion was pressed beneath the water's surface, dragged under the elephant's knees, and trodden into the mud, and in a short time the lion sire was dead.

The elephant laughed triumphantly, and cried, "Ho, ho! Am I not strong, Ma Lion? Did you ever see the likes of me before? Two of you! Young Lion and Pa Lion are now killed! Come, Ma Lion, had you not better try now, just to see if you won't have better luck? Come on, old woman, just once."

The lioness fiercely answered, while she retreated from the pool, "Rest where you are. I am going to find my brother, and will be back shortly."

The elephant trumpeted his scorn of her and her kind, and seizing the carcase of her lord, flung it on shore after her, and declared his readiness to abide where he was, that he might make mash of all the lion family.

In a short time the lioness had found her brother, who was a mighty fellow, and full of fight. As they advanced near the pool together, they consulted as to the best means of getting at the elephant. Then the lioness sprang forward to the edge of the pool. The elephant retreated a short distance into deeper water. Upon this move the lioness crept along the pool's shore, and pretended to lap the water. The elephant moved towards her. The lion, her brother, waited for his chance, and finally, with a great roar, sprang upon the elephant's shoulders, and commenced tearing away at the very place which had been torn by lion sire.

The elephant backed quickly into deep water as he had done before, and submerged himself, but the lion maintained his hold and bit deeper. The elephant then sank down until there was nothing to be seen but the tip of his trunk. The lion, to avoid suffocation, relaxed his hold and swam vigorously towards shore. The elephant rose up, and as the lion was stepping on shore, he seized him, and drove one of his tusks through his adversary's body. As he was in the act, the lioness sprang upon the elephant's neck, and bit and tore so furiously that he fell dead, and with his fall crushed the dying lion.

Soon after the close of the terrible combat, the second elephant came up, and discovered the lioness licking her chops and paws, and said, "Hello, it seems there has been quite a quarrel here lately. Three lions are dead, and here lies one of my own kind, stiffening."

"Yes," replied lioness, gloomily, "the rogue elephant killed my cub while the little fellow was asleep in the woods. He then killed my husband and brother, and I killed him, but I do not think the elephant has gained much by fighting with us. I did not have much trouble in killing him. Should you meet any friends of his, you may warn them to leave the lioness alone, or she may be tempted to make short work of them."

The elephant, though a patient person generally, was annoyed at this, and gave her a sudden kick with one of his hind feet, which sent her sprawling a good distance off, and asked, "How do you like that, Ma Lion?"

"What do you mean by that?" demanded the enraged lioness.

"Oh, because I hate to hear so much bragging."

"Do you also wish to fight?" she asked.

"We should never talk about doing an impossible thing, Ma Lion," he answered. "I have travelled many years through these woods, and I have never fought yet. I find that when a person minds his own business he seldom comes to trouble, and when I meet one who is even stronger than myself I greet him pleasantly, and pass on, and I should advise you to do the same, Ma Lion."

"You are saucy, Elephant. It would be well for you to think upon your stupid brother there, who lies so stark under your nose, before you trouble with your insolence the one who slew him."

"Well, words never yet made a plantation. It is the handling of a hoe that makes fields. See here, Ma Lion, if I talked to you all day I could not make you wise. I will just turn my back to you. If you bite me, you will soon learn how weak you are."

The lioness, angered still more by the elephant's contempt, sprang at his shoulders, and clung to him, upon which he rushed at a stout tree, and pressing his shoulders against it, crushed the breath out of her body, and she ceased her struggles. When he relaxed his pressure, the body fell to the ground, and he knelt upon it, and kneaded it until every bone was broken.

While the elephant was meditatively standing over the body, and thinking what misfortunes happen to boasters, a man came along, carrying a spear, and seeing that the elephant was unaware of his presence, he thought what great luck had happened to him.

Said he, "Ah, what fine tusks he has. I shall be rich with them, and shall buy slaves and cattle, and with these I will get a wife and a farm," saying which he advanced silently, and when he was near enough, darted his spear into a place behind the shoulder.

The elephant turned around quickly, and on beholding his enemy rushed after and overtook him, and mauled him, until in a few moments he was a mangled corpse.

Soon after a woman approached, and seeing four lions, one elephant, and her husband dead, she raised up her hands wonderingly and cried, "How did all this happen?"

The elephant, hearing her voice, came from behind a tree, with a spear quivering in his side, and bleeding profusely. At the sight of him the woman turned round to fly, but the elephant cried out to her, "Nay, run not, woman, for I can do you no harm. The happy days in the woods are ended for all the tribes. The memory of this scene will never be forgotten. Animals will be henceforth at constant war one with another. Lions will no more greet elephants, the buffaloes will be shy, the rhinoceroses will live apart, and man when he comes within the shadows will think of nothing else than his terrors, and he will fancy an enemy in every shadow. I am sorely wounded, for your man stole up to my side and drove his spear into me, and soon I shall die."

When she had heard these words the woman hastened home, and all the villagers, old and young, hurried into the woods, by the pool, where they found four lions, two elephants, and one of their own tribe lying still and lifeless.

The words of the elephant have turned out to be true, for no man goes now-a-days into the silent and deserted woods but he feels as though something were haunting them, and thinks of goblinry, and starts at every sound. Out of the shadows which shift with the sun, forms seem crawling and phantoms appear to glide, and we are in a fever almost from the horrible illusions of fancy. We breathe quickly and fear to speak, for the smallest vibration in the silence would jar on our nerves. I speak the truth, for when I am in the woods near the night, there swims before my eyes a multitude of terrible things which I never see by the light of day. The flash of a fire-fly is a ghost, the chant of a frog becomes a frightful roar, the sudden piping of a bird signals murder, and I run. No, no. No woods for me when alone.

Dog And The Kingship

This tale has been edited and adapted from Kate Douglas Wiggin and Nora Archibald Smith's collection, The Talking Beasts, A Book of Fable and Wisdom, and illustrated by Harold Nelson. The book was published in 1922.

Some people wanted to invest Mister Dog with the honour of their kingship. They sought out all the things of royalty, the cap, the sceptre, the rings, and the skin of mulkaka.

When everything was ready they said, "The day has come to install Mister Dog as our king."

The headmen all came in their full number and regalia. They sent for the players of drum and marimba. They spread coarse mats and fine mats. Where the lord was going to sit, they laid down a coarse mat. They then spread a fine mat on top of that. They set a chair on top of the fine mat.

They said, "Let the lord sit down."

He sat down. The people serve the celebratory food and drink. He, Mister Dog, on seeing the breast of a fowl, felt the pangs of great greed grasp him. He stood up in haste, took the breast of the fowl, and ran into the bush.

The people said, "The lord, whom we are crowning today, has run away with the breast of the fowl into the bush!"

The people packed everything away and went home. Mister Dog lost his chance to be their king because he was, at heart, a thief.

I have told my little tale and I am finished.

King Gumbi And His Lost Daughter

This tale has been edited and adapted from Henry Morton Stanley's book, My Dark Companions, published in 1893 by Sampson, Lowe, Marston and Company, London.

It was believed in the olden time that if a king's daughter had the misfortune to be guilty of ten mistakes, she should suffer for half of them, and her father would be punished for the rest. Now, King Gumbi had lately married ten wives, and all at once this old belief of the elders about troubles with daughters came into his head, and he issued a command, which was to be obeyed upon pain of death, that if any female children should be born to him they should be thrown into the Lualaba, and drowned, "for," said he, "the dead are beyond temptation to err, and I shall escape mischief."

To avoid the reproaches of his wives, on account of the cruel order, the king thought he would absent himself, and he took a large following with him and went to visit other towns of his country. Within a few days after his departure there were born to him five sons and five daughters. Four of the female infants were at once disposed of according to the king's command, but when the fifth daughter was born, she was so beautiful, and had such great eyes, and her colour was mellow, so like a ripe banana, that the chief nurse hesitated, and when the mother pleaded so hard for her child's life, she made up her mind that the little infant should be saved. When the mother was able to rise, the nurse hastened her away secretly by night. In the morning the queen found herself in a dark forest, and, being alone, she began to talk to herself, as people generally do, and a grey parrot with a beautiful red tail came flying along, and asked, "What is it you are saying to yourself, O Miami?"

She answered and said, "Ah, beautiful little parrot, I am thinking what I ought to do to save the life of my little child. Tell me how I can save her, for Gumbi wishes to destroy all his female children."

The parrot replied, "I grieve for you greatly, but I do not know. Ask the next parrot you see," and he flew away.

A second parrot still more beautiful came flying towards her, whistling and screeching merrily, and the queen lifted her voice and cried, "Ah, little parrot, stop a bit, and tell me how I can save my sweet child's life. For cruel Gumbi, her father, wants to kill it."

"Ah, mistress, I may not tell, but there is one comes behind me who knows. Ask him," and he also flew to his day's haunts.

Then the third parrot was seen to fly towards her, and he made the forest ring with his happy whistling, and Miami cried out again, "Oh, stay, little parrot, and tell me in what way I can save my sweet child, for Gumbi, her father, vows he will kill it."

"Deliver it to me," answered the parrot. "But first let me put a small banana stalk and two pieces of sugar-cane with it, and then I shall carry it safely to its grandmamma."

The parrot relieved the queen of her child, and flew through the air, screeching merrier than before, and in a short time had laid the little princess, her banana stalk, and two pieces of sugar-cane in the lap of the grandmamma, who was sitting at the door of her house, and he said, "This bundle contains a gift from your daughter, wife of Gumbi. She bids you be careful of it, and let none out of your own family see it, lest she should be slain by the king. And to remember this day, she requests you to plant the banana stalk in your garden at one end, and at the other end the two pieces of sugar-cane, for you may need both."

"Your words are good and wise," answered granny, as she received the babe.

On opening the bundle the old woman discovered a female child, exceedingly pretty, plump, and yellow as a ripe banana, with large black eyes, and such smiles on its bright face that the grandmother's heart glowed with affection for it.

Many seasons came and went by. No stranger came round to ask questions. The banana flourished and grew into a grove, and each sprout marked the passage of a season, and the sugar-cane likewise throve prodigiously as year after year passed and the infant grew into girlhood. When the princess had bloomed into a beautiful maiden, the grandmother had become so old that the events of long ago appeared to her to be like so many dreams, but she still worshipped her child's child, cooked for her, waited upon her, wove new grass mats for her bed, and fine grass-cloths for her dress, and every night before she retired she washed her dainty feet.

Then one day, before her ears were quite closed by age, and her limbs had become too weak to bear her about, the parrot who brought the child to her, came and rested upon a branch near her door, and after piping and whistling its greeting, cried out, "The time has come. Gumbi's daughter must depart, and seek her father.

Furnish her with a little drum, teach her a song to sing while she beats it, and send her forth."

Then granny purchased for her a tiny drum, and taught her a song, and when she had been fully instructed she prepared a new canoe with food, from the bananas in the grove, and the plot of sugar-cane, and she made cushions from grass-cloth bags stuffed with silk-cotton floss for her to rest upon. When all was ready she embraced her grand-daughter, and with many tears sent her away down the river, with four women servants.

Granny stood for a long time by the riverbank, watching the little canoe disappear with the current, then she turned and entered the doorway, and sitting down closed her eyes, and began to think of the pleasant life she had enjoyed while serving Miami's child, and while so doing she was so pleased that she smiled, and as she smiled she slept, and never woke again.

But the princess, as she floated down, bathed her eyes which had smarted with grief, and began to think of all that granny had taught her, and began to sing in a fluty voice, as she beat her tiny drum:

"List, all you men, to the song I sing.

I am Gumbi's child, brought up in the wild.

And home I return, as you all will learn,

When this my little drum

Tells Gumbi I have come, come, come."

The sound of her drum attracted the attention of the fishermen who were engaged with their nets, and seeing a strange canoe with only five women aboard floating down the river, they drew near to it, and when they saw how beautiful the princess was, and noted her graceful, lithe figure clad in robes of fine grass-cloths, they were inclined to lay their hands upon her. But she sang again:

"I am Gumbi's child,

Make way for me.

I am homeward bound,

Make way for me."

Then the fishermen were afraid and did not molest her. But one desirous of being the first to carry the news to the king, and obtain favour and a reward for it, hastened away to tell him that his daughter was coming to visit him.

The news plunged King Gumbi into a state of wonder, for as he had taken such pains to destroy all female children, he could not imagine how he could be the father of a daughter. Then he sent a quick-footed and confidential slave to inquire, who soon returned and assured him that the girl who was coming to him was his own true daughter. Then he sent a man who had grown up with him, who knew all that had happened in his court, and he also returned and confirmed all that the slave had said.

Upon this he resolved to go himself, and when he met her he asked, "Who are you, child?"

And she replied, "I am the only daughter of Gumbi."

"And who is Gumbi?"

"He is the king of this country," she replied.

"Well, but I am Gumbi myself, and how can you be my daughter?" he asked.

"I am the child of your wife, Miami, and after I was born she hid me that I might not be cast into the river. I have been living with grandmamma, who nursed me, and by the number of banana-stalks in her garden you may tell the number of the seasons that have passed since my birth. One day she told me the time had come, and she sent me to seek my father, and I embarked in the canoe with four servants, and the river bore me to this land."

"Well," said Gumbi, "when I return home I shall question Miami, and I shall soon discover the truth of your story, but meantime, what must I do for you?"

"My grandmamma said that you must sacrifice a goat to the meeting of the daughter with the father," she replied.

Then the king requested her to step on the shore, and when he saw the flash of her yellow feet, and the gleams of her body, which were like shining bright gum, and gazed on the clear, smooth features, and looked into the wondrous black eyes, Gumbi's heart melted and he was filled with pride that such a surpassingly beautiful creature should be his own daughter.

But she refused to set her feet on the shore until another goat had been sacrificed, for her grandmother had said ill-luck would befall her if these ceremonies were neglected.

Therefore the king commanded that two goats should be slain, one for the meeting with his daughter, and one to drive away ill-luck from before her in the land where she would first rest her feet.

When this had been done, she said, "Now, father, it is not meet that your recovered daughter should soil her feet on the path to her father's house. You must lay a grass-cloth along the ground all the way to my mother's door."

The king thereupon ordered a grass-cloth to be spread along the path towards the women's quarters, but he did not mention to which doorway. His daughter then moved forward, the king by her side, until they came in view of all the king's wives, and then Gumbi cried out to them, "One of you, I am told, is the mother of this girl. Look on her, and be not ashamed to own her, for she is as perfect as the egg. At the first sight of her I felt like a man filled with pleasantness, so let the mother come forward and claim her, and let her not destroy herself with a lie."

Now all the women bent forward and longed to say, "She is mine, she is mine!" but Miami, who was ill and weak, sat at the door, and said, "Continue the matting to my doorway, for as I feel my heart is connected with her as by a cord, she must be the child whom the parrot carried to my mother with a banana stalk and two pieces of sugar-cane."

"Yes, yes, you must be my own mother," cried the princess, and when the grass-cloth was laid even to the inside of the house, she ran forward, and folded her arms around her.

When Gumbi saw them together he said, "Truly, equals always come together. I see now by many things that the princess must be right. But she will not long remain with me, I fear, for a king's daughter cannot remain many moons without suitors."

Now though Gumbi considered it a trifle to destroy children whom he had never seen, it never entered into his mind to hurt Miami or the princess. On the contrary, he was filled with a gladness which he was never tired of talking about. He was even prouder of his daughter, whose lovely shape and limpid eyes so charmed him, than of all his tall sons. He proved this by the feasts he caused to be provided for all the people. Goats were roasted and stewed, the fishermen brought fish without number, the peasants came loaded with weighty bunches of bananas, and baskets of yams, and manioc, and pots full of beans, and vetches, and millet and corn, and honey and palm-oil, and as for the fowls, who could count them? The people also had plenty to drink of the juice of the palm, and thus they were made to rejoice with the king in the return of the princess.

It was soon spread throughout Manyema that no woman was like to Gumbi's daughter for beauty. Some said that she was of the colour of a ripe banana, others that she was like fossil gum, others like a reddish oil-nut, and others again that her face was more like the colour of the moon than anything else. The effect of this reputation was to bring nearly all the young chiefs in the land as suitors for her hand. Many of them would have been pleasing to the king, but the princess was averse to them, and she caused it to be made known that she would marry none save the young chief who could produce matako brass rods by polishing his teeth. The king was very much amused at this, but the chiefs stared in surprise as they heard it.

The king mustered the choicest young men of the land, and he told them it was useless for anyone to hope to be married to the princess unless he could drop brass rods by rubbing his teeth. Though they held it to be impossible that anyone could do such a thing, yet every one of them began to rub his teeth hard, and as they did so, brass rods were seen to drop on the ground from the mouth of one of them, and the people gave a great shout for wonder at it.

The princess was then brought forward, and as the young chief rose to his feet he continued to rub his teeth, and the brass rods were heard to tinkle as they fell to the ground. The marriage was therefore duly proceeded with, and another round of feasts followed, for the king was rich in flocks of goats, and sheep, and in well-tilled fields and slaves.

But after the first moon had waned and gone, the husband said, "Come, now, let us depart, for Gumbi's land is no home for me."

And unknown to Gumbi they prepared for flight, and stowed their canoe with all things needful for a long journey, and one night soon after dark they embarked, and paddled down the river. One day the princess, while she was seated on her cushions, saw a curious nut floating near the canoe, upon which she sprang into the river to obtain it. It eluded her grasp. She swam after it, and the chief followed her as well as he was able, crying out to her to return to the canoe, as there were dangerous animals in the water. But she paid no heed to him, and continued to swim after the nut, until, when she had arrived opposite a village, the princess was hailed by an old woman, who cried, "Ho, princess, I have got what you seek. See." And she held the nut up in her hand. Then the princess stepped on shore, and her husband made fast his canoe to the bank.

"Give it to me," demanded the princess, holding out her hand.

"There is one thing you must do for me before you can obtain it."

"What is that?" she asked.

"You must lay your hands upon my bosom to cure me of my disease. Only thus can you have it," the old woman said.

The princess laid her hands upon her bosom, and as she did so the old woman was cured of her illness.

"Now you may depart on your journey, but remember what I tell you. You and your husband must cling close to this side of the river until you come abreast of an island which is in the middle of the entrance to a great lake. For the shore you seek is on this side. Once there you will find peace and rest for many years. But if you go to the other side of the river you will be lost, you and your husband."

Then they re-embarked, and the river ran straight and smooth before them. After some days they discovered that the side they were on was uninhabited, and that their provisions were exhausted, but the other side was cultivated, and possessed many villages and plantations. Forgetting the advice of the old woman, they crossed the river to the opposite shore, and they admired the beauty of the land, and joyed in the odours that came from the gardens and the plantations, and they dreamily listened to the winds that crumpled and tossed the great fronds of banana, and fancied that they had seen no sky so blue. And while they thus dreamed, the river current was bearing them both swiftly along, and they saw the island which was at the entrance to the great lake, and in an instant the beauty of the land which had charmed them had died away, and they now heard the thunderous booming of waters, and saw them surging upward in great sweeps, and one great wave curved underneath them, and they were lifted up, up, up, and dropped down into the roaring abyss, and neither chief nor princess was ever seen again. They were both swallowed up in the deep.

The moral of the story is that of a warning. People should not follow their inclinations. Did not the girl find her father? Did not her father welcome her, and pardon the mother for very joy? Was not her own choice of a husband found for her? Was not the young chief fortunate in possessing such a beautiful wife? Why should they have become discontented? Why not have stayed at home instead of wandering into strange lands of which they knew nothing? Did not the old woman warn them of what would happen, and point to them how they might live in peace once again? But it was all to no purpose. We never know the value of anything until we have lost it. Ruin follows the wilful always. They left their home and took to the river, the river was not still, but moved on, and as their heads were already full of their own thoughts, they could not keep good advice.

A Fernando Po Legend

This tale has been edited and adapted from Mary H. Kingsley's book, Travels in West Africa.. The book was published in 1897.

The first man called all people to one place. His name was Raychow.

"Hear this, my people" said he, "I am going to give a name to every place, for I am King in this River."

One day he came with his people to the Hole of Wonga Wonga, which is a deep pit in the ground from which fire comes at night. Men spoke to them from the Hole, but they could not see them.

Raychow said to his son, "Go down into the Hole", and his son went.

The son of the King of the Hole came to him and challenged him to a contest of throwing the spear. If he lost he should be killed, but if he won he should go back in safety. He won.

Then the son of the King of the Hole said, "It is strange you should have won, for I am a spirit. Ask whatever you wish.'"

The King's son asked for a remedy for every disease he could remember. And the spirit gave him the medicines, and when he had done so, he said, "There is one sickness you have forgotten. It is the Krawkraw, and of that you shall die."

A tribe named Ndiva was then strong, and they gave Raychow's son a canoe and forty men, to take him back to his father's town, and when he saw his father he did not speak.

His father said, "My son, if you are hungry eat."

He did not answer.

His father said, "Do you wish me to kill a goat?"

He did not answer.

His father said, "Do you wish me to give you new wives?"

He still did not answer.

Then his father said, "Do you want me to build you a fetish hut?"

Then he answered, "Yes," and the hut was built, and the medicines he had brought back from the Hole were put into it.

"Now," said the son of King Raychow, "I go to make Moondah enter the Orongo." So he went and dug a canal and when this was finished all his men were dead.

Then he said, "I will go and kill river-horse in the Benito." He killed four, and as he was killing the fifth, the people descended from the mountains against him. So he made fetish on his great war-spear and sang:

"My spear, go kill these people,

Or these people will kill me"

The spear went and killed the people who were attacking him, except for a few who got into canoes and fled to Fernando Po.

Then their King said, "My people shall never wear cloth till we have conquered the M'pongwe."

To this day the Fernando Poians go naked and hate the M'pongwe with a special hatred."

The Story Of Maranda

This tale has been edited and adapted from Henry Morton Stanley's book, My Dark Companions, published in 1893 by Sampson, Lowe, Marston and Company, London.

Maranda's father was named Sukila, and he lived in the village of Chief Busandiya. Sukila owned a fine large canoe and many paddles, which he had carved with his own hand. He also possessed several long nets which he himself also made, besides spears, knives, a store of grass-cloths, and a few slaves. He was highly respected by his countrymen, and sat by the chief's side in the council place.

As the girl grew to be fit for marriage, Mafala, a Basoko warrior, thought she would suit him as a wife, and went and spoke of it to Sukila, who demanded a slave girl, six long paddles ornamented with ivory caps, six goats, as many grass-cloths as he had fingers and toes, a new shield, two axes, and two field-hoes. Mafala tried to reduce the demand, and walked backwards and forwards many times to smoke pipes with Sukila, and get him to be less exacting. But the old man knew his daughter was worth the price he had put upon her, and that if he refused Mafala, she would not remain long without a suitor. For a girl like Maranda is not often seen among the Basokos. Her limbs were round and smooth, and ended in thin, small hands and feet. The young men often spoke about Maranda's light, straight feet, and quick-lifting step. A boy's arm could easily enclose the slim waist, and the manner in which she carried her head, and the supple neck and the clear look in her eyes belonged to Maranda only.

Mafala, on the other hand, was curiously unlike her. He always seemed set on something, and the lines between the eyebrows gave him a severe face, not pleasant to see, and you always caught something in his eyes that made you think of the glitter which is in a serpent's eye.

Perhaps that was one reason why Sukila did not care to have him for his daughter's husband. At any rate, he would not abate his price one grass-cloth, and at last it was paid, and Maranda passed over from her father's house into that of her husband.

Soon after, the marriage Maranda was heard to cry out, and it was whispered that she had learned much about Mafala in a few days, and that blows as from a rod had been heard. Half a moon passed away, and then all the village knew that Maranda had fled to Busandiya's house, because of her husband's ill-treatment. Now the custom in such a case is that the father keeps his daughter's dowry, and if it be true that a wife finds life with her husband too harsh to be borne, she may seek the chief's protection, and the chief may give her to another husband who will treat her properly.

But before the chief had chosen the man to whom he would give her, Mafala went to a crocodile, for it turned out that he was a Mganga, a witch-man who had dealings with reptiles on land, as well as with the monsters of the river,, and he bargained with it to catch her as she came to the river to wash, and carry her up to a certain place on the riverbank where there was a tall tree with a large hole in it.

The crocodile bided his chance, and one morning, when Maranda visited the water, he seized her by the hand, and swept her onto his back, and carried her to the hiding-place in the hollow tree. He then left her there, and swam down opposite the village, and signalled to Mafala that he had performed his part of the bargain.

On the crocodile's departure Maranda looked about the hole, and saw that she was in a kind of pit, but a long way up the hollow narrowed like the neck of a gourd, and she could see foliage and a bit of sky. She determined to climb up, and though she scratched herself very much, she finally managed to reach the very top, and to crawl outside into the air. The tree was very large and lofty, and the branches spread out far, and they were laden with heavy jackfruit of which elephants are so fond. At first she thought that she could not starve because of so many of these big fruit. Then, as they were large and heavy, she conceived the idea that they might be useful to defend herself, and she collected a great number of them, and laid them in a heap over some sticks she had laid across the branches.

By-and-by Mafala came, and discovered her high up among the foliage, and after jeering at her, began to climb the tree. But when he was only half-way up, Maranda lifted one of the ponderous fruits and flung it on his head, and he fell to the ground with his senses all in a whirl and his back greatly bruised. When he recovered he begged the crocodile to help him, and the crocodile tried to climb up, but when he had ascended but a little way, Maranda dropped one of the elephant fruits fairly on his snout, which sent him falling backwards. Mafala then begged two great serpents to ascend and bring her down, but Maranda met them with the heavy fruit one after another, and they were glad to leave her alone. Then the man departed to seek a leopard, but while he was absent Maranda, from her tree, saw a canoe on the river with two young fishermen in it, and she screamed loudly for help. The fishermen paddled close ashore and found that it was Sukila's daughter, the wife of Mafala, who was alone on a tall tree. They waited long enough to hear her story, and then returned to the village to obtain assistance.

Busandiya was much astonished to hear the fishermen's news, and forthwith sent a war-canoe full of armed men, led by the father, Sukila, to rescue her. By means of rattan-climbers they contrived to reach her, and to bring her down safely. While some of the war-party set out to discover Mafala, the others watched for the crocodile and the two serpents. In a short time the cruel man was seen and caught, and he was brought to the river-side, bound with green withies. His legs and his arms were firmly tied together, and, after the Basoko had made Maranda repeat her story from the beginning, and Sukila had told the manner of the marriage, they searched for great stones, which they fastened to his neck. And, lifting him into the war-canoe, they paddled into the middle of the stream, where they sang a death-chant, after which they dropped Mafala overboard and he was never heard of more. That is all there is of the story of Maranda.

The Story Of Kitinda And Her Wise Dog

This tale has been edited and adapted from Henry Morton Stanley's book, My Dark Companions, published in 1893 by Sampson, Lowe, Marston and Company, London.

Kitinda, a woman of the Basoko, near the Aruwimi river, possessed a dog who was remarkable for his intelligence. It was said that he was so clever that strangers understood his motions as well as though he talked to them, and that Kitinda, familiar with his ways and the tones of his whines, his yelps, and his barks, could converse with him as easily as she could with her husband.

One market-day the mistress and her dog agreed to go together, and on the road she told him all she intended to do and say in disposing of her produce in exchange for other articles which she needed in her home. Her dog listened with sympathy, and then, in his own manner, he conveyed to her how great was his attachment to her, and how there never was such a friend as he could be, and he begged her that, if at any time she was in distress, she would tell him, and that he would serve her with all his might. "Only," he said, "were it not that I am afraid of the effects of being too clever, I could have served you oftener and much more than I have done."

"What do you mean?" said Kitinda.

"Well, you know, among the Basoko, it is supposed, if one is too clever, or too lucky, or too rich, that it has come about through dealings in witchcraft, and people are burned in consequence. I do not like the idea of being burned, and therefore I have refrained often from assisting you because I feared you could not contain your surprise, and would chat about it to the villagers. Then someday, after some really remarkable act of cleverness of mine, people would say, `Ha! This is not a dog. No dog could have done that! He must be a demon, or a witch in a dog's hide!' and of course they would take me and burn me."

"Why, how very unkind of you to think such things of me! When have I chatted about you? Indeed I have too many things to do, my housework, my planting and marketing so occupy me, that I could not find time to gossip about my dog."

"Well, it is already notorious that I am clever, and I often tremble when strangers look at and admire me for fear some muddle-headed fellow will fancy that he sees something else in me more than unusual intelligence. What would they say, however, if they really knew how very sagacious I am? The reputation that I possess has only come through your affection for me, but I assure you that I dread this excess of affection lest it should end fatally for you and for me."

"But are you so much cleverer than you have already shown yourself? If I promise that I will never speak of you to any person again, will you help me more than you have done, if I am in distress?"

"You are a woman, and you could not prevent yourself talking if you tried ever so hard."

"Now, look here, my dog. I vow to you that no matter what you do that is strange, I wish I may die, and that the first animal I meet may kill me if I speak a word. You shall see now that Kitinda will be as good as her word."

"Very well, I will take you at your word. I am to serve you every time you need help, and if you speak of my services to a soul, you are willing to lose your life by the first animal you may meet."

Thus they made a solemn agreement as they travelled to market.

Kitinda sold her palm-oil and fowls to great advantage that day, and in exchange received sleeping-mats, a couple of carved stools, a bag of cassava flour, two large well-baked and polished crocks, a bunch of ripe bananas, a couple of good plantation hoes, and a big strong basket.

After the marketing was over she collected her purchases together and tried to put them into the basket, but the big crocks and carved stools were a sore trouble to her. She could put the flour and hoes and the bananas on top with the mats for a cover very well, but the stools and the crocks were a great difficulty.

Her dog in the meantime had been absent, and had succeeded in killing a young antelope, and had dragged it near her. He looked around and saw that the market was over, and that the people had returned to their own homes, while his mistress had been anxiously planning how to pack her property.

He heard her complain of her folly in buying such cumbersome and weighty things, and ask herself how she was to reach home with them.

Pitying her in her trouble, the dog galloped away and found a man empty-handed, before whom he fawned and whose hands he licked, and being patted he clung to his cloth with his teeth and pulled him gently along, wagging his tail and looking very amiable. He continued to do this until the man, seeing Kitinda fretting over her difficulty, understood what was wanted, and offered to carry the stools and crocks at each end of his long staff over his shoulders for a few of the ripe bananas and a lodging. His assistance was accepted with pleasure, and Kitinda was thus enabled to reach her home, and on the way was told by the man how it was that he had happened to return to the marketplace.

Kitinda was very much tempted there and then to dilate upon her dog's well-known cleverness, but remembered in time her promise not to boast of him. When, however, she reached the village, and the housewives came out of their houses, burning to hear the news at the market, in her eagerness to tell this one and then the other all that had happened to her, and all that she had seen and heard, she forgot her vow of the morning, and forthwith commenced to relate the last wonderful trick of her dog in dragging a man back to the marketplace to help her when she thought that all her profit in trade would be lost, and when she was just about to smash her nice crocks in her rage.

The dog listened to her narrative, viewed the signs of wonder stealing over the women's faces, heard them call out to their husbands, saw the men advancing eagerly towards them, saw them all look at him narrowly, heard one man exclaim, "That cannot be a dog! It is a demon within a dog's hide. He…"

But the dog had heard enough. He turned, and ran into the woods, and was never more seen in that village.

The next market-day came round, and Kitinda took some more palm-oil and a few fowls, and left her home to dispose of them for some other domestic needs. When about half-way, her dog came out of the wood, and after accusing her of betraying him to her stupid countrymen, thus returning evil for good, he sprang upon her and tore her to pieces.

The Ladder

This tale has been edited and adapted from Mary H. Kingsley's book, Travels in West Africa.. The book was published in 1897.

Once upon a time there was direct intercourse between the gods, the spirits that live in the sky, and men. In this time, when there was no trouble or serious disturbance upon earth, it was because there was a ladder that reached from heaven to the earth. The ladder was made like the one you get palm-nuts with, *only long, long*. This ladder reached from earth to heaven so the gods could go up and down it and attend personally to mundane affairs.

But one day a cripple boy started to go up the ladder, and he had got a long way up when his mother saw him, and worried to death that her son would fall, she went up in pursuit.

The gods, horrified at the prospect of having boys and women invading heaven, threw down the ladder, and have since left humanity severely alone.

The Story Of The Prince Who Insisted On Possessing The Moon

This tale has been edited and adapted from Henry Morton Stanley's book, My Dark Companions, published in 1893 by Sampson, Lowe, Marston and Company, London.

The country now inhabited by the Basoko tribe was formerly known as Bandimba. A king called Bahanga was its sole ruler. He possessed a houseful of wives, but all his children were unfortunately of the female sex, which he considered to be a great grievance, and of which he frequently complained. His subjects, on the other hand, were blessed with more sons than daughters, and this fact increased the king's grief, and made him envy the meanest of his subjects. One day, however, he married Bamana, the youngest daughter of his principal chief, and finally he became the father of a male child, and was very happy, and his people rejoiced in his happiness.

The prince grew up to be a marvel of strength and beauty, and his father doted on him so much, that he shared his power with the boy in a curious manner. The king reserved authority over all the married people, while the prince's subjects consisted of those not yet mated. It thus happened that the prince ruled over more people than his father, for the children were, of course, more numerous than the parents. But with all the honour conferred upon him the prince was not happy. The more he obtained, the more he wished to possess. His eyes had but to see a thing to make him desire its exclusive possession. Each day he preferred one or more requests to his father, and because of his great love for him, the king had not the heart to refuse anything to him. Indeed, he was persuaded to bestow so many gifts upon his son that he reserved scarcely anything for himself.

One day the prince was playing with the youth of his court, and after the sport retired to the shade of a tree to rest, and his companions sat down in a circle at a respectful distance from him. He then felt a gush of pride stealing over him as he thought of his great power, at the number and variety of his treasures, and he cried out boastfully that there never was a boy so great, so rich and so favoured by his father, as he had become. "My father," said he, "can deny me nothing. I have only to ask, and it is given to me."

Then one little slender boy with a thin voice said, "It is true, prince. Your father has been very good to you. He is a mighty king, and he is as generous as he is great. Still, I know of one thing that he cannot give you, and it is certain that you will never possess it."

"What thing is that which I may not call my own, when I see it, and what is it that is not in the king's power to give me?" asked the prince, in a tone of annoyance.

"It is the moon," answered the little boy, "and you must confess yourself that it is beyond the king's power to give that to you."

"Do you doubt it?" asked the prince. "I say to you that I shall possess it, and I will go now and claim it from my father. I will not give him any peace until he gives it to me."

Now it so happens that such treasures as are already ours, we do not value so much as those which we have not yet got. So it was with this spoiled prince. The memory of the many gifts of his father faded from his mind, and their value was not to be compared with this new toy, the moon, which he had never thought of before and which he now so ardently coveted.

He found the king discussing important matters with the old men.

"Father," said he, "just now, while I was with my companions I was taunted because I did not have the moon among my toys, and it was said that it was beyond your power to give it to me. Now, prove this boy a liar, and procure the moon for me, that I may be able to show it to them, and glory in your gift."

"What is it you say, my son, you want the moon?" asked the astonished king.

"Yes. Do get it for me at once, won't you?"

"But, my child, the moon is a long way up. How shall we be ever able to reach it?"

"I don't know, but you have always been good to me, and you surely would not refuse me this favour, father?"

"I fear, my own, that we will not be able to give you the moon."

"But, father, I must have it. My life will not be worth living without it. How may I dare to again face my companions after my proud boast before them of your power and goodness? There was but one thing that yonder pert boy said I might not have, and that was the moon. Now my soul is bent upon possessing this moon, and you must obtain it for me or I shall die."

"Nay, my son, speak not of death. It is an ugly word, especially when connected with my prince and heir. Do you not know yet that I live only for your sake? Let your mind be at rest. I will collect all the wise men of the land together, and ask them to advise me. If they say that the moon can be reached and brought down to us, you shall have it."

Accordingly the great state drum was sounded for the general palaver, and a score of criers went through the towns beating their little drums as they went, and the messengers hastened all the wise men and elders to the presence of the king.

When all were assembled, the king announced his desire to know how the moon could be reached, and whether it could be shifted from its place in the sky and brought down to the earth, in order that he might give it to his only son the prince. If there was any wise man present who could inform him how this could be done, and would undertake to bring it to him, he would give the choicest of his daughters in marriage to him and endow him with great riches.

When the wise men heard this strange proposal, they were speechless with astonishment, as no one in the Basoko Land had ever heard of anybody mounting into the air higher than a tree, and to suppose that a person could ascend as high as the moon was, they thought, simple madness. Respect for the king, however, held them mute, though what their glances meant was very clear.

But while each man was yet looking at his neighbour in wonder, one of the wise men, who appeared to be about the youngest present, rose to his feet and said, "Long life to the prince and to his father, the king! We have heard the words of our king, Bahanga, and they are good. I, even I, his slave, am able to reach the moon, and to do the king's pleasure, if the king's authority will assist me."

The confident air of the man, and the ring of assurance in his voice made the other wise men, who had been so ready to believe the king and prince mad, feel shame, and they turned their faces to him curiously, more than half willing to believe that after all the thing was possible. The king also lost his puzzled look, and appeared relieved.

"Say on. How may you be able to perform what you promise?"

"If it please the king," answered the man, boldly, "I will ascend from the top of the high mountain near the Cataract of Panga. But I shall first build a high scaffold on it, the base of which shall be as broad as the mountain top, and on that scaffold I will build another, and on the second I shall build a third, and so on and so on until my shoulder touches the moon."

"But is it possible to reach the moon in this manner?" asked the king doubtingly.

"Most certainly, if I were to erect a sufficient number of scaffolds, one above another, but it will require a vast quantity of timber, and a great army of workmen. If the king commands it, the work will be done."

"Be it so, then," said the king. "I place at your service every able-bodied man in the kingdom."

"Ah, but all the men in your kingdom are not sufficient, O king. All the grown-up men will be wanted to fell the trees, square the timber and bear it to the works, and every grown-up woman will be required to prepare the food for the workmen, and every boy must carry water to satisfy their thirst, and bark rope for the binding of the timbers, and every girl, big and little, must be sent to till the fields to raise cassava for food. Only in this manner can the prince obtain the moon as his toy."

"I say, then, let it be done as you think it ought to be done. All the men, women, and children in the kingdom I devote to this service, that my only son may enjoy what he desires."

Then it was proclaimed throughout the wide lands of the Bandimba that all the people should be gathered together to proceed at once with the work of obtaining the moon for the king's son. And the forest was cut down, and while some of the workmen squared the trees, others cut deep holes in the ground, to make a broad and sure base for the lower scaffold, and the boys made thousands of rope coils to lash the timbers together, out of bark, fibre of palm, and tough grass, and the girls, big and little, hoed up the ground and planted the cassava shrubs and cuttings from the banana and the plantain, and sowed the corn, and the women kneaded the bread and cooked the greens, and roasted green bananas for food for the workmen. And all the Bandimba people were made to slave hard every day in order that a spoiled boy might have the moon for his toy.

In a few days the first scaffolding stood up as high as the tallest trees, in a few weeks the structure had grown until it was many arrow-flights in height, in two months it was so lofty that the top could not be seen with the naked eye. The fame of the wonderful wooden tower that the Bandimba were building was carried far and wide, and the friendly nations round about sent messengers to see and report to them what mad thing the Bandimba were about, for rumour had spread so many contrary stories among people that strangers did not know what to believe. Some said it was true that all the Bandimba had become mad, but some of those who came to see with their own eyes, laughed, while others began to feel anxious. All, however, admired the bigness, and wondered at the height of the tower.

In the sixth month the top of the highest scaffold was so high that on the clearest day people could not see half-way up, and it was said to be so tall that the chief engineer could tell the day he would be able to touch the moon.

The work went on, and at last the engineer passed the word down that in a few days more it would be finished. Everybody believed him, and the nations round about sent more people to be present to witness the completion of the great tower, and to observe what would happen. In all the land, and the countries adjoining it, there was found only one wise man who foresaw, if the moon was shifted out of its place what damage would happen, and that probably all those foolish people in the vicinity of the tower would be destroyed. Fearing some terrible calamity, he proposed to depart from among the Bandimba before it should be too late. He then placed his family in a canoe, and, after storing it with sufficient provisions, he embarked, and in the night he floated down the river Aruwimi and into the big river, and continued his journey night and day as fast as the current would take him, far, far below any lands known to the Bandimba. A week later, after the flight of the wise man and his family, the chief engineer sent down word to the king that he was ready to take the moon down.

"It is well," replied the king from below. "I will ascend, that I may see how you set about it."

Within twenty days the king reached the summit of the tower, and, standing at last by the side of the engineer, he laid his hand upon the moon, and it felt exceedingly hot. Then he commanded the engineer to proceed to take it down. The man put a number of cool bark coils over his shoulder and tried to dislodge it. But, as it was firmly fixed, he used such a deal of force that he cracked it, and there was an explosion, the fire and sparks which scorched him. After the engineer of the works, the first who died were the king and the prince whose folly had brought ruin on the land. Then the timber on which the king and his chiefs had been standing began to burn fiercely, and many more bursting sounds were heard, and fire and melted rock ran down through the scaffolding in a steady stream, until all the woodwork was ablaze, and the flames soared upward among the uprights and trestles of the wood in one vast pile of fire, and every man, woman, and child was utterly consumed in a moment.

And the heat was so great that it affected the moon, and a large portion of it tumbled to the earth, and its glowing hot materials ran over the ground like a great river of fire, so that most of the country of the Bandimba was burnt to ashes. On those who were not smothered by the smoke, nor burnt by the fire, and who fled from before the burning river, the effect was very wonderful. Such of them as were grown up, male and female, were converted into gorillas, and all the children into different kinds of long-tailed monkeys.

The old man who told me this story ended by saying to us, who listened with open mouth to his words, "Friends, if you doubt the truth of what I have said, all you have to do is to look at the moon when it is full, and you may then see on a clear night a curious dark portion on its face, which often appears as though there were peaky mountains in it, and often the dark spots are like some kind of homed animals, and then again, you will often fancy that on the moon you see the outlines of a man's face, but those dark spots are only the holes made in the moon by the man who forced his shoulders through it. By this you will know that I have not lied to you. Now ever since that dreadful day when the moon burst and the Bandimba country was consumed, parents are not in the habit of granting children all they ask for, but only such things as their age and experience warn them are good for their little ones. And when little children will not be satisfied by such things, but fret and pester their parents to give them what they know will be harmful to them, then it is a custom with all wise people to take the rod to them, to drive out of their heads the wicked thoughts."

The Origin Of Disease

This tale has been edited and adapted from Mary H. Kingsley's book, Travels in West Africa.. The book was published in 1897. This is a Timneh tale.

Once upon a time God was very friendly with men, and when He thought a man had lived long enough on earth, He sent a messenger to him telling him to come up into the sky, and stay with Him.

Once, though, there was a man who, when the messenger of God came, did not want to leave his wives, his slaves, and his riches, and so the messenger had to go back without him. God was very cross and sent another messenger for him, who was called Disease, but the man would not come for him either, and so Disease sent back word to God that he must have help to bring the man

God sent another messenger whose name was Death. Disease and Death together got hold of the man, and took him to God. And God said in future He would always send these messengers to fetch men.

How Kimyera Became King Of Uganda

This tale has been edited and adapted from Henry Morton Stanley's book, My Dark Companions, published in 1893 by Sampson, Lowe, Marston and Company, London.

Many ages ago Uni reigned as king over Unyoro, a great country which lies to the north and west of Uganda. One day he took to wife Wanyana, a woman of the neighbouring kingdom, who on the first night she had been taken into the inner harem manifested a violent aversion for his person. At that time a man named Kalimera, who was a dealer in cattle, was visiting the court, and had already resided some months there as an honoured guest of the king, on account of his agreeable manners, and his accomplishments on the flute. During his stay he had not failed to note the beauty of the young women who were permitted to crowd around him while he played, but it had long been observed that he had been specially attracted by the charms of Wanyana. It was whispered by a few of the more maliciously disposed among the women that a meeting had taken place, and that an opportunity had been found by them to inform each other of their mutual passion. However that may be, King Uni, surprised at the dislike which she manifested towards him, forbore pressing her for the time, trustfully believing that her sentiments would change for the better after a more intimate acquaintance with him. Meantime he built for her a separate apartment, and palisaded its court closely around with thick cane. His visits were paid to her on alternate days, and each time he brought some gift of bead or bark-cloth, or soft, furry hide, in the hope of winning her favour.

In time she discovered that she was pregnant, and, fearing King Uni's wrath, she made a compact with him that if he would abstain from visiting her for one month she would repay his kindness with all affection. Uni gladly consented to this proposal, and confined his attentions to sending his pages with daily greetings and gifts. Meantime she endeavoured through her own servants to communicate with Kalimera, her lover, but, though no effort on her part was wanting, she could gain no news of him, except a report that soon after she had entered the harem of Uni, Kalimera had disappeared.

In a few days she was delivered of a fine male child, but as she would undoubtedly be slain by the king if the child was discovered, she departed by night with it, and laid it, clad in fur adorned with fine bead-work, at the bottom of a potter's pit. She then hastened to a soothsayer in the neighbourhood, and bribed him to contrive in some way to receive and rear her child until he could be claimed. Satisfied with his assurance that the child would be safe, Wanyana returned to her residence at the court in the same secret manner that she had left it.

Next morning Mugema, the potter, was seen passing the soothsayer's door, and was hailed by the great witch-finder.

"Mugema," said he, "your pots are now made of rotten clay. They are not at all what they used to be. They now crumble in the hand. Tell me why this is?"

"Ah, doctor, it is just that. I thought to bribe you to tell me, only I did not wish to disturb you."

"It is well, Mugema. I will tell you why. You have an enemy who wishes evil to you, but I will defeat his projects. Haste you to your pit, and whatever living thing you find there, keep it, and rear it kindly. While it lives you are safe from all harm."

Wondering at this news, Mugema departed from the soothsayer's house, and proceeded to the pit where he obtained his clay. Peering softly over the edge of the pit, he saw a bundle of bark-cloth and fur. From its external appearance he could not guess what this bundle might contain, but, fearing to disturb it by any precipitate movement, he silently retreated from the pit, and sped away to tell his wife, as he was in duty bound, and obtain her advice and assistance, for the wife in all such matters is safer than the man.

His wife on hearing this news cried out at him, saying, "Why, what a fool you are! Why did you not do as the soothsayer commanded you? Come, I will go with you at once, for my mind is troubled with a dream which I had last night, and this thing you tell me may have a weighty meaning for us both."

Mugema and his wife hurried together towards the clay-pit, and as her husband insisted on it, she crept silently to its edge to look down. At that moment the child uttered a cry and moved the clothes which covered it.

"Why, it is a babe," cried the woman, "just as I found it in my dream. Hurry, Mugema. Descend quickly, and bring it up to me, and take care not to hurt it."

Mugema wondered so much at his wife's words that he almost lost his wits, but being pushed into the pit he mechanically obeyed, and brought up the bundle and its living occupant, which he handed to his wife without uttering a word.

On opening the bundle there was discovered the form of a beautiful and remarkably lusty child, of such weight, size, and form, that the woman exclaimed, "Oh! Mugema, was ever anybody's luck like this of ours? My very heart sighed for a child that I could bring up to be our joy, and here the good spirits have given us the pick of all the world. Mugema, your fortune is made."

"But whose child is it?" asked Mugema, suspiciously.

"How can I tell you that? Had you not brought the news to me of it being in the pit, I should have been childless all my life. The soothsayer who directed you here is a wise man. He knows the secret, I warrant him. But come, Mugema, drop these silly thoughts. What say you? `Shall we rear the child, or leave it here to perish?"

"All right, wife. If it prove of joy to you, I shall live content."

Thus it was that the child of Wanyana found foster-parents, and no woman in Unyoro could be prouder of her child than Mugema's wife came to be of the foundling. The milk of woman, goat, and cow was given to him, and he throve prodigiously, and when Mugema asked the soothsayer what name would be fittest for him, the wise man said, "Call him Kimyera, the mighty one."

Some months after this, when Kimyera was about a year old, Wanyana came to the potter's house to purchase pots for her household, and while she was seated in the porch selecting the soundest among them, she heard a child crying within.

"Ah, has your wife had a child lately? I did not observe or hear when I last visited you that she was likely to become a mother."

"No, princess," replied Mugema, "that is the cry of a child I discovered in the clay-pit about a year ago."

Wanyana's heart gave a great jump, and for a moment she lost all recollection of where she was. Recovering herself with a great effort, she bade Mugema tell her all about the incident, but while he related the story, she was busy thinking how she might assure herself of his secrecy if she declared herself to be the mother of the child.

Mugema, before concluding his story, did not fail to tell Wanyana how for a time he had suspected his wife of having played him falsely, and that though he had no grounds for the suspicion further than that the clay-pit was his own and the child had been found in it, he was not quite clear in his mind yet, and he would be willing to slave a long time for any person who could thoroughly disabuse his mind of the doubt, as, with that exception, his wife was the cleverest and best woman in Unyoro.

Wanyana, perceiving her opportunity, said, "Well, much as I affected not to know about the child, I know whose child it is, and who placed it in the pit."

"You, princess!" he cried.

"Yes, and, if you will take an oath upon the great Muzimu to keep it secret, I will disclose the name of the mother."

"You have my assurance of secrecy upon the condition that the child is not proved to be my wife's. Whosoever else's it may be, matters not to me. The child was found, and is mine by right of the finder. Now name the mother, princess."

"Wanyana!"

"Yours?"

"Even so. It is the offspring of fond love, and Kalimera of Uganda is his father. The young man belongs to one of the four royal clans of Uganda, called the Elephant clan. He is the youngest son of the late king of Uganda. To him, on his father's death, fell his mother's portion, a pastoral district rich in cattle not far from the frontier of Unyoro. It was while he drove fat herds here for sale to Uni that he saw and loved me, and I knew him as my lord. Dreading the king's anger, he fled, and I was left loveless in the power of Uni. One night the child was born, and in the darkness I crept out of the king's court, and bore the babe to your pit. To the wise man I confided the secret of that birth. You know the rest."

"Princess, my wife never appeared fairer to me than she does now, and I owe the clear eye to you. Rest in peace. My wife loves the babe, let her nurse it until happier times, and I will guard it safe as though it were my own. Aye, the babe, I feel assured, will pay me well when he is grown. The words of the wise man come home to me now, and I see whereby good luck shall come to all. If bone and muscle can make a king, Kimyera's future is sure. But come in to see my wife, and to her discretion and wisdom confide your tale frankly."

Wanyana soon was hanging over her child, and, amid tears of joy, she made Mugema's wife acquainted with his birth, and obtained from her earnest assurance that he would be tenderly cared for, and her best help in any service she could perform for Kimyera and his mother.

Great friendship sprang up between Princess Wanyana and the potter Mugema and his wife, and she found frequent excuses for visiting the fast-growing child.

Through the influence of the princess, the potter increased in riches, and his herds multiplied, and when Kimyera was grown tall and strong, he was entrusted by his foster-father with the care of the cattle, and he gave him a number of strong youths as assistants. With these Kimyera indulged in manly games, until he became wonderfully dexterous in casting the spear, and drawing the bow, and in wrestling. His swiftness exceeded that of the fleetest antelope. No animal of the plain could escape him when he gave chase. His courage, proved in the defence of his charge, became a proverb among all who knew him. If the cry of the herdsman warned him that a beast sought to prey upon the cattle, Kimyera never lost time to put himself in front, and, with spear and arrow, he often became victor.

With the pride becoming the possessor of so many admirable qualities, he would drive his herds right through the corn-fields of the villagers, and to all remonstrances he simply replied that the herds belonged to Wanyana, favourite wife of Uni. The people belonged to her also, as well as their corn, and who could object to Wanyana's cattle eating Wanyana's corn?

As his reputation for strength and courage was well known, the villagers then submissively permitted him to do as he listed.

As he grew up in might and valour, Uni's regards cooled towards Wanyana, and, as she was not permitted that freedom formerly enjoyed by her, her visits to Kimyera ceased. Mugema sympathised with the mother, and contrived to send Kimyera with pots to sell to the people of the court, with strict charge to discover every piece of news relating to the Princess Wanyana. The mother's heart dilated with pride every time she saw her son, and she contrived in various ways to lengthen the interview. And each time he returned to his home he carried away some gift from Wanyana, such as leopard-skins, strings of beast claws, beads, and crocodile-teeth, girdles of white monkey-skin, parcels of ground ochre, or camwood, or rare shells, to show Mugema and his wife. And often he used to say, "Wanyana bade me ask you to accept this gift from her as a token of her esteem," showing them similar articles.

His mother's presents to him in a short time enabled him to purchase two fine large dogs, one was black as charcoal, which was named by him Msigissa, or "Darkness," the other was white as a cotton tuft, and called Sema-gimbi, or "Wood-burr." You must know that it is because of the dog Darkness, that the Baboon clan of Uganda became so attached to black dogs, by which they perpetuate the memory of Kimyera.

When he had become the owner of Darkness and Wood-burr, he began to absent himself from home for longer periods, leaving the herds in charge of the herdsmen. He explored the plains, and hills, and woods to a great distance from his home. Sometimes he would be absent for weeks, causing great anxiety to his kind foster-parents. The further he went the more grew his passion to know what lay beyond the furthest ridge he saw, which, when discovered, he would be again tempted to explore another that loomed in the far distance before him. With every man he met he entered into conversation, and obtained a various knowledge of things of interest relating to the country, the people, and the chiefs. In this manner before many months he had a wide knowledge of every road and river, village and tribe, in the neighbouring lands.

On his return from these daring excursions, he would be strictly questioned by Mugema and his wife as to what he had been doing, but he evaded giving the entire truth by rehearsing the hunting incidents that attended his wanderings, so that they knew not the lands he had seen, nor the distances that he travelled. However, being uneasy in their minds they communicated to Wanyana all that was related to them and all they suspected. Wanyana then sought permission to pay a visit to the potter and his wife, and during the visit she asked Kimyera, "Pray tell me, my son, where do you travel on these long journeys of your to seek for game?"

"Oh! I travel far through woods, and over grassy hills and plains."

"But is it in the direction of sunrise, or sunset, is it north or is it south of here?"

To which he replied, "I seek game generally in the direction where the sun rises."

"Ah!" said Wanyana. "In that way lies Ganda, where your father lives, and where he came in former days to exchange cattle for salt and hoes."

"My father! What may be my father's name, mother?"

"Kalimera."

"And where did he live?"

"His village is called Willimera, and is near the town of Bakka."

"Bakka! I know the town, for in some of my journeys I entered a long way into Uganda, and have chased the leopard in the woods that border the stream called Myanja, and over the plains beyond the river many an antelope has fallen a victim to my spear."

"It is scarcely credible, my son."

"Nay, but it is true, mother."

"Then you must have been near Willimera in that case, and it is a pity that you should not have seen your father, and been received by him."

A few days later Kimyera slung his knitted haversack over his shoulder, and with shield, two spears, and his faithful dogs Darkness and Wood-burr, he strode out of the potter's house, and set his face once more towards the Myanja river. At the first village across the stream he questioned the natives if they knew Willimera, and was told that it was but eight hours east. The next day he arrived, and travelled round the village, and rested that night at the house of one of the herdsmen of Kalimera. He made himself very agreeable to his host, and from him he received the fullest information of all matters relating to his father.

The next day he began his return to Unyoro, which he reached in two weeks. He told Mugema and his foster-mother of his success, and they sent a messenger to apprise Wanyana that Kimyera had returned home.

Wanyana, impatient to learn the news, arrived that night at Mugema's house, and implored Kimyera to tell her all that he had heard and seen.

"In brief, it is this," replied Kimyera. "I now know to a certainty where Kalimera lives. I have gone round the village, I know how many natives are in it, how many herds of cattle, and how many herdsmen and slaves he has. Kalimera is well. All these I learned from one of his chief herdsmen with whom I rested a night. I came here straight to let you and my foster-parents know it."

"It is very well, my son. Now, Mugema, it is time to move," she said to the potter. "Uni daily becomes more intolerable to me. I never have yet mated with him as his wife, and I have been true to the one man who seemed to me to be the comeliest of his kind. Now that I know Kalimera lives, my heart has gone to him, though my body is here. Mugema, speak, my friend."

"Wanyana, my wit is slow and my tongue is heavy. You know my circumstances. I have one wife, but many cattle. The two cows, Namala and Nakaombeh, you gavest me first, I possess still. Their milk has always been abundant and sweet. Namala has sufficed to nourish Kimyera into perfect lustiness and strength. Nakaombeh gives more than will feed my wife and me. Let Kimyera take his flute, his dogs, Darkness and Wood-burr, his spears and shield. Sebarija, my cowherd, who taught Kimyera the flute, will also take his flute and staff, and drive Namala and Nakaombeh. My wife will carry a few furs, some of the spoils won by Kimyera's prowess. And, I and my family will follow Wanyana."

"A true friend you have been to me and mine, Mugema! We will leave before dawn. In Willimera you shall receive tenfold what you leave here. The foundling of the clay-pit has grown tall and strong, and at last he has found the way to his father and his father's kindred."

And as Wanyana advised, the journey was undertaken that night, and before the sun arose Wanyana, Mugema and his wife, the slave Sebarija driving the two cows, Namala and Nakaombeh, were far on their way eastward, Kimyera and his two dogs, Darkness and Wood-burr, preceding the emigrants and guiding the way.

The food they took with them sustained them for two days, but on the third day they saw a lonely buffalo, and Kimyera, followed by Mugema and Sebarija, chased him. The buffalo was uncommonly wild, and led them a long chase, far out of sight of the two women.

Then Mugema reflected that they had done wrong in thus leaving the two women alone, and called out to Sebarija to hurry back, and to look after the women and two cows. Not long after, Darkness fastened his fangs in the buffalo, until Wood-burr came up and assisted him to bring it to the ground, and there they held him until Kimyera gave him his death-stroke. The two men loaded themselves with the meat, and returned to the place where they had left, but alas! they found no traces of the two women, nor of Sebarija and the two cows.

Day after day Kimyera and Mugema hunted all around the country for news of the missing party, until, finally, to their great sorrow, they were obliged to abandon the search, and came to the conclusion that it was best for them to continue their journey and trust to chance for the knowledge they desired.

Near Ganda another buffalo was sighted by Kimyera, and, bidding Mugema remain at the first house he came to, he went after it with his dogs. The buffalo galloped far, and near noon he stood still under the shelter of a rock. Kimyera bounded to the top, and, exerting all his strength, he shot his spear clean through the back of the animal. That rock is still shown to strangers as the place where Kimyera killed the first game in Uganda, and even the place where he stood may be seen by the marks of his feet which were, impressed on it. While resting on the rock he saw a woman pass nearby with a gourd of water. He called out to her, and begged for a drop to allay his thirst. She smilingly complied, as the stranger was comely and his manner pleasant. They entered into conversation, during which he learned that she belonged to Ganda, and served as maid to Queen Naku, wife of Sebwana, and that Naku was kind to strangers, and was famed for her hospitality to them.

"Do you think she will be kind to me?" asked Kimyera. "I am a native of Unyoro, and I am seeking a house where I may rest."

To which the maid replied, "It is the custom of Naku, and, indeed, of all the princes of Ganda, to entertain the stranger since, in the far olden times, the first prince settled in this land in which he was a stranger. But what may that be which is secured in your girdle?"

"That is a reed flute on which I imitate when alone the songs of such birds as sound sweetest to me."

"And are you clever at it?" asked the maid.

"Be you judge," he said, and forthwith blew on his flute until the maid marvelled greatly.

When he had ended, she clapped her hands gaily and said,

"You will be more than welcome to Naku and her people. Haste and follow me that I may show you to her, for your fortune is made."

"Nay. I have a companion not far from here, and I must not lose him. But you may say you have met a stranger who, when he has found his friend, will present himself before Queen Naku and Sebwana before sunset."

The maid withdrew and Kimyera rose, and cutting a large portion of the meat he retraced his steps, and sought and found Mugema, to whom he told all his adventures.

After washing the stains of travel and refreshing themselves, they proceeded into the village to the residence of the queen and her consort Sebwana. Naku was prepared by the favourable reports of the maid to receive Kimyera kindly, but when she saw his noble proportions and handsome figure she became violently in love with him, and turning to Sebwana she said, "See now, we have guests of worth and breeding. They must have travelled from a far land, for I have heard of no tribe which could boast of such a youth as this. Let us receive him and his old friend nobly. Let a house close by our own be made ready for his lodging, and let it be furnished with abundance of food, with banana wine and milk, bananas and yams, water and fuel, and let nothing be lacking to show our esteem for them." Sebwana gave orders accordingly and proceeded to select a fit house as a lodging for the guests.

Then Naku said, "I hear that you are skilled in music. If that is the instrument in your girdle with which you have delighted my maid, I should be pleased to hear you."

"Yes, Queen Naku, it is my flute, and if my music will delight you, my best efforts are at your service."

Then Kimyera, kneeling on the leopard-skins placed for the convenience of himself and Mugema, took out his flute, and after one or two flourishes, poured forth such melodious sounds that Naku, unable to keep her eyes open, closed them and lay down with panting breasts, while her senses were filled as it were with dreams of happier lands, and faces of brighter people than ever she knew in real life. As he varied the notes, so varied the gladsome visions of her mind. When the music gently vibrated on her ears, her body palpitated under the influence of the emotions which swayed her. When they became more enlivened she tossed her arms about, and laughed convulsively, and when the notes took a solemn tone, she sighed and wept as though all her friends had left her only their tender memory.

Grieved that Naku should suffer, Kimyera woke the queen from her sorrowful condition with tones that soon started her to her feet, and lo, all at once, those who were present joined in the lively dance, and nothing but gay laughter was heard from them. Oh, it was wonderful what quick changes came over people as they heard the flute of Kimyera. When he ceased people began to look at one another in a foolish and confused way, as though something very strange had happened to them.

But Naku quickly recovered, and went to Kimyera, smiling and saying, "It is for you to command, O Kimyera. To resist your flute would be impossible. Again welcome to Ganda, and we shall see if we cannot keep you and your flute amongst us."

She conducted Kimyera and his foster-father Mugema to their house. She examined carefully the arrangements made by the slaves, and when she found anything amiss she corrected it with her own hands. Before she parted from them she called Mugema aside, and questioned him further respecting the youth, by which means she obtained many interesting particulars concerning him.

On arriving at her own house she called all the pages of the court to her, and gave orders that if Sebwana told them to convey such and such things to the strangers next day, that none of them should do so, but carry them to the rear court where only women were admitted.

In consequence of this command Mugema and Kimyera found themselves deserted next day, and not one person went near them. Mugema therefore sought an interview the day after with Queen Naku and said, "The custom of this country seems strange to us, O Queen. On the first day we came your favours showered abundance on us, but on the next not a single person showed his face to us. Had we been in a wilderness we could not have been more alone. It is possible that we may have offended you unknown to ourselves. Pray acquaint us with our offence, or permit us to depart at once from Ganda."

"Nay, Mugema, I must ask you to be patient. Food you shall have in abundance, through my women, and much more is in store for you. But come, I will visit the young stranger, and you shall lead me to him."

Kimyera had been deep in thought ever since he had parted from Naku, and he had not observed what Mugema had complained of, but on seeing Naku enter his house, he hasted and laid matting on the floor, and, covering it with leopard-skins, begged Naku to be seated on them. He brought fresh banana-leaves in his arms, and spread them near her, on which he arranged meat and salt, and bananas and clotted milk, and kneeled before her like a ready servitor.

Naku observed all his movements, her admiration for his person and graces of body becoming stronger every minute. She peeled a mellow banana and handed it to him, saying, "Let Kimyera taste and eat with me, and I will then know that I am in the house of a friend."

Kimyera accepted the gift with thanks, and ate the banana as though he had never eaten anything so delicious in his life. Then he also peeled a beautiful and ripe banana, and, presenting it to her on a fragment of green leaf with both hands, said to her, "Queen Naku, it is the custom of my country for the master of the house to wait upon his guests. Wherefore accept, O Queen, this banana as a token of friendship from the hands of Kimyera."

The queen smiled, bent forward with her eyes fixed on his own, and took the yellow fruit, and ate it as though such sweetness was not known in the banana land of Ganda.

When she had eaten she said, "List, Kimyera, and you, Mugema, listen well, for I am about to utter weighty words. In Ganda, since the death of my father, there has been no king. Sebwana is my consort by choice of the elders of the land, but in name only. He is really only my kate-kiro, my minister. But I am now old enough to choose a king for myself, and according to custom, I may do so. Wherefore I make known to you, Mugema, that I have already chosen my lord and husband, and he by due right must occupy the chair of my father, the old king who is dead. I have said to myself since the day before yesterday that my lord and husband shall be Kimyera."

Both Kimyera and Mugema prostrated themselves three times before Naku, and, after the youth had recovered from his confusion and surprise, he replied, "But, Queen Naku, have you thought what the people will say to this? May it not be that they will ask, `who is this stranger that he should reign over us?' and they will be angry with me and try to slay me?"

"Nay. For you are my father's brother's son, as Mugema told me, and my father having left no male heirs of his body, his daughter may, if she choose, ally herself with a son of his brother. Kalimera is a younger brother of my father. You see, therefore, that you, Kimyera, have a right to the king's chair, if I, Naku, will it to be so."

"And how, Naku, do you propose to act? In your cause my arm is ready to strike. You have but to speak."

"In this way. I will now leave you, for I have some business for Sebwana. When he has gone I will then send for you, and you, when you come to me, must say, `Naku, I have come. What can Kimyera do for Queen Naku?' And I will rise and say, `Kimyera, come and sit in your father's brother's chair.' And you will step forward, bow three times before me, then six times before the king's chair, and, with your best spear in hand and shield on arm, you will proceed to the king's chair, and turning to the people who will be present, say in a loud voice thus, 'People of Ganda, I am Kimyera, son of Kalimera, by Wanyana of Unyoro. I hereby declare that with her own free will I this day do take Naku, my father's brother's daughter, to wife, and seat myself in the king's chair. Let all obey, on pain of death, the king's word.'"

"It is well, Naku. Be it according to your wish," replied Kimyera.

Naku departed and proceeded in search of Sebwana. And, when she found him, she affected great distress and indignation.

"How is this, Sebwana? I gave orders that our guests should be tenderly cared for and supplied with every needful thing. But I find, on inquiring this morning, that all through yesterday they were left alone to wonder at our sudden disregard for their wants. Haste, my friend, and make amends for your neglect. Go to my fields and plantations, collect all that is choicest for our guests, lest, when they leave us, they will proclaim our unkindness."

Sebwana was amazed at this charge of neglect, and in anger hastened to find out the pages. But the pages, through Naku's good care, absented themselves, and could not be found. So that old Sebwana was obliged to depend upon a few unarmed slaves to drive the cattle and carry the choicest treasures of the queen's fields and plantations for the use of the strangers.

Sebwana having at last left the town, Naku returned to Kimyera, whom she found with a sad and disconsolate aspect.

"Why, what ails you, Kimyera?" she asked. "The chair is now vacant. Arm you and follow me to the audience court."

"Ah, Naku! I but now remembered that as yet I know not whether my mother and good nurse are alive or dead. They may be waiting for me anxiously somewhere near the Myanja, or their bones may be bleaching on one of the great plains we traversed in coming here."

"Nay, Kimyera, my lord, this is not a time for mourning. Bethink you of the present needs first. The chair of the king awaits you. Rise, and occupy it, and tomorrow all Ganda is at your service to find your lost mother and nurse. Come, delay not, lest Sebwana return and take vengeance on us all."

"Fear not, Naku, it was but a passing fit of grief which filled my mind. Sebwana must needs be strong and brave to dispossess me when Naku is on my side," saying which Kimyera dressed himself in war-costume, with a crown of cock's tail feathers on his head, a great leopard skin hanging from his neck down his back, a girdle of white monkey-skin round his waist, his body and face brilliantly painted with vermilion and saffron. He then armed himself with two bright shining spears of great length, and bearing a shield of dried elephant hide, which no ordinary spear could penetrate, he strode after Queen Naku towards the audience court in the royal palace. Mugema, somewhat similarly armed, followed his foster-son.

As Kimyera strode proudly on, the great drum of Ganda sounded, and its deep tones were heard far and wide. Immediately the populace, who knew well that the summons of the great drum announced an important event, hastily armed themselves, and filled the great court. Naku, the queen, they found seated in a chair alongside of the king's chair, which was now unfilled, and in front of her was a tall young stranger, who prostrated himself three times before the queen. He was then seen bowing six times before the empty king's chair. Rising to his feet, he stepped towards it, and afterwards faced the multitude, who were looking on wonderingly.

The young stranger, lifting his long spears and raising his shield in an attitude of defence, cried out aloud, so that all heard his voice, "People of Ganda! I am Kimyera, son of Kalimera, by Wanyana of Unyoro. I hereby declare that with her own free will I this day do take Naku, my father's brother's daughter, to wife, and seat myself in the king's chair. Let all obey, on pain of death, the king's word."

On concluding this address, he stepped back a pace, and gravely sat in the king's chair. A loud murmur rose from the multitude, and the shafts of spears were seen rising up, when Naku rose to her feet, and said, "People of Ganda, open your ears. I, Naku, the legitimate queen of Ganda, hereby declare that I have found my father's brother's son, and I, this day, of my own free will and great love for him, do take him for my lord and husband. By full right Kimyera fills the king's chair. I charge you all henceforth to be loyal to him, and him only."

As she ended her speech the people gave a great shout of welcome to the new king, and they waved their spears, and clashed them against their shields, thus signifying their willing allegiance to King Kimyera.

The next day great bodies of strong men were despatched in different directions for the king's mother and his nurse, and for Sebarija and the two cows, Namala and Nakaombeh. If alive they were instructed to convey them with honour and care to Ganda, and if any fatal misadventure had happened to them, their remains were to be borne with all due respect to the king.

Sebwana, meanwhile, had started for the plantations, and hearing the thunder of the great drum, divined that Naku had deposed him in favour of the young stranger. To assure himself of the fact, he sent a confidential slave to discover the truth of the matter, while he sought a place where he could await, unobserved, the return of his messenger. When his slave came back to him he learned what great event had occurred during his short absence, and that his power had been given to another. Knowing the fate attending those thus deposed, he secretly retired to the district that had given him birth, where he lived obscure and safe until he died at a good old age.

After some days Sebarija and Mugema's wife, and the two cows Namala and Nakaombeh, were found by the banks of Myanja, near a rocky hill which contained a cave, where they had retired to seek a dwelling-place until news could be found of Mugema and Kimyera. But Wanyana, the king's mother, while gathering fuel near the cave during the absence of Sebarija and the potter's wife, had been fatally wounded by a leopard, before her cries brought Sebarija to her rescue. A short time after she had been taken into the cave she had died of her wounds, and her body had been folded in such furs and covering as her friends possessed, that Kimyera, on his return, might be satisfied of the manner of her death.

Kimyera, accompanied by his wife Naku and old Mugema, set out from Ganda with a great escort to receive the long-lost couple and the remains of Wanyana. Mugema rejoiced to see his old wife once more, though he deeply regretted the loss of his friend the princess. As for the king, his grief was excessive, but Naku, with her loving ways, assisted him to bear his great misfortune. A period of mourning, for an entire moon, was enjoined on all the people, after which a great mound was built at Kagoma over the remains of the unfortunate princess, and Sebarija was duly installed as keeper of the monument. Ever since that day it has become the custom to bury the queen-mothers near the grave of Wanyana, and to appoint keepers of the royal cemetery in memory of Sebarija, who first occupied that post.

While he lived Sebarija was honoured with a visit, on the first day of every alternate moon, from Kimyera, who always brought with him a young buffalo as a gift to the faithful cowherd. During these days the king and Sebarija were accustomed to play their flutes together as they did in the old time, and their seats were on mats placed on top of the mound, while the escort and servants of the king and queen sat all around the foot of it, and this was the manner in which Wanyana's memory was honoured during her son's life.

Kimyera finally settled with Queen Naku at Birra, where he built a large town. Mugema and his wife, with their two cows Namala and Nakaombeh, lived near the palace for many years, until they died.

Darkness and Wood-burr accompanied the king on many a hunt in the plains bordering the Myanja, in the woods of Ruwambo, and along the lakelands which look towards Bussi, and they in their turn died and were honourably interred with many folds of bark-cloth. Queen Naku, after giving birth to three sons, died during the birth of her fourth child, and was buried with great honour near Birra, and finally, after living to a great old age, the hunter king, Kimyera, died, mourned by all his people.

The Hen And The Cat

This tale has been edited and adapted from Kate Douglas Wiggin and Nora Archibald Smith's collection, The Talking Beasts, A Book of Fable and Wisdom, and illustrated by Harold Nelson. The book was published in 1922.

A Cat arose in her house, went to a Hen and said to her, "Let us be friends!"

The Hen replied to the Cat, "Do you like me for a friend?"

The Cat said, "Yes," and went away.

After having been at home for a while, she sent her child to the Hen, saying, "Go and tell the Hen to rise up early tomorrow morning, and to come and accompany me to a neighbouring town."

The child arose, went to the Hen's house and saluted her.

The Hen arose, and asked it, "You child of the Cat, do you come to me in peace?"

The Cat's child replied, "I come in peace. My mother has sent me to you."

The Hen said to the Cat's child, "Say what your mother has sent you for. Let me know."

After the Cat's child had told it to the Hen, it said, "I will go," and the Cat's child set out and went home.

When it was gone the Hen arose, called a child of hers, and said, "Go and ask the Cat at what time we shall go to the neighbouring town?"

The child had already started, she called it back again, saying, "Come back, I will tell you something."

The child returned, and when it had come to its mother, she said to it, "When you go to the Cat, open your ears and hear well what she says, and come and tell me."

The child went to the Cat, and saluted her, and when the Cat arose and came out to it, the Hen's child was standing there. The Cat asked the Hen's child, "Why did your mother send you to me?"

The Hen's child said, "My mother said I must come and ask you how early we shall go to the neighbouring town?"

The Cat said to the Hen's child, "Go and tell your mother to arise and come at the cockcrowing. For what should eat her?"

The Hen's child returned to its mother, and said to her, "Behold I went to the Cat's place where you sent me, and am come back."

The Hen said to her child, "What did the Cat say? Let me hear what word she spoke?"

Her child answered and said to her, "My mother, the word which the Cat spoke is this, 'Go and tell your mother to come to me when the cock crows, that we may go. For what should eat her?'"

Its mother, the Hen, said to her child, "My child, lie down in your house, for I have heard what the Cat said."

The child of the Hen obeyed her mother, went and lay down, and also her mother lay down. They slept their sleep until the cock crowed. When the Cat heard the cock crow, she arose, got ready and waited for the Hen, thinking, "May she come that we may go!"

The cock crowed a second time, and the Cat looked out on the way where the Hen was to come from, thinking, "May she come that we may go!"

The Hen did not get up at home and day came on. When it became day, the Cat arose in her house, went to the Hen's home, and said to her, "Hen, you sent your child to me, and asked at what time you should rise up, and I said to your child, 'Go and tell your mother to come when the cock crows, that we may go.' Did it not tell you what I said ? Why are you are still sitting at home although it has become day?"

The Hen said to the Cat, "Sister Cat, if you wish to have me for a friend, I must never get up in my house and come out at night."

The Cat said to the Hen, "What are you afraid of that you say, 'I will never come out at night'? What is there in the way?"

The Hen listened to what the Cat said, got herself ready and called her children, saying, "Come and let us accompany the Cat to a neighbouring town!"

All the children arose and when they had set out on their way, the Cat went in front, and having gone on a little, she seized two of the children of the Hen, and the Hen saw that the cat was seizing two of her children. So she said to the Cat, "Sister Cat, we have scarcely set out on our way and you have seized two of my children!"

The Cat replied, "Your two children which I took have not strength enough to walk. Therefore did I take them to my bosom that we may go on."

The Hen said to the Cat, "If you act like this, then I and you must dissolve our friendship."

The Cat replied, "If you will not have a friend, I shall let you go home."

So, as the Hen began to go home, the Cat made a bound, and seized the Hen's head, whereupon the Hen cried for help. All the people of the town heard her, arose, ran, and when they came to the place, , the Cat was holding the Hen's head tight. When the Cat saw the people of the town, she left the Hen, ran away, and entered the forest.

There the Hen was standing and the people of the town said to her, "Foolish one, did you, a Hen, arise and go to befriend a Cat? If we had not heard your screams, and come to you, she would have killed you and carried away all your children into her forest."

The Hen said to the people of the town, "God bless you, you have taken me out of the Cat's mouth."

The people of the town said to her, "Today our Lord has delivered you, but for the future make no more friendship with the Cat. The Cat is too cunning for you, so beware of the Cat in future!"

I have heard old people say, that on that day the cats and the fowls dissolved their friendship.

The Legend Of The Leopardess And Her Two Servants, Dog And Jackal

This tale has been edited and adapted from Henry Morton Stanley's book, My Dark Companions, published in 1893 by Sampson, Lowe, Marston and Company, London.

Long ago, in the early age of Uganda, a leopardess, in want of a servant to do chores in her den, was solicited by a jackal to engage him to perform that duty. As Jackal had a very suspicious appearance, with his ears drawn back, and his furtive eyes, and a smile which always seemed to be a leer, the Leopardess consulted with Dog, whom she had lately hired as her steward, as to the propriety of trusting such a cunning-looking animal.

Dog trotted out to the entrance of the den to examine the stranger for himself, and, after close inspection of him, asked Jackal what work he could do. Jackal replied humbly and fawningly, and said that he could fetch water from the brook, collect fuel, sweep out the house, and was willing, if necessary, to cook now and then, as he was not a novice in the art of cooking. And, looking at Leopardess, he said, "I am very fond of cubs, and am very clever in nursing them."

Mistress Leopardess, on hearing this, seemed to be impressed with the abilities of Jackal, and, without waiting for the advice of Dog, engaged him at once, and said, "Jackal, you must understand that my custom is to feed my servants well. What is left from my table is so abundant that I have heard no complaints from any who have been with me. Therefore you need fear no starvation, but while you may depend upon being supplied with plenty of meat, the bones must not be touched. Dog shall be your companion, but neither he nor anyone else is permitted to touch the bones."

"I shall be quite content, Mistress Leopardess. Meat is good enough for me, and for good meat you may depend upon it I shall give good work."

The household of Mistress Leopardess was completed. She suffered no anxiety, and enjoyed herself in her own way. The chase was her great delight. The forest and plains were alive with game, and each morning at sunrise it was her custom to set out for the hunt, and scarcely a day passed but she returned with sufficient meat to fatten her household. Dog and Jackal expressed themselves delighted with the luscious repasts which they enjoyed, and a sleek roundness witnessed that they fared nobly. But as it frequently happens with people who have everything they desire, Dog, in a short while, became nicer and more fastidious in his tastes. He hankered after the bones which were forbidden him, and was heard to sigh deeply whenever Mistress Leopardess collected the bones and stored them in the interior, and his eyes became filled with tears as he eyed the rich morsels stowed away.

His feelings at last becoming intolerable, he resolved to appeal to his mistress one day, as she appeared to be in a more amiable mood than usual, and said, "Mistress, thanks to you, the house is always well supplied with meat, and none of your servants have any reason to think that they will ever suffer the pangs of hunger. But, speaking for myself, mistress mine, I wish for one thing more, if you will be so good as to grant it."

"And what may that be, greedy one?" asked Leopardess.

"Well, you see, mistress, I fear you do not understand the nature of dogs very well. You must know dogs delight in marrow, and often prefer it to meat. The latter by itself is good, but however plentiful and good it may be, without an occasional morsel of marrow it is apt to pall. Dogs also love to sharpen their teeth on bones and screw their tongues within the holes for the sake of the rich juice. By itself, marrow would not fatten my ribs, but meat with marrow is most delectable. Now, good mistress, seeing that I have been so faithful in your service, so docile and prompt to do your bidding, will you not be gracious enough to let me gnaw the bones and extract the marrow?"

"No," roared Leopardess decisively, "that is positively forbidden, and let me warn you that the day you venture to do so, a strange event will happen suddenly, which shall have most serious consequences to you and to all in this house.

"And you, Jackal, bear what I say well in mind," she continued, turning to that servile subordinate.

"Yes, mistress. I will, most certainly. Indeed, I do not care very greatly for bones," said Jackal, "and I hope my friend and mate, Dog, will remember, good mistress, what you say."

"I hear, mistress," replied Dog, "and since it is your will, I must needs obey."

The alarming words of Leopardess had the effect of compelling Dog and Jackal for a while to desist from even thinking of marrow, and the entreaty of Dog appeared to be forgotten by Leopardess, though Jackal was well aware, by the sparkles in the covetous eyes of Dog when any large bone was near him, how difficult it was for him to resist the temptation. Day after day Leopardess sallied out from her den, and returned with kids, goats, sheep, antelopes, zebra, and often a young giraffe, and one day she brought a great buffalo to her household, and cubs and servants came running to greet her, and praise her successful hunting.

On this day Dog undertook to prepare the dinner. The buffalo-meat was cooked in exquisite fashion, and when it was turned out of the great pot, steaming and trickling over everywhere with juice, Dog caught sight of a thigh-bone and yellow marrow glistening within. The temptation to steal it was too great to resist. He contrived to drop the bone back again into the pot, furnished the tray quickly with the meat, and sent Jackal with it to Leopardess, saying that he would follow with the kabobs and stew. As soon as Jackal had gone out of the kitchen, Dog whipped the bone out of the pot and slyly hid it. Then, loading stew and kabobs on a tray, he hurried after Jackal, and began officiously bustling about, fawning upon Leopardess, stroking the cubs as he placed them near their mamma around the smoking trays, scolding Jackal for his laziness, and bidding him hurry up with the steaks. All of which, of course, was due to his delight that he had a rare treat in store for himself snugly hidden away.

Leopardess was pleased to bestow a good many praises upon Dog's cooking, and the cubs even condescended to smile their approval for the excellent way in which their wants were supplied.

Towards evening Mistress Leopardess went out again, but not before reminding Jackal of his duties towards the cubs, and bidding him, if it were late before she returned, on no account to leave them alone in the dark. Dog smilingly followed his mistress to the door, wishing her, in the most fawning manner, every success. When he thought that his mistress was far enough, and Jackal quite occupied with the cubs, Dog hastened to the kitchen, and, taking up his bone, stole out of the house, and carried it to a considerable distance off. When he thought he was safe from observation, he lay down, and, placing the bone between his paws, was about to indulge his craving for marrow, when the bone was seen to fly away back to the den. Wondering at such a curious event, furious at his disappointment, and somewhat alarmed as he remembered Leopardess's warning words, he rushed after it, crying, "Jackal, Jackal! Shut the door. The bone is coming. Jackal, please shut the door."

Jackal fortunately was at the door, squatting on his haunches, having just arrived there from nursing the cubs, and saw the bone coming straight towards him, and Dog galloping and crying out to shut the door. Quickly perceiving that Dog had at last allowed his appetite to get the better of his duty, and having, truth to say, a fellow-feeling for his fellow-servant, Jackal closed the door just in time, for in about a second afterwards the bone struck the door with a tremendous force, dinting it deeply.

Then Jackal turned to Dog, on recovering from his astonishment, and angrily asked, "Oh, Dog, do you know what you are doing? Have you no sense? You came near being the death of me this time.

I'll tell you what, my friend, if Mistress Leopardess hears of this, your life is not worth a feather."

"Now don't, please, good Jackal, don't say anything of it this time. The fright I have had is quite sufficient to keep me from touching a bone again."

"Well, I am sure I don't wish you any harm, but for your life's sake do not be so dull as to forget the lesson you have learned."

Soon after Leopardess returned with a small antelope for the morrow's breakfast, and cried out to Jackal, as was usual with her on returning from the hunt, "Now, my Jackal, bring the cubs here. My dugs are so heavy. How are the little ones?"

"Ah, very well, ma'am, poor little dears, they have been in a sweet sleep ever since you went out."

A few days later, Leopardess brought a fat young zebra, and Jackal displayed his best skill in preparing it for dinner. Dog also assisted with wise suggestions in the preparation of certain auxiliaries to the feast. When all was ready, Dog laid the table, and as fast as Jackal brought the various dishes, Dog arranged them in the most tempting manner on fresh banana-leaves, spread over the ample plateau. Just before sitting down to the meal, Leopardess heard a strange noise without, and bounded to the door, growling angrily at being disturbed. Dog instantly seized the opportunity of her absence to extract a great bone from one of the trays, and stowed it in a recess in the wall of the passage leading from the kitchen. Presently Leopardess came back, and when the cubs were brought the meal was proceeded with in silence. When they had all eaten enough, the good effect of it was followed by commendations upon the cooking, and the juicy flavour of the meat, and how well Jackal had prepared everything. Neither was Dog forgotten by the mistress and her young ones, and he was dismissed with the plenteous remnants of the feast for himself and mate, with the courteous hope that they would find enough and to spare.

In the afternoon Leopardess, having refreshed herself with a nap, sallied out once more, enjoining Jackal, as she was going out of the den, to be attentive to her little ones during her absence.

While his friend Jackal proceeded towards the cubs, Dog surreptitiously abstracted his bone from the cavity in the passage wall, and trotted out unobserved. When he had arrived at a secluded place, he lay down, and, seizing the bone between his paws, was about to give it a preliminary lick, when again, to his dismay and alarm, the bone flew up and away straight for the door. Dog loped after it as fast as his limbs could carry him, crying out, "Oh, Jackal, Jackal, good Jackal! Shut the door. Hurry up. Shut the door, good Jackal."

Again Jackal heard his friend's cry, and sprang up to close the door, and the instant he had done so the bone struck it with dreadful force. Turning to the crestfallen and panting Dog, Jackal said sternly, "You are a nice fellow, you are. I well see the end of you. Now listen, this is the last time that I shall help you, my friend. The next time you take a bone you will bear the consequences, so look out."

"Come, Jackal, now don't say any more. I will not look at a bone again, I make you a solemn promise."

"Keep to that, and you will be safe," replied Jackal.

Poor Dog, however, was by no means able to adhere to his promise, for a few days afterwards Leopardess brought a fat young eland, and he found an opportunity to abstract a fine marrowbone before serving his generous mistress. Late in the afternoon, after dinner and siesta, Leopardess, before going out, repeated her usual charge to

Jackal, and while the faithful servant retired to his nursing duties, greedy Dog sought his bone, and stole out to the forest with it. This time he went further than usual. Jackal meanwhile finding the cubs indisposed for sleep, led them out to the door of the den, where they frisked and gambolled about with all the liveliness of cubhood. Jackal was sitting at a distance from the door when he heard the cries of Dog. "Oh, Jackal, Jackal, good Jackal! Shut the door quickly. Look out for the bone. It is coming. Shut the door quickly."

"Ha, ha! Friend Dog! At it again, eh?" said the Jackal. "It is too late, too late, Doggie dear, the cubs are in the doorway." He looked up, however, and saw the bone coming with terrific speed. He heard it whiz as it flew close over his head, and almost immediately after it struck one of the cubs, killing it instantly.

Jackal appeared to quickly realise the consequences of Dog's act, and his own carelessness, and feeling that henceforth Leopardess's den would be no home for him, he resolved to escape. Just then Dog came up, and when he saw the dead cub he set up a piteous howl.

"Aye," said Jackal. "You fool, you begin to see what your greed has brought upon us all. Howl on, my friend, but you will howl differently when Mistress Leopardess discovers her dead cub. Consider how all this will end. Our mighty mistress, if she catches you, will make mincemeat of you. Neither may I stay longer here. My home must be a burrow in the wild wood, or in the rocky cave in future. What will you do?"

"I, Jackal? I know not yet. Go, if you will, and starve yourself. I trust to find a better home than a cramped burrow, or the cold shelter of a cave. I love warmth, and kitchen fires, and the smell of roast meats too well to trust myself to the chilly covert you propose to seek, and my coat is too fine for rough outdoor life."

"Hark!" cried Jackal. "Do you hear that? That is the mistress's warning note! Fare you well, Doggie. I shall dream of you tonight lying stark under the paw of the Leopardess."

Jackal waited to say no more, but fled from the scene, and from that day to this Jackal has been a vagabond. He loves the darkness, and the twilight. It is at such times you hear his yelp. He is very selfish and cowardly. He has not courage enough to kill anything for himself, but prefers to wait, licking his chops, until the lion or the leopard, who has struck the game, has gorged himself.

As for Dog he was sorely frightened, but after a little deliberation he resolved to face the matter out until he was certain of the danger. He conveyed the cubs, living and dead, quickly within, and then waited with well-dissembled anxiety the coming of his mistress.

Leopardess shortly arrived, and was met at the door by the obsequious Dog with fawning welcome.

"Where is Jackal?" asked Leopardess as she entered.

"I regret to say he has not returned yet from a visit which he said he was bound to pay his friends and family, whom he had not seen for so long," replied Dog.

"Then you go and bring my little ones to me. Poor little dears, they must be hungry by this, and my milk troubles me," commanded the mistress.

Dog departed readily, thinking to himself, "I am in for it now." He soon returned, bearing one of the cubs, and laid it down.

"Bring the other one, quickly," cried Leopardess.

"Yes, ma'am, immediately," he said.

Dog took the same cub up again, but in a brief time returned with it. The cub, already satisfied, would not touch the teat.

"Go and bring the other one, stupid," cried Leopardess, observing that it would not suck.

"This is the other one, mistress," he replied.

"Then why does it not suck?" she asked.

"Perhaps it has not digested its dinner."

"Where is Jackal? Has he not yet returned? Jackal!" she cried. "Where are you, Jackal?"

From the jungle out-doors Jackal shrilly yelped, "Here I am, mistress!"

"Come to me this instant," commanded Leopardess.

"Coming, mistress, coming," responded Jackal's voice faintly, for at the sound of her call he had been alarmed and was trotting off.

"Why, what can be the matter with the brute, trifling with me in this manner? Here, Dog, take this cub to the crib."

Dog hastened to obey, but Leopardess, whose suspicions had been aroused, quietly followed him as he entered the doorway leading into the inner recess of the house where the crib was placed. Having placed the living near the dead cub in the crib, Dog turned to leave, when he saw his dreaded mistress in the doorway, gazing with fierce distended eyes, and it flashed on him that she had discovered the truth, and fear adding speed to his limbs he darted like an arrow between her legs, and rushed out of the den. With a loud roar of fury Leopardess sprang after him, Dog running for dear life. His mistress was gaining upon him, when Dog turned aside, and ran round the trees. Again Leopardess was rapidly drawing near, when Dog shot straight away and increased the distance between them a little. Just as one would think Dog had no hope of escaping from his fierce mistress, he saw a wart-hog's burrow, into which he instantly dived. Leopardess arrived at the hole in the ground as the tail of Dog disappeared from her sight. Being too large of body to enter, she tore up the entrance to the burrow, now and then extending her paw far within to feel for her victim. But the burrow was of great length, and ran deep downwards, and she was at last obliged to desist from her frantic attempts to reach the runaway.

Reflecting awhile, Leopardess looked around and saw Monkey nearby, sitting gravely on a branch watching her.

"Come down, Monkey," she imperatively commanded, "and sit by this burrow and watch the murdering slave who is within, while I procure materials to smoke him out."

Monkey obeyed, and descending the tree, took his position at the mouth of the burrow. But it struck him that should Dog venture out, his strength would be unable to resist him. He therefore begged Leopardess to stay a moment, while he went to bring a rock with which he could block the hole securely. When this was done Leopardess said, "Now stay here, and do not stir until I return. I will not be long, and when I come I will fix him."

Leopardess, leaving the burrow in charge of Monkey, commenced to collect a large quantity of dry grass, and then proceeded to her house to procure fire wherewith to light it, and suffocate Dog with the smoke.

Dog, soon after entering the burrow had turned himself round and faced the hole, to be ready for all emergencies. He had heard Leopardess give her orders to Monkey, had heard Monkey's plans for blockading him, as well as the threat of Leopardess to smoke him out. There was not much hope for him if he stayed longer.

After a little while he crept close to the rock that blocked his exit, and whispered, "Monkey, let me out, there's a good fellow."

"It may not be," replied Monkey.

"Ah, Monkey, why are you so cruel? I have not done any harm to you. Why do you stand guard over me to prevent my escape?"

"I am simply obeying orders, Dog. Leopardess said, 'Stay here and watch, and see that Dog does not escape;' and I must do so or harm will come to me, as you know."

Then said Dog, "Monkey, I see that you have a cruel heart, too, though I thought none but the Leopard kind could boast of that. May you feel some day the deep despair I feel in my heart. Let me say one word more to you before I die. Put your head close to me that you may hear it."

Monkey, curious to know what the last word could be about, put his face close between the rock and the earth and looked in, upon which Dog threw so much dust and sand into his cunning eyes as almost to blind him.

Monkey staggered back from the entrance, and while knuckling his eyes to nib the sand out, Dog put his fore-feet against the rock and soon rolled it away. Then, after a hasty view around, Dog fled like the wind from the dangerous spot.

Monkey, after clearing his eyes from the dirt thrown in them, and reviewing his position, began to be concerned as to his own fate. It was not long before his crafty mind conceived that it would be a good idea to place some soft nuts within the burrow, and roll back the stone into its place.

When Leopardess returned with the fire she was told that Dog was securely imprisoned within, upon which she piled the grass over the burrow and set fire to it.

Presently a crackling sound was heard within.

"What can that be?" demanded Leopardess.

"That must surely be one of Dog's ears that you heard exploding," replied Monkey.

After a short time another crackling sound was heard.

"And what is that?" asked Leopardess.

"Ah, that must be the other ear of course," Monkey answered.

But as the fire grew hotter and the heat increased within there were a great many of these sounds heard, at which Monkey laughed gleefully and cried, "Ah ha! Do you hear? Dog is splitting to pieces now. Oh, he is burning up finely. Every bone in his body is cracking. Ah, but it is a cruel death, though, is it not?"

"Let him die," fiercely cried Leopardess. "He killed one of my young cubs, one of the loveliest little fellows you ever saw."

Both Leopardess and Monkey remained at the burrow until the fire had completely died out, then the first said, "Now, Monkey, bring me a long stick with a hook at the end of it, that I may rake Dog's bones out and feast my eyes upon them."

Monkey hastened to procure the stick, with which the embers were raked out, when Leopardess exclaimed, "What a queer smell this is! It is not at all like what one would expect from a burnt dog."

"Ah," replied Monkey, "Dog must be completely burnt by this. Of that there can be no doubt. Did you ever burn a dog before that you know the smell of its burnt body so well?"

"No," said the Leopardess, "but this is not like the smell of roast meat. Rake out all the ashes that I may see the bones and satisfy myself."

Monkey, compelled to do as he was commanded, put in his stick, and drew out several half-baked nuts, the shells of which were cracked and gaping open. These Leopardess no sooner saw than she seized Monkey, and furiously cried, "You wretch, you have deceived and trifled with me! You have permitted the murderer of my cub to escape, and your life shall now be the forfeit for his."

"Pardon, mighty Leopardess, but let me ask how you propose to slay me?"

"Why, miserable slave, how else should I kill you but with one scratch of my claws?"

"Nay, then, great Queen, my blood will fall on your head and smother you. It is better for yourself that you should toss me up above that thorny bough, so that when I fall upon it the thorns may penetrate my heart and kill me."

No sooner had Monkey ended, than fierce Leopardess tossed Monkey upward as he had directed, but the latter seized the bough and sat up, and from this he sprang upward into another still higher, and there from branch to branch and from tree to tree until he was safe from all possible pursuit.

Leopardess perceived that another of her intended victims had escaped, and was furious with rage. "Come down this instant," she cried to Monkey, hoping he would obey her.

"Nay, Leopardess. It has been told me, and the forest is full of the report, that your cruelty has driven from you Jackal and Dog, and that they will never serve you again. Cruel people never can reckon upon friends. I and my tribe, so long servants to you, will henceforth be strangers to you. Fare you well."

A great rustling was heard in the trees overhead as Monkey and his tribe migrated away from the district of the cruel Leopardess who, devoured with rage, was obliged to depart with not one of her vengeful thoughts gratified.

As she was returning to her den, Leopardess remembered the Oracle, who was her friend, who would no doubt, at her solicitations, reveal the hiding-places of Jackal and Dog. She directed her steps to the cave of the Oracle, who was a nondescript practising witchcraft in the wildest part of the district.

To this curious being she related the story of the murder of her cub by Jackal and Dog, and requested him to inform her by what means she could discover the criminals and wreak her vengeance on them.

The Oracle replied, "Jackal has gone into the wild wood, and he and his family henceforward will always remain there, to degenerate in time into a suspicious and cowardly race. Dog has fled to take his shelter in the home of man, to be his companion and friend, and to serve man against you and your kind. But lest you accuse me of ill-will to you, I will tell you how you may catch Dog if you are clever and do not allow your temper to exceed your caution.

"Not far off is a village belonging to one of the human tribes, near which there is a large ant-hill, where moths every morning flit about in the sunshine of the early day. About the same time Dog leaves the village to sport and gambol and chase the moths. If you can find a lurking-place not far from it, where you can lie silently in wait, Dog may be caught by you in an unwary moment while at his daily play. I have spoken."

Leopardess thanked the Oracle and retired brooding over its advice. That night the moon was very clear and shining bright, and she stole out of her den, and proceeding due west as she was directed, in a few hours she discovered the village and the ant-hill described by the Oracle. Near the mound she also found a thick dense bush, which was made still more dense by the tall wild grass surrounding it. In the depths of this she crouched, waiting for morning.

At dawn the village wherein men and women lived was astir, and at sunrise the gates were opened. A little later Dog signalled himself by his well-known barks as he came out to take his morning's exercise. Unsuspicious of the presence of his late dread mistress he bounded up the hill and began to circle around, chasing the lively moths. Leopardess, urged by her anger, did not wait until Dog, tired with his sport, would of his own accord stray among the bushes, but uttering a loud roar sprang out from her hiding-place. Dog, warned by her voice, which he well knew, put his tail between his legs and rushed through the open gates and alarmed his new masters, who came pouring from their houses with dreadful weapons in their hands, who chased her, and would have slain her had she not bounded over the fence. Thus Leopardess lost her last chance of revenging the death of her cub, but as she was creeping homeward her mortification was so great that she vowed to teach her young eternal hostility towards Dog and all his tribe. Dog also, convinced that his late mistress was one who nourished an implacable resentment when offended, became more cautious, and a continued life with his new masters increased his attachment for them.

When he finally married, and was blessed with a progeny, he taught his pups various arts by which they might ingratiate themselves more and more with the human race. He lived in comfort and affluence to a good old age, and had the satisfaction to see his family grow more and more in the estimation of their generous masters, until dogs and men became inseparable companions.

Leopardess and her cub removed far away from the house associated with her misfortune, but though Time healed the keen sore of her bereavement by blessing her annually with more cubs, her hate for Dog and his kind was lasting and continues to this day. And thus it was that the friendly fellowship which reigned between the forest animals during the golden age of Uganda was broken for ever.

For proof of the truth of what I have said consider the matter in your own minds. Regard the Ape who, upon the least alarm springs up the tree, and stays not until he has secured himself far from reach. Think of the Jackal in his cheerless solitude deep in the bowels of the earth, or in the farthest rocky recess that he can discover, ever on the watch against some foe, too full of distrust to have a friend, the most selfish and cowardly of the forest community. The Leopard is the enemy at all times, night and day, of every animal, unless it be the lion and the elephant. As for the Dog, where is the man who is not acquainted with his fidelity, his courage in time of danger, his watchful care of his interests by night, and his honest love for the family which feeds him? My story is here ended.

The Stork And The Toad

This tale has been edited and adapted from Kate Douglas Wiggin and Nora Archibald Smith's collection, The Talking Beasts, A Book of Fable and Wisdom, and illustrated by Harold Nelson. The book was published in 1922.

A Stork went and laid eggs in a tree, then brooded and hatched young ones. Then she left and went to seek food for her little ones, but she did not get any food, and all her little ones were crying for hunger. The Stork did not know what to do. So she arose one day, went to her friend, and said, "My friend, I am come to you."

Her friend said, "Why have you come to me?"

She replied to her friend, "My children are hungry, and I have no food. Therefore, I have come to you. Teach me a device!"

Her friend said to her, "Arise in the morning, go to the brook, and see whether there are Toads in it. Then come back, and on the following morning go again, and lie down by the side of the brook. Stretch out your legs and your wings, shut your eyes, keep quite silent, and lie in one place until the Toads come out in the morning, and, after seeing you, go home and call all their people to come, to take you by the wing and to drag you away. But do not you speak to them. Stay perfectly quiet."

She listened to what her friend said, and at night-quiet she arose, and went to the brook, when all the Toads were singing, but as soon as they saw her, they went and hid themselves at the bottom of the water. So the Stork went home and slept, and having slept she arose up early and went back again to the brook, without being observed by the Toads. She went softly, and lay down by the side of the water, pretending to be dead. She stretched out her legs, her wings, and her mouth, and shut her eyes. Thus she lay, until at break of day when one Toad arose, and, finding that it was day, came forth and saw the Stork lying there as if dead. He went back, and called all the Toads, saying, "Come, behold, I have seen something dead lying at the door of our house, and when I had seen it I came back to call you."

So all the Toads arose and followed him, and having come out, they all saw a Stork lying at the door of their house, but they did not know that the Stork was more cunning than themselves. They returned home, called a council together and said, "What shall we do? Someone who came, we do not know where, has died before the gate of our town."

All their great men answered, and said, "Arise all of you, go out, drag this dead body far away, and leave it there." So they all arose, went out, and, taking the Stork by its wings and legs, dragged it away. The Stork was cunning. She saw them without their knowing it. They sang, as they dragged her away:

"Drag her and leave her!

Drag her and leave her!"

The Stork did not speak to them, as they all dragged her away, although she saw them. Now, when they had carried her far away, the Stork opened her eyes,. When the Toads saw this they all began to run away. As soon as the Stork saw that the Toads had begun to run away, she arose, and pursued them. Having overtaken one, she took and swallowed it, and went on taking and swallowing them. The Toads kept running, but by the time they would have got home the Stork had swallowed them all, one by one. She filled her bag, and then started on her way home.

As soon as her children saw her, they all ran to their mother, saying, "Our mother has brought us food." When they came their mother threw all the Toads in her bag down to her children, and her children ate them, so that their hunger was appeased.

The Stork arose, went to her friend, and said, "My friend, what you told me yesterday is excellent. I went and lay down by the side of the brook, and when the Toads saw me in the morning, they thought I was dead. They came, dragged me along, and when they had carried me far away, not knowing that I was wiser than they and thinking that I was dead, I opened my eyes to look at them. But on seeing me open my eyes, they all began to run away. Then I arose, pursued them, and when I had overtaken one, I took and swallowed it. And when I had overtaken a second I took and swallowed it. So by the time they would have reached home I had swallowed them all, and filled my bag with them. I brought them to my children, and when my children were around me, I threw the Toads before them out of the bag and they ate them, that their hunger was appeased."

She also thanked her friend, saying, "God bless you. You have taught me an excellent trick."

Thus the Stork and her friend devised a plan, and thus they were able to maintain their children while the Toads were sitting in their houses. So now, when the Toads are croaking in a brook, and they see anyone come, they are all quite silent, supposing that a Stork is coming.

This fable of the Stork and Toads, which I heard, is now finished.

How The Dog Outwitted The Leopard

This tale has been edited and adapted from Henry Morton Stanley's book, My Dark Companions, published in 1893 by Sampson, Lowe, Marston and Company, London.

In the early time there was a dog and a leopard dwelling together in a cave like chums. They shared and fared alike. Exact half of everything and equal effort were the terms upon which they lived. Many and many a famous raid among the flocks and fowls in the human villages they made. The leopard was by far the strongest and boldest, and was most successful in catching prey. Dog lived so well on the spoils brought home by his friend that he became at last fat and lazy, and he began to dislike going out at night in the rain and cold dew, and to hide this growing habit from Leopard he had to be very cunning. He always invented some excuse or another to explain why he brought nothing to the common larder, and finally he hit upon a new plan of saving himself from the toil and danger.

Just before dusk one day, Leopard and Dog were sociably chatting together, when Leopard said that he intended that night to catch a fine fat black goat which he had observed in the nearest village to their den. He had watched him getting fatter every day, and he was bent upon bringing him home.

"Black is it?" cried Dog. "That is strange, for that is also the colour of the one I purposed to catch tonight."

The two friends slept until most of the night was gone, but when there were signs that morning was not far off they silently loped away to their work.

They parted at the village which Leopard had selected to rob, Dog whispering "Good luck" to him. Dog trotted off a little way and sneaked back to watch his friend.

Leopard stealthily surveying the tall fence, saw one place which he could leap over, and at one spring was inside the village. Snuffing about, he discovered the goat-pen, forced an entrance, and seizing his prize by the neck, drew it out. He then flung it over his shoulders, and with a mighty leap landed outside the fence.

Dog, who had watched his chance, now cried out in an affected voice, "Hi, hi, wake up! Leopard has killed the goat. There he is. Ah, ah! Kill him, kill him!"

Alarmed at the noise made, and hearing a rustle in the grass near him, Leopard was obliged to abandon his prize, and to save his own life, dropped the goat and fled.

Dog, chuckling loudly at the success of his ruse, picked the dead goat up, and trotted home to the den with it.

"Oh, see, Leopard!" cried he, as he reached the entrance, "What a fat goat I've got at my village. Is it not a heavy one? But where is yours? Did you not succeed after all?"

"Oh! I was alarmed by the owners in the village, who pursued me and yelled out, `Kill him, kill him!' and there was something rustling in the grass close by, and I thought that I was done for, but I dropped the goat and ran away. I dare say they have found the animal by this, and have eaten our meat. Never mind, though, better luck next time. I saw a fine fat white goat in the pen, which I am sure to catch tomorrow night."

"Well, I am very sorry, but cheer your heart. You shall have an equal share with me of this. Let us bestir ourselves to cook it."

They gathered sticks and made a fire, and began to roast it. When it was nearly ready Dog went outside, and took a stick and beat the ground, and whined out, "Oh! Please, I did not do it. It was Leopard that killed the goat. Oh! Don't kill me. It was Leopard who stole it."

Leopard, hearing these cries and the blows of the stick, thought to himself, "Ah! The men have followed us to our den, and are killing Dog. Then they will come and kill me if I do not run." He therefore ran out and escaped.

Dog, on seeing him well away, coolly returned to the den and devoured the whole of the meat, leaving only the bones.

After a long time Leopard returned to the den, and found Dog moaning piteously. "What is the matter, my friend?" he asked.

"Ah! Oh! Don't touch me. Don't touch me, I beg of you. I am so bruised and sore all over! Ah! My bones! They have half killed me," moaned Dog.

"Poor fellow! Well, lie still and rest. There is nothing like rest for a bruised body. I will get that white goat the next time I try."

After waiting two or three days, Leopard departed to obtain the white goat. Dog sneaked after him, and served his friend in the same way, bringing the white goat himself, and bragging how he had succeeded, while pretending to pity Leopard for his bad luck.

Three times running Dog served him with the same trick, and Leopard was much mortified at his own failure. Then Leopard thought of the Muzimu, the oracle who knows all things, and gives such good advice to those who are unfortunate and ask for his help, and he resolved, in his distress, to seek him.

In the heart of the tall, dark woods, where the bush is most dense, where vines clamber over the clumps, and fold themselves round and round the trees, and hang in long coils by the side of a cool stream, the Muzimu resided.

Leopard softly drew near the sacred place and cried, "Oh! Muzimu, have pity on me. I am almost dying with hunger. I used to be bold and strong, and successful, but now, of late, though I catch my prey as of old, something always happens to scare me away, and I lose the meat I have taken. Help me, O Muzimu, and tell how my good luck may return."

After a while the Muzimu answered in a deep voice, "Leopard, your ill-luck comes from your own folly. You know how to catch prey, but it takes a dog to know how to eat it. Go. Watch your friend, and your ill-luck will fly away."

Leopard was never very wise, though he had good eyes, and was swift and brave, and he thought over what the Muzimu said. He could not understand in what way his good luck would return by watching his friend, but he resolved to follow the advice of the Muzimu.

The next night Leopard gave out that he was going to seize a dun-coloured goat, and Dog said, "Ah! That is what I mean to do too. I think a dun-coated goat so sweet."

The village was reached, a low place was found in the palings, and Leopard, as quick as you could wink, was over and among the goats.

With one stroke he struck his victim dead, threw it over his shoulders, and, with a flying leap, carried it outside. Dog, who was hiding near the place, in a strange voice cried, "Ah! Here he is, the thief of a Leopard! Kill him! Kill him!"

Leopard turning his head around, saw him in the grass and heard him yelp, "Awu-ou-ou! Awu-ou-ou! Kill him! Kill him!" Leopard dropped the goat for an instant and said, "Ah, it is you, my false friend, is it? Wait a bit, and I will teach you how you may steal once too often."

With eyes like balls of fire, he rushed at him, and would have torn him into pieces, but Dog's instinct told him that the game he had been playing was up, and burying his tail between his hind legs, he turned and fled for dear life. Round and round the village he ran, darting this way and that, until, finding his strength was oozing out of him, he dashed finally through a gap in the fence, straight into a man's house and under the bed, where he lay gasping and panting. Seeing that the man, who had been scared by his sudden entry, was about to take his spear to kill him, he crawled from under the bed to the man's feet, and licked them, and turned on his back imploring mercy. The man took pity on him, tied him up, and made a pet of him. Ever since Dog and Man have been firm friends, but a mortal hatred has existed between Dog and Leopard. Dog's back always bristles straight up when his enemy is about, and there is no truer warning of the Leopard's presence than that given by Dog, while Leopard would rather eat a dog than a goat any day. That is the way, as I heard it in Unyoro, that the chumship between Leopard and Dog was broken up.

The Rat And The Toad

This tale has been edited and adapted from Kate Douglas Wiggin and Nora Archibald Smith's collection, The Talking Beasts, A Book of Fable and Wisdom, and illustrated by Harold Nelson. The book was published in 1922.

The Toad said to the Rat, "I can do more than you."

The Rat replied to the Toad, "You do not know how to run. Having flung you anywhere you stop there. This is all. And will you say that you can do more than I?"

When the Toad had heard the words of the Rat he said to him, "If, according to your opinion, I cannot do more than you, you shall see what I will begin to do tomorrow, and if you begin and do the same, without anything happening to you, you can do more than I."

The Rat agreed to the Toad's proposal, and went to see the Toad.

The Toad prepared himself, and when the sun reached about the middle, between the horizon and the zenith, the great men felt its heat, and went to sit down in the shade of a tree. The Toad on seeing this, arose, went to where the men were sitting, and passed through the midst of them. When the men observed him they said, "If you touch him, your hand will become bitter." So no one touched him, and the Toad passed through and went home.

Then the Toad said to the Rat, "Did you see me? Now if you can do what I do, arise, and begin to do it. I will see!"

The Rat, attending to what the toad said, got ready and the following morning, when the sun had gained strength and the great men had stood up and got under the shade of a tree, the Rat saw them sitting there, and went to do what the Toad had done, but when he came to where the men were sitting, and just went to pass through the midst of them, they saw him, and they all took sticks, and sought to kill him. One man attempting to kill him with a stick, struck at him, but did not hit him well, the stick touching him only a little on the back. So he ran away to the Toad.

On his arrival the Rat said to the Toad, "Brother Toad, as you went to where the people were sitting no one said a word to you, and you came home again with a sound skin. But when I went, and they saw me, and just as I went to pass through them they all took sticks, and sought to kill me, and one man taking a stick and striking at me to kill me, our Lord helped me, that the stick hit me only a little on the back. So I ran away, and came to you. I disputed with you, thinking that I could do what you do, but now today I have experienced something. Tomorrow let us begin again and when I have the experience of tomorrow, I shall be able to give you an answer."

The Toad said to the Rat, "The things of today are passed. Tomorrow, when the great men have gone and sat down under the tree, I will get ready. When you see that I can pass through the midst of them, and they will not say a word to me, you also shall do what I did."

So the Rat then went to watch the Toad. As soon as the Toad saw the great men sitting under the tree, he again began, saying to the Rat, "Look at me, as I go to the place where the great men are sitting, with a sound skin, but if, on my return from them, if you see the mark of a stick on any part of my body, you have spoken the truth, and can do more than I."

The Toad got ready, and on coming to where the men were sitting no one said anything to him. So he passed through the midst of them, and went again to the Rat, saying, "Look at me! Look at my whole body! Can you see the mark of a stick? If you see one, then tell me of it!"

When the Rat had looked at the Toad's whole body and not seen any mark of a stick he said to the Toad, "Brother Toad, I have looked at your whole body, and not seen any marks of a stick, you are right."

The Toad said to the Rat. "As you dispute with me, and maintain that you can do what I do, get up again, and go to where the great men are sitting, and if on seeing you, these men do not say anything to you, so that I see you come back to me again with a sound skin, then I know that you can do more than I."

The Rat, attending to what the Toad said, arose, got himself ready, and when he saw the great men sitting under the tree, he went toward them. But on observing him, they said, "Here comes a Rat," and every man took a stick, and pursued him in order to kill him. So he ran away, and as he ran, a man with a stick pursued him, saying, "I will not let this Rat escape."

The Rat ran until his strength failed him. The man pursued him with his stick, to kill him, and having come near to him, he took his stick, and struck at him, but the stick did not hit him, and God saved him, by showing him a hole into which he crept. When the man saw that he had gotten into the hole, he went back and returned home. The Rat, on seeing that the man had gone home, came again out of the hole, and went to the Toad, saying to him, "Brother Toad, I indeed at first disputed with you, saying that I could do more than you, but, as for my disputing with you, you in truth can do more than I. When the people saw you, they did not say a word to you, but when they saw me, they wished to kill me. If our Lord had not helped me and showed me a hole, they, on seeing me, would not have left, but killed me. You surpass me in greatness."

At that time the Rat entreated our Lord and he placed it in a hole, but the Toad he placed in the open air. The Rat does not come out by day, before anyone. As to the time when it comes out at night, it stretches its head out of the hole, and when it does not see anybody it comes out to seek its food.

As for the Toad, it comes out by day and by night, at any time, whenever it likes. It comes out and goes about, and not anything likes to molest it. It is bitter, and no one eats it on account of its bitterness. The Toad is left alone. Therefore it goes about wherever it likes.

The Rat does not come out of its hole and walk about except at night.

What the Toad and the Rat did, this I heard, and have told to you. This fable of the Toad and the Rat is now finished.

The Legend Of The Cunning Terrapin And The Crane

This tale has been edited and adapted from Henry Morton Stanley's book, My Dark Companions, published in 1893 by Sampson, Lowe, Marston and Company, London.

A Terrapin and a Crane were one time travelling together very sociably. They began their conversation by the Terrapin asking, "How is your family today, Miss Crane?"

"Oh, very well. Mamma, who is getting old, complains now and then, that's all."

"But do you know that it strikes me that she is very fat?" said Terrapin. "Now a thought has just entered my head, which I beg to propose to you. My mother, too, is ailing, and I am rather tired of hearing her complaints day after day, but she is exceedingly lean and tough, though there is plenty of her. I wonder what you will say to my plan? We are both hungry. So let us go and kill your mother, and eat her, and tomorrow, you will come to me, and we will kill my mother. We thus shall be supplied with meat for some days."

Replied the Crane, "I like the idea greatly, and agree to it. Let us go about it at once, for hunger is an exacting mistress, and the days of fasting are more frequent than those of fulness."

The matricides turned upon their tracks, and, arriving at the house of Mrs Crane, the two cruel creatures seized upon Mamma Crane, and put her to death. They then plucked her clean, and placed her body in the stew-pot, and both Terrapin and Crane feasted.

Terrapin then crawled home, leaving Crane to sleep, and the process of digestion. But, alas! Crane soon became very ill. Whether some qualms of conscience disturbed digestion or not, I cannot say, but she passed a troublesome night, and for several days afterwards she did not stir from her house.

Terrapin, on reaching the house of its mamma, which was in the hollow of a tree, cried out, "Tu-no-no-no!" upon which Mrs Terrapin said, "Oh, that is my child," and she let down a cord, to which young Terrapin made himself fast, and was assisted to the nest where the parent had already prepared a nice supper for him.

Several days later, Terrapin was proceeding through the woods to the pool where he was accustomed to bathe, when at the water-side he met Miss Crane apparently quite spruce and strong again.

She hailed Terrapin and said, "Oh, here you are, at last. I have been waiting to see you for some time."

"Yes," replied Terrapin, "here I am, and you, how do you feel now? My neighbours told me you were very ill."

"I am all right again," said Miss Crane, "but I think my old ma disagreed with me, and I was quite poorly for some days, but I am now anxious to know when you are going to keep your part of the bargain which we made."

"What, you mean about the disposing of my old ma?"

"Yes, to be sure," answered Crane, "I feel quite hungry."

"Well, well. Bargains should always be kept, for if the blood-oath be broken misfortune follows. Your mother's death rests on my head, and I mean to return your hospitality with interest, otherwise, may my shell be soon empty of its tenant. Stay here awhile and I will bring her."

So saying, Terrapin departed, and crept to where he had secretly stowed a quantity of india-rubber, in readiness for the occasion. After taking out quite a mass of it, he returned to the pond, where Miss Crane stood on one leg, expectant and winking pleasantly.

"I fear, sister Crane," said Terrapin, as he laid his burden down, "that you will find my old ma tough. She turned out to be much leaner than I anticipated. There is no more fat on her bones, than there is on my back. But now, fall to, and welcome. There is plenty there. I am not hungry myself, as I have just finished my dinner."

Miss Crane, with her empty stomach, was not fastidious, and stepped out eagerly to the feast so faithfully provided, and began to tear away at what Terrapin had brought. The rubber, however, stretched by the greedy Crane, suddenly flew from her foot, and rebounding, struck her in the face a smart blow.

"Oh! oh!" cried Crane, confused with the blow. "Your old ma is most tough."

"Yes, she is. I suspected she would prove a little tough," answered Terrapin, with a chuckle. "But don't be bashful. Eat away, and welcome."

Again Miss Crane tugged at the rubber to tear it, but the more it was stretched, the more severe were the shocks she received, and her left eye was almost blinded.

"Well, I never," exclaimed Miss Crane. "She is too tough altogether."

"Try again," cried Terrapin. "Try again. Little by little, it is said, a fly eats a cow's tail. You will get a rare and tender bit in time."

Miss Crane thus pressed, did so, and seizing a piece lay back, and drew on it so hard that when the rubber at last slipped, it bounded back with such force, that she was sent sprawling to the ground.

"Why, what is the matter?" asked Terrapin, pretending to be astonished. "She is tough, I admit, but our family are famous for toughness. However, the tougher it is, the longer it lasts on the stomach. Try again, sister Crane. I warrant you will manage it next time."

"Oh, bother your old ma. Eat her yourself. I have had enough of that kind of meat."

"You give it up, do you?" cried Terrapin. "Well, well, it is a pity to throw good meat away. Maybe, if I keep it longer it will get tenderer by and by."

They thus parted, Terrapin bearing his share of rubber away in one direction, and Miss Crane sadly disgusted, striding grandly off in another, but looking keenly about for something to satisfy her hunger.

When she had gone a great distance a parrot flew across her path, and perching on a branch near her, cried out, "Oh, royal bird, say since when has rubber become the food of the bird-king's family?"

"What do you mean, Parrot?" she asked.

"Well, I saw you tearing at a piece of rubber just now, and when you marched off Terrapin carried it away, and I heard him say, because he has a habit of speaking his thoughts aloud, 'Oh, how stupid my sister Crane is! She thinks my ma is dead. Ho, ho, ho! What a stupid!'. And all the way he chuckled and laughed as though he was filled with plantain wine."

"Is his ma not dead then?" asked Miss Crane.

"Dead! Not a bit of it," replied Parrot. "I saw old Ma Terrapin but a moment ago as I flew by her tree, waiting for her son, and the cord is ready for his cry of `Tu-no-no-no. Ano-no-no. We-no-no-no!'"

"Ah, Parrot, your words are good. When we know what another is saying behind our backs, we discover the workings of his heart. The words of Terrapin are like the bush that covers the trap. Good-bye, Parrot. When we next meet, we shall have another story to tell."

On the next day, Terrapin observed Miss Crane approaching his house, and he advanced a little way to meet her.

"Well, sister Crane, I hope you are all right this morning?" he asked.

"Oh yes, so, brother Terrapin. But you must excuse me just now. I've heard bad news from my family. A brother and sister of mine are suddenly taken ill, and I am bound to go and visit them," answered Crane.

"Ah, Miss Crane, that reminds me of my own brother and sister, who are much younger than I am, but very soft and tender. What do you say now to making another bargain?" asked Terrapin with a wink.

"You are very good, Terrapin. I will think of it as I go along. I shall be back before noon tomorrow, and we will talk of a trade then." They were very civil to one another as they parted. Terrapin went for his usual walk to the pond, Miss Crane proceeded to visit her family, but muttered, "Ha, ha, Terrapin, you are great at a trade, but you will not make another with me in a hurry till our first one is squared."

After she had gone a little way she turned suddenly round and came back to the foot of Terrapin's tree, and cried, "Tu-no-no-no. Ano-no-no-no. We-no-no-no!"

"Ah, that is my child's voice," said Ma Terrapin to herself, and let down the cord.

Miss Crane caught hold and climbed up towards the nest. Ma Terrapin craned her neck out far to welcome her child, but before she could discover by what means little Terrapin had changed its dress, Miss Crane struck Ma Terrapin with her long sharp bill in the place where the neck joins the shoulder, and in a short time Ma Terrapin was as dead as Miss Crane's own mother.

The body was rolled from the nest, and it went falling down, and Miss Crane slid quickly after it.

In a quiet place screened by thick bushes Miss Crane made a great fire, with which Ma Terrapin's thick shell was cracked. She then scooped out the flesh, and carried it to her own home, and stowed it in a big black pot.

On the next day as Miss Crane was standing on one leg by the pond, with her head half buried in her feathers, who should come along but Terrapin, crying bitterly, and saying, "Ah, my ma is dead. My old ma has been killed. Who will assist me now?"

Miss Crane affected to be asleep, but heard every word. When, however, Terrapin was near, she woke up suddenly and said, cheerfully, "Ah! It is Terrapin, my little brother Terrapin. How do you do today?"

Now as Terrapin had already slain his mother, according to his own confession, it struck him that it would not do to accuse Miss Crane of the murder, because by doing so he would expose his breach of faith with her, but the scent of the roasted flesh of Ma Terrapin came strong just then, and he knew that it was Crane who, discovering his trick, had killed her.

He managed, however, to reply briskly, "Sissy, dear, I am but tolerable. But how is your family today?"

"My brother and sister are much improved, Terrapin. They are both as fat as tallow. By-the-bye, what about that trade you proposed to me?"

"I am ready, Miss Crane, for a trade any day. When shall it be?"

"No time so good as the present, and if you jog along to the other end of the pond, I will fix my house here, and soon catch up with you."

Terrapin professed great delight, and toddled along, but when he had gone a little way his bad habit of thinking aloud came on him, and he was heard to say, "My poor ma! My poor ma is dead! O you wicked Crane! I know by the scent of the meat that you have killed my ma. What can I do now?"

Miss Crane knew then that she had been discovered, and she began to think that it was time to remove to another district, for Terrapin had many friends in the woods, such as rabbits, jackals, lions, and serpents, and if Terrapin moaned so loud, all the people of the woods would know what she had done, and many would no doubt assist him to punish her. Casting about in her mind for the best place, she remembered an extremely tall tree which was not far from Terrapin's house, a very lofty clean-shafted tree, on the top of which she would be safe from surprise.

There she hastily removed her belongings, and soon established herself comfortably. She had also provided herself with a store of strong sticks to be used as weapons in case of necessity.

Terrapin meanwhile crawled along, loudly moaning his lamentations. Suddenly Rabbit popped out of the woods, and stood in his path. He soon was made aware of Terrapin's bereavement, and strongly sympathised with him. Terrapin related the story in such a way that made Miss Crane appear to be a murderess, against whom the people of the woods should take vengeance.

"Then," said Rabbit, "that must be Miss Crane, who is building her house on the very top of that tall tree near your place."

"Is she?" asked Terrapin. "I did not know that. She was to have met me here, but I see she knows that she is detected, and is already taking measures to protect herself. But, Rabbit, you who are always wise, tell me how I may avenge myself?"

"There is only one way that I know of," answered Rabbit, dubiously. "Go to the Soko, the Gorilla, but he is a hard dealer who will make you pay handsomely for his help. Soko is the king of the ape kind. If you pay him well, he will fasten a cord to Crane's nest, up which you can climb when she is absent. Once there, lie quietly, and when she alights seize her."

The plan pleased Terrapin immensely, and possessing a comfortable property upon the loss of his mother, he thought he had sufficient to purchase Soko's assistance.

Through the good offices of Rabbit negotiations were entered into with Soko, who agreed for a potful of good nuts, ten bunches of ripe bananas, one hundred eggs, and sundry other trifles, to hang a stout rattan climber to Crane's nest, long enough to reach the ground.

The royal bird was soon informed of the conspiracy against her by the Parrot, who loves to carry tales, and Miss Crane resolved to be absent from home while Soko was fastening the climber, but commissioned her friend the Parrot to observe the proceedings, and to report to her when Soko had completed his task.

Soko performed his part expeditiously. Terrapin tested the strength of the rattan, and had to confess that Soko had earned his pay, and Rabbit accompanied Terrapin and Soko to Terrapin's house to see the Soko receive his commission.

As they departed Parrot flew to inform Miss Crane, who immediately returned to her house to await her enemy.

Not long after Terrapin came to the foot of Crane's tree and commenced to climb up. He had nearly reached the top when Miss Crane stood up and delivered such a thwacking blow on Terrapin's back that it caused him to lose his hold and fall to the ground. When Terrapin recovered his senses, he heard Miss Crane cry out, "Ha! Brother Terrapin, that was a nasty fall. You remember the rubber, don't you? There is nothing like the advice you gave me. Try again, Terrapin, my brother. Try again."

"You killed my ma, did you not?" asked Terrapin.

"I thought you told me that you had killed her according to agreement. Then how can you say that I killed her?" asked Miss Crane.

"That was not my ma I gave you. It was only a lump of rubber."

"Ho, ho! You confess it then? Well, we are now quits. You induced me to kill my ma, and as you could not keep your part of the bargain, I saved you the trouble. My ma was as much to me as your ma was to you. We have both lost our ma's now. So let us call it even, and be friends again."

Terrapin hesitated, but the memory of his ma's loss soon produced the old bitterness, and he became as unforgiving as ever. Miss Crane must, however, be persuaded that the matter was forgiven, otherwise he would never have the opportunity to avenge his ma's death.

"All right, Crane," he answered, "but let me come up, and embrace you over it, or do you descend and let us shake hands."

"Come up, by all means, Terrapin. I am always at home to friends," said Miss Crane.

Terrapin upon this began to climb, but as he was ascending he foolishly began to think aloud again, and he was heard saying, "Oh, yes, sister Crane. Just wait a little, and you will see. He, he, he!"

Miss Crane, who was quietly listening, heard Terrapin's chuckle and muttering, and prepared to receive him properly. When he was within reach, she cried, "Hold hard, Terrapin," and at once proceeded to shower mighty blows on his back, then laid the stick on his feet so sharply that, to protect them, he had to withdraw them into his shell, in doing which he lost his hold and fell to the ground with such force that to anything but a terrapin the great fall would have been instantly fatal.

"Try again, Terrapin. Try again, my brother. Another time and you will succeed," cried Miss Crane, mockingly.

Terrapin slowly recovered his faculties from the second fall, and exclaimed, "Ah, Crane, Crane. If I heed you a second time, call me fool. Yesterday and today you triumphed, tomorrow will be my turn."

"Kwa-le, kwa-le," Miss Crane shrilly cried. "My tree will stand tomorrow where it stood today. You know the way to it. If not, your hate will find it."

Terrapin toddled away upon this to seek the Lion, to whom, when he had found him, he pleaded so powerfully that the Lion pitied him greatly, and answered, "I may not help you in this matter, for I was not made to climb trees. Go you, and tell Jackal your story, and he will be able to advise you."

Acting on the friendly advice, Terrapin sought out the Jackal, to whom he repeated his lamentable tale. The Jackal rewarded him with a sympathetic sigh, and said, "Friend Terrapin, my teeth are sharp and my feet are swift, but, though I am so happily endowed, I have no wings to fly. Go and seek Elephant. His strength is so great that perhaps he will be able to pull the tree down for you."

Terrapin proceeded on his way to search out the Elephant, and, after much patient travel, discovered him brooding under a thick shade. To him at once Terrapin unburdened his breast of its load of grief, and appealed piteously for his assistance.

"Little Terrapin," replied the kindly Elephant, "your tale is dour. But though I am strong, there are some things that I cannot do. Miss Crane's house is built on one of the biggest trees of the forest, and it would require two score of elephants to drag it down. It is wisdom, and not strength, that you need. Go you and seek Serpent, and he will assist you."

There Terrapin went to seek Serpent, and, after long seeking, found him coiled, in many shining folds, in the fork of a sturdy tree.

"Ah, Serpent," he cried, "you are a kinsman of mine, and I have long sought you. I am in dire distress, my friend," and he proceeded to inveigh against Miss Crane passionately, and concluded by invoking his assistance. "Help me this day," cried Terrapin, "and you shall be my father and my mother, and all my nearest relations in one."

"It is well," replied the Serpent, in his slow, deliberate manner. "Miss Crane shall die, and here I make a pact with you. There shall be no enmity for all future time between your family and mine. Go now, and rest in peace, for the fate of Crane is fixed."

In the darkness of the night Serpent roused himself from his sleep and, uncoiling himself, descended the tree and glided noiselessly along the ground towards Miss Crane's tree. The tall clean shaft could not arrest those spiring movements, and the Serpent steadily ascended until he gained the fork. There, by an almost imperceptible motion, he advanced towards the nest. Poor Miss Crane was fast asleep, dreaming of the fall of Terrapin, while the Serpent folded his extremity around a stout branch and stood up prepared to strike. Quick as one could wink the Serpent flung himself upon the bird-queen, and in a moment she lay crushed and mangled. Then, seizing her body with his jaws, the Serpent slid down the shaft of the tree and sought Terrapin's house, and laid her remains before him. Terrapin was overjoyed, and invited Serpent to share with him the dainty feast which the body of Miss Crane supplied.

From that day to this Serpent and Terrapin have remained close friends, and neither has ever been known to break the solemn agreement that was made between them on that day that Terrapin solicited the help of Serpent against the bird-queen.

The Lion And The Wild Dog

This tale has been edited and adapted from Kate Douglas Wiggin and Nora Archibald Smith's collection, The Talking Beasts, A Book of Fable and Wisdom, and illustrated by Harold Nelson. The book was published in 1922.

The Lion said to the Wild Dog that he did not fear anyone in the forest except these four, viz., tree-leaves, grass, flies, and earth, and when the Wild Dog said, "There is certainly one stronger than you," the Lion replied to the Wild Dog, "I kill the young ones of the elephant, the wild cow, and the leopard, and bring them to my children to be eaten. If I give one roar, all the beasts of the forest tremble, every one of them, on hearing me roar. None is greater than I within this forest."

The Wild Dog said to the Lion, "As you say that you fear not any one in this forest, so let us go and show me your house, and I will come and call you, in order to show you a place where a black bird comes to eat, as soon as I shall see him again."

The Lion took the Wild Dog with him and showed him his house, and then the Wild Dog went home.

The next day, when a hunter was come to the forest the Wild Dog, on seeing him, went to the Lion's house, and said to the Lion, "Brother Lion, come, and follow me, and I will show you something which I have seen."

The Lion arose and followed the Wild Dog, and when they were close to where the hunter was, the hunter saw them and prepared himself. He had put on his forest garment, had sewn the bill of a long bird to his cap, and put it on his head, and he walked as a bird. The Wild Dog, seeing him, said to the Lion, "Brother Lion, yonder is that black bird. Go and catch him, and when you have caught him, please give me one of his legs, for I want it for a charm."

The Lion attended to what the Wild Dog said, and went softly to where the bird was, but the Wild Dog ran back.

The Lion went, thinking, "I will kill the bird," but he did not know that on seeing him the hunter had prepared himself, and taken out his arrow. So, as he thought, "I will go and seize the bird," and was close to the hunter, the hunter shot an arrow at the Lion and hit him. Then the Lion fell back, and having got up and fallen down three times, the arrow took effect and he felt giddy. In the same moment the hunter had made himself invisible using magic tricks, so that Lion saw him no more. Then the Lion recovered his courage and went very gently home.

On his arrival at home the Wild Dog said to him, "Brother Lion, as you said to me that you are not afraid of any one in the world except our Lord, tree-leaves, grass, flies, and dirt, why did you not catch that black bird which I showed you, and bring it to your children?"

The Lion replied, "This man's strength is greater than mine."

Then the Wild Dog said again, "You said that you fear no one, except grass, flies, earth and tree-leaves. You fear, lest when you enter the forest, that the leaves of trees should touch you, or lest grass should touch your body, or lest flies should sit on your skin. You also fear to lie upon the bare earth, and you fear our Lord, who created you, all these you fear, 'but not any other I fear within this forest,' you said, and yet I showed you a bird, which you could not kill, but you left it, and ran home. Now tell me how this bird looks?"

The Lion answered and said to the Wild Dog, "Wild Dog, what you said is true, and I believe it. A man is something to be feared. If we do not fear a man neither shall we fear our Lord who created us."

Now all the wild beasts which God has created hunt for their food in the forest, and eat it, but as soon as they see one man standing, they do not stop and wait, but run away. Now the following beasts are dangerous in the forest, viz., the leopard, the lion, the wild cow, the wild dog and the hyena, but when they see a man, they do not stop and wait. As for the dispute which the Lion and the Wild Dog had, the Wild Dog was right, and the Lion gave him his right. Then they shook hands again, and each went and ran to his own home. This fable, which I heard, respecting the Wild Dog and the Lion, is now finished.

The Legend Of Kibatti The Little Who Conquered All The Great Animals

This tale has been edited and adapted from Henry Morton Stanley's book, My Dark Companions, published in 1893 by Sampson, Lowe, Marston and Company, London.

On a day ages ago the great animals of the world, consisting of the elephant, the rhinoceros, the buffalo, the lion, the leopard, and hyena, assembled in council in the midst of a forest not far from a village on the frontier of Uganda. The elephant being acknowledged by general consent as the strongest, presided on the occasion.

Waving his trunk, and trumpeting to enjoin silence, he said, "Friends, we are gathered together today to consider how we may repay in some measure the injuries daily done to us and our kin by the sons of men. Not far from here is situated a village, where the vicious two-footed animals issue out to make war upon all of us, who possess double the number of feet they have. Without warning of hostility or publishing of cause, they deliberately leave their conical nests, day by day, with fell intent against any of us whom they may happen to meet during the shining of the sun. Wherefore we are met upon common grounds to devise how we may retaliate upon them the wanton outrages they daily perpetrate upon our unfortunate kind. Personally, I have many injuries to the elephants of my tribe to remember, and which I am not likely to forget. It was only a week ago that a promising child of my sister fell into a deep pit and was impaled on a short stake set in the bottom of it, and but a few days before my youngest brother fell head-foremost into a horribly deep excavation that was dug, and which was artfully concealed by leaves and grass, whereby none but those, like me, experienced in their guileful arts, could have escaped. You have all, I daresay, been similarly persecuted, and have deep injuries to revenge. I wait to hear what you propose. Brother Rhinoceros, you are the next to me in bigness and strength, speak."

"Well, brother Elephant and friends, the words we have heard are true. The son of man is, of all creatures that I know, the most wanton in offence against us of the four-footed tribes. Not a day passes but I hear moan and plaint from some sufferer. Not long ago, a cousin, walking quietly through a wood not far from here, caught his foot in a vine that lay across the path, and almost immediately after a hardened and pointed stake was precipitated from above deep into the jointure of the neck with the spine, which killed him instantly, of course. I have, by wonderful good luck, escaped thus far, but it may be my fate to fall tomorrow through some foul practice. So, I think it would be good if we set about doing what we decide to do immediately. I propose that early in the morning, before a glint of sunshine be seen, we set upon the piratical nest and utterly destroy it. I am so loaded with hate of them, that I could dispose of the half of the rascals myself before they could recover their wits. But if any of you here has a better plan, I lend my ears to the hearing of it, my heart to the approval of it, and my strength and fury to the doing of it, without further speech. I have spoken."

"Now, friend Lion," said the Elephant, turning solemnly to him, "it is your turn, and say freely what your wit conceives in this matter. Your courage we all know, and none of us doubt that your mind is equal to it."

"Truly, friend Elephant, and you others, the business we are met to consider is pressing. The sons of men are crafty, and their guile is beyond measure. The four-footed tribes have much cause of grievance against me and mine. However, none can accuse me or my family of having taken undue advantage of those whom we meditate striking. We always give loud warning, as you all know, and afterwards strike. For if we did not do this, few of even the strongest would escape our vengeance. But these pestilent, two-footed beasts, by net, trap, falling stake, pit, or noose, are unceasing in their secret malice, and there is no safety in the plain, bush, or rock-fastness against their wiles. For what I and my kin do there is good motive, that of providing meat for ourselves and young, but it passes my wit to discover what the son of man can want with all he destroys. Even our bones, as, for instance, your long teeth, O Elephant, they carry away with them, and even mine. I have seen the younglings of mankind dangle the teeth of my sister round their necks, and my hide appears to be so precious that the king of the village wears it over his dirty black loins.

"Your tribe, O Elephant, have not much cause of complaint against me, and you, Rhinoceros, it would tax your memory to accuse me of anything against your family. Brother Leopard will hold me and mine guiltless of harm to him. So also must my cousin Hyena. Friend Buffalo and our family have sometimes a sharp quarrel, but there is no malice in it, I swear. Whereas the son of man, friends, is the common enemy of us all, it is either our flesh, or our fur, or our hide, or our teeth that he is wanting, and his whole thought is bent upon destruction pure and simple. If you would follow me, I would glory in leading you even now against the community, and I give you my word that few would escape my paw and claw. However, as our object is to destroy all, that none may escape, I agree with my friend Rhinoceros that night-time at its blackest is safest. So, believe me that I am so sharp set for revenge, and I feel so hollow, that nothing but the half of all of them will satisfy my thirst for their blood. I have ended my say."

"Now, friend Leopard, you had better follow your cousin, and we will feel obliged to you for the benefit of your advice," said the Elephant.

Leopard gave his tail a quick twirl, and licked his chops and spoke, saying, "All that you, my friends and cousin, have said, I heartily agree and bear witness to. The spite of the son of man towards us is limitless. It is remarkable, too, for its cold-bloodedness and lack of passion. We have our own quarrels in the woods, as you all know, and they are sharp and quick while they last, but there is no premeditation or malignity in what we do to one another, but Man, to whom we would rather give a wide berth, if possible, pursues each of us as if his existence depended upon the mere slaying, though I observe that he has abundance of fruit, which ought to satisfy any reasonable being of the ape tribe.

"So, as I have many sharp reasons for retaliation on him for his countless offences against me and my kin, I gladly attended this council, and I will go as far as any of you, and further if I can, to return some of this spite on him and his tribe. I propose that night at its darkest is best for our plan. While the human folk are indulging in dreams of slaughter of us, I vote that we turn their dreams into action against themselves. The elephant, and rhinoceros, and buffalo are strong. Let each lead his tribe to attack, overturn, and trample down their nests. We, with our families, will range round and slaughter every one that escapes them. Those are my words."

"Now, friend Buffalo, what say you?" demanded the Elephant. "You are a staunch friend and stout foe. We cannot but listen with respect to such a one as you."

"Ah, friend Elephant, and you chiefs of tribes, every sentiment of hostility against the vile and spiteful sons of man that you have expressed finds an echo in my innards. If wrong has been done to any here, magnify that wrong tenfold in order that you may understand the intensity of the hate I bear the remorseless destroyers of my kith and kin. Ask me not how I would slay them, my fury is so great that I am unfit to devise. You do the devising, and give the method to me. All I can think of now is the pleasure I shall feel when my horns are warmed in the bodies of the base and treacherous creatures who have murdered wife, brother, sister, and child of mine, besides a countless number of my kindred by lance and line, spear and snare, sword and stake, trick and trap. I will lead my herd into the midst of the vicious community with a joy that only my hate can match. That is all I have to say."

"Now, my good friend Hyena. You are the only one left whose sentiments are as yet unknown. Speak, and let us hear wisdom from you in this matter."

The Hyena uttered a mocking laugh, and said, "My kind friends and cousins, The night suits me well, for I am in my element then. I may say that I have a large family which is always hungry. It will be a laughing matter to them indeed to hear of your good purpose. It has been long delayed, this signal measure of just vengeance upon those who have outdone in cold cruelty all that generations of the four-footed tribe of the fiercest kind have done. Bird and beast, from the smallest to the greatest, have fallen victims to man's lust for destruction. True, my kind are often indebted to man for bones and refuse, but what we have eaten has been sorely against his good will, and we therefore owe him no gratitude. The young of the human community will be juicy morsels for my tribe, when the signal is given for the attack. With all my heart I say let it be tonight. I have said my say."

The Elephant then said, "Friends, chiefs of the most powerful tribes of the forest, let it be tonight, as you say. Let each go and muster his forces, and let the attack be in the following manner. Half-way betwixt dawn and midnight I will lead my troop from the Uganda side. The Rhinoceros will lead his from the Katonga side. The Buffalo will range his tribe along that side facing Unyoro. Behind my troop the Hyena and his families shall follow to finish those who may be but bruised by our heavy hoofs. Let Leopard place his fellows and kin in rear of the Rhinoceros troop. Lion and his great tribe are needed in rear of Buffalo's forces, for they are apt in their fury to overlook the crafty bipeds. Our object is to make a complete job of it. The sooner we part now, the fitter each will be for the perfect consummation of his long-deferred revenge."

It was well past midnight when the four-footed forces were gathered around the doomed village, and, at the shrill trumpet-note of the King Elephant, the several chiefs led their respective troops at the charge. The elephants tore on resistlessly, trampling down the doomed cages of the human folk flat and level with the ground. The rhinoceros and his host pushed on with noses low down, and tossed the human nests as we would kick an empty egg-basket. The buffaloes bellowed in unison, and, closing their eyes, threw themselves upon the huts, and gored everything within reach of their horns. Then the fierce carnivora, all excitement at the prospect of the bloody feast, roared, snarled, and laughed as they tore the mangled victims piecemeal. Ah, poor village, and poor people! In a short time the dreaming souls dreamed no more, but were gone past recall into the regions where dreams are unknown, all excepting one clever boy named Kibatti, and his parents, who survived the calamity. These happened to live in a tiny hut close hidden by a grove of bananas on the edge of the forest, and Kibatti about midnight had been disturbed in his sleep by a pressure on his stomach which woke him, and denied him further sleep. He therefore sat sorrowing over the red embers of his fire, when he heard the hollow tramp of large animals, and pricking his ears, he heard trampling in another direction. Whereupon his suspicions that something unusual was about to happen grew on him, so that he woke his parents, and bade them listen to the rumbling sounds that could be heard by such experienced hunters all around them.

"Father, come, delay not! Make mother rise at once. This night my sleep has been broken as a warning to me that mischief is brewing. Let us ascend the big tree nearby and observe."

"Child, you are right," said his father, after listening a moment, "the demons of the wilderness are gathered against the village, for human enemies make no such stir as this. We will ascend the great tree at once." Thereupon he drew his wife out.

Kibatti wriggled himself through the burrow under the milkweed hedge into the banana-grove, and having gained its deep shadows, raced for the great tree, closely followed by his parents. A large vine hung pendant, and up this vine Kibatti climbed, his mother after him, the old man last. Not a moment too soon, for just then the trumpet-note of the King Elephant was heard, and afterwards such a concert of noises that neither Kibatti nor his aged father had ever heard the like before. In the starlight they saw the huge forms of all kinds of furious animals pass and repass below them, but clinging closely to the shelter of the giant limbs of the tree, they, from their safe perch, witnessed the dreadful ending of their friends and relatives.

When he fully realised the catastrophe and its completeness, Kibatti suggested to his parents that they should ascend to the very highest fork, lest they should be observed in the morning, and on climbing up they found a snug hiding-place far above, hidden all round by the thick, fleshy leaves of the tree. There they remained quiet until morning, when the boy's restless curiosity became so strong that he resolved to gratify it. Grasping close a great limb of the tree, he descended as far as the lower fork and looked down. He saw all the huts smashed, and the bones of his tribe white and gleaming, scattered about. The fences were all levelled, but the elephants, under their leader, were re-setting the poles round about. The lions were pacing watchfully around, the rhinoceroses and buffaloes were herded separately, gazing upon the elephants, the leopards were lying down under the trees in scattered groups, the hyenas were crunching bones, for these last never know when they have eaten enough.

Kibatti kept his post all day. By night the poles fenced the village round about as before, and in the dusk he saw the gathering together of all the creatures in a circle round the King Elephant, to hear his rumbling voice delivering an harangue to the motley allies. When it was ended the lions roared, the rhinoceroses snorted, the buffaloes bellowed, the hyenas laughed, and the shrill trumpetings of the elephants announced that the meeting was over. What occurred after, Kibatti did not stay to learn, but climbed aloft to give the news to his anxious parents.

Said he, "It appears to me, father, that they are going to build the village up again, for they have already fenced it around even better, as I think, than it was before. Those animals have clever leaders, that is certain, but I am not a man-son if Kibatti does not get the better of some of them."

"Oh, you are clever, my child, that is true," said the old man. "Whatever you undertake to do, done it is. I have found out that long ago. If wit will get us out of this place of danger, I have a conviction it will be by yours, and not by mine, or by my old woman's."

"I do not purpose to leave the tree just yet, father," replied Kibatti. "If we keep quiet, we could not find a safer place than here. The tree is so tall that they cannot hear us talk unless they set their ears to listen at the foot of it, and against all that may happen we must provide ourselves."

"Give your confidence to me, boy, and let me judge of your plan," said the father.

"Well, my idea is this. Tonight they will all start off, some to catch the lesser prey, others to graze and feed. The leaders, of course, will remain behind. I propose, after getting three or four winks of sleep, to go down to the gate and discover how things are. If possible, I will try and get my net-ropes. They will be useful for my purpose. We may trap some game, you know."

"I see, I see, my boy. That is a good idea. Shall I help you?"

"Not tonight, father, except you keep watch until yonder bright star stands overhead."

The old man agreed to keep watch until the star approached the zenith. A little after midnight Kibatti was waked, and having given his father injunctions to go to sleep, he descended. He proceeded straight to his house, and among the wreckage he found his strong nets and their ropes, and his sharp hunting-knife, besides his father's five spears and his own quiver. These weapons he conveyed directly to the tree, and bore them up to the lower fork. This done, he re-descended the tree and crawled away to a bit of marsh-land not far off, where there was a crane's nest which contained some eggs. He took these in his hand, and went around through the bushes to the Unyoro Road. All this had been done very quickly, because, being a hunter, he knew the neighbourhood well, and while watching the animals in the village, his mind had been busy forming his plans. Now when he came to the Unyoro Road, he stood straight up and strode rapidly in the direction of the village which had been that of his tribe. Arriving near it he crawled up to the gate and looked in, then traced the fence all around until he came back to the same gate.

Kibatti now stood up and hailed the animals, crying loud, "Hullo, hullo there! Are you all asleep? Will you not let a poor benighted stranger in? The night is cold, and I am hungry."

King Buffalo, who was on guard, trotted up to the gate, and looking out saw a small boy who was naked, except for a scant robe which descended from his shoulders.

"Who are you?" demanded the buffalo in his gruffest voice.

Kibatti answered in the thin voice of a fatherless and starving orphan. "It is I, Kibatti the Little, from Unyoro."

"What do you want?"

"Only a little fire to roast my eggs, and a place to sleep. I am a forest-boy, and live alone in Unyoro. My parents are both dead, and I have no home. If you will give me work I will stay with you. For then I shall have plenty to eat. If not, let me sleep here tonight, and in the morning I will go."

"What work can you do?"

"Not much, but I can fetch water and fuel."

"Wait a minute, I will see if our people will let you in."

The buffalo moved away and woke up the rhinoceros, the elephant, the lion, the leopard, and hyena, and told them that there was a little forest-boy seeking a night's lodging. At first the general belief was, that he belonged to the tribe which had owned the village, but the buffalo denied that this boy could have known of the country, as he had come boldly up to the gate from the Unyoro road. Besides, was it likely that a small boy, knowing what had happened, would ever have come back when those who had destroyed the village were in possession of it? This last remark settled the matter.

King Elephant said, "As you will, Buffalo. Even if the matter were otherwise, a small boy can do no harm. Let him in. We will give him plenty of work."

King Buffalo opened the gate and allowed Kibatti to enter, and introduced him to his friends, King Elephant and the rest, all of whom smiled as they saw his slender and small form, the only human amongst them. Buffalo took very kindly to his protege and showed him around, while Kibatti amused him with his innocent unsophisticated prattle, which convinced the kingly bovine that little Kibatti was indeed a wild-wood waif.

"And where do you all sleep?" asked Kibatti of Buffalo.

"I sleep here, near the gate, King Elephant rests near that big tree. King Lion prefers lying near that great log there, Brother Rhinoceros throws himself down on the edge of the banana-grove, Leopard curls himself near the fence, and Hyena snores stupidly near his pile of bones."

After a little while Buffalo lay down near the gate for a little rest. Kibatti stretched himself near him, but not to sleep. His eyes were quite open, and he soon saw Buffalo's nose rest upon the ground and his head sway from side to side. Kibatti then untied a cord, and stealthily passing it round the four legs of the buffalo, drew the other end round the neck in a slip noose without waking him. He then crawled off towards the elephant, and tied his four legs together, gently tightening the slip noose, and fastening the rope three or four times running round, and brought them all together. To the rhinoceros he did the same. He then went out of the gate and brought his bundle of nets. He took one up, fastened one end to the fence, and drawing it lightly like a curtain over the form of the sleeping lion, just hung it on splinters and projections of the fence. In like manner he secured a net over the leopard, and another over the hyena. Clever little Kibatti did all of this without waking any of them. He then stole out of the gate a second time, and made his way to the tree where his parents were sleeping.

"Come, father," he said, "the kings of the herds are trapped and netted. Bring down mother to the lower fork, and come, hasten with me with a bundle of spears, two bows, and quivers full of arrows, for we must finish the game before morning."

Completely armed with spears and arrows, Kibatti led his father to the gate, and stealthily entered the fenced enclosure, and they stood over the still-sleeping buffalo. Kibatti gave his father a sharp-pointed spear, and gently laying his finger on the vital spot, between neck and head, showed him where to strike. The father lifted his right arm high up, and with one stroke severed the spinal cord. A shiver passed through King Buffalo's body, and he rolled over stone dead.

Then Kibatti and his father approached King Lion, who lay lengthways near the log by the fence, with his side exposed. Kibatti pointed to his own left side behind the shoulder-blade, and father and son drew their bows and drove two arrows into Lion's heart, who sprang up and threw himself like a ball into the net, which closed round him taut, and he presently lay still and lifeless. In the same manner father and son despatched Leopard and Hyena. There then only remained Rhinoceros and Elephant.

They chose to attack the first-named beast, who was still lying down on his side, unconscious of the tragic fate of his confederates.

Kibatti pointed to the enemy's fore-shoulder and touched his father with his finger two inches below the shoulder-blade. His father understood, and launched his spear straight into the body with such force that the blade was buried. King Rhinoceros, feeling the iron in his vitals, snorted and struggled to stand, but in doing so tightened the cords, and fell back rolling half over. Kibatti drew his bow and buried an arrow close to his father's buried spear. Meantime, King Elephant had taken the alarm, and, struggling with his bonds, had capsized himself on the ground.

Kibatti gave vent to a war whoop and cried, "Never mind, father, let the rhinoceros die. Let us away to the elephant while he is helpless."

They sprang to the prostrate beast, and they shot their arrows first to every vital point exposed, and then launched their spears with such good effect that before long the last of the kings of the beasts had ended his life.

Kibatti and his father then flew to where the old woman crouched in the fork of the tree, and taking her with them, they left the ruined village, and sought a home in another district, where, because of the terrible revenge they had taken on the forest lords, they were held by their fellow-creatures all their lives in great esteem.

How Sense Was Distributed

This tale has been edited and adapted from Kate Douglas Wiggin and Nora Archibald Smith's collection, The Talking Beasts, A Book of Fable and Wisdom, and illustrated by Harold Nelson. The book was published in 1922.

In the beginning not one of all the beasts of the forest was endowed with sense, when they saw a hunter come to them intending to kill them, they stood and looked at the hunter, and so the hunter killed them. Day after day he killed them. Then our Lord sent one who put all the sense into a bag, tied it, carried it, and put it down under a large tree.

The Weasel saw the man put the bag down, and afterward went, called the Hare, and said to him, "Brother Hare, I saw a man put something down under a tree, but as I went to take it, I could not. So let us go and if you take it I will show it to you that you may do so."

When the Weasel and the Hare had gone together to where the bag was, the Weasel said to the Hare, "Behold, here is the thing which I could not take and for which I called you here."

But as the Hare went and attempted to take it, he could not, so he left it and went away.

When he was gone the Weasel went again to take hold of the bag, but as he attempted to take it, it was too heavy. So the Weasel did not know what to do. Then came a Pigeon, who sat upon a tree, and said something to the Weasel. The Weasel heard it say, "Lean it over and take it." And again, "Bend it and take it."

As soon as he had heard this, he dragged the bag along and thus brought it and leaned it against a tree, and caused it to stand in an inclined position. Then having gone to the bottom of it, he bowed down, put his head to the bag, and as he drew the bag toward him it rested upon his head. This being done, he pressed himself upon the ground, rose up and stood there with the bag on his head. After this he went his way home, and on putting the bag down upon the ground and untying it, the Weasel saw that there was no other thing in the bag, but pure sense.

So he went and called the Hare again, and when the Hare was come, he said to him, "Brother Hare, there was not a single other thing in that bag but pure sense, God has loved us so that today we have obtained sense, but do not tell it to anybody, then I will give you a little, and what remains I will hide in my hole until someone comes and begs of me, and then I will give him also a little."

So he took one sense and gave to the Hare, saying, "If you take home this one sense, which I give you, it will preserve you. When you sleep by day open your eyes. Then if one comes to you, thinking, 'I have got meat, I will take it,' and sees that your eyes are open, he will think that you are not asleep, will leave you alone and go. But when you go and lie down without sleeping, then shut your eyes, and if one sees you, and sees that your eyes are shut, when he comes close to you, saying, 'I have got meat, I will take it,' then you will see him, rise up and run away into your forest. This one sense will be enough for you, but what remains I will keep in my own house." The Hare took his one sense and went home.

Now if one sees a Hare lying with his eyes open, it sleeps, but if its eyes are closed it is awake, and does not sleep. By this one sense the Hare is preserved.

The Weasel took all the sense that was left and hid it in his house. The Weasel surpasses all the beasts of the field in sense. When you see the Weasel, and say, "There the King of Sense has come out," and drive it before you, saying, "I will catch it," it runs into its hole. And if you begin to dig up the hole, it comes out behind you, and runs until you see it no more. This is why now if one sees a Weasel, one calls it "The King of Sense."

Amongst all the beasts of the field he distributed sense only little by little, and this is what they now have. This tale, showing how sense came abroad in the world is now finished.

The Partnership Of Rabbit And Elephant, And What Came Of It

This tale has been edited and adapted from Henry Morton Stanley's book, My Dark Companions, published in 1893 by Sampson, Lowe, Marston and Company, London.

In Willimesi, Uganda, a Rabbit and an Elephant, coming from different directions, met on a road one day, and being old friends, stopped to greet one another, and chat about the weather and the crops, and to exchange opinions on the state of trade. Finally the Rabbit proposed that the Elephant should join him in a partnership to make a little trading expedition to the Watusi shepherds, "because," said he, "I hear there are some good chances to make profit among them. Cloth, I am told, is very scarce there, and I think we might find a good bargain awaiting us." The Elephant was nothing loth, and closed with the offer of his little friend, and a couple of bales of assorted goods were prepared for the journey.

They set out on particularly good terms with each other, and Rabbit, who had a good store of experiences, amused the Elephant greatly. By-and-by the pair of friends arrived at a river, and the Elephant, to whom the water was agreeable, stepped in to cross it, but halted on hearing Rabbit exclaim, "Why, Elephant, you surely are not going to cross without me? Are we not partners?"

"Of course we are partners, but I did not agree to carry you or your pack. Why don't you step right in? The water is not deep, it scarcely covers my feet."

"But, you stupid fellow, can you not see that what will scarcely cover your feet is more than enough to drown me, and I can't swim a bit. And, besides, if I get my fur wet I shall catch the ague, and how ever am I to carry my pack across?"

"Well, I cannot help that. It was you who proposed to take the journey, and I thought a wise fellow like you would have known that there were rivers running across the road, and that you knew what to do. If you cannot travel, then good-bye. I cannot stop here all day," and the Elephant walked on across to the other side.

"Surly rascal," muttered Rabbit. "All right, my big friend, I will pay you for it some time."

Not far off, however, Rabbit found a log, and after placing his pack on it, he paddled himself over, and reached the other bank safely, but to his grief he discovered that his bale had been wetted and damaged.

Rabbit wiped the water up as much as possible, and resumed the journey with the Elephant, who had looked carelessly on the efforts of his friend to cross the river.

Fortunately for Rabbit, the latter part of the journey did not present such difficulties, and they arrived in due time among the Watusi shepherds.

Now at a trade Elephant was not to be compared with Rabbit, for he could not talk so pleasantly as Rabbit, and he was not at all sociable. Rabbit went among the women, and laughed and joked with them, and said so many funny things, that they were delighted with him, and when at last the trade question was cautiously touched upon, a chief's wife was so kind to him, that she gave a mighty fine cow in exchange for his little bale of cloth. Elephant, on the other hand, went among the men, and simply told them that he had come to buy cattle with cloth. The Watusi shepherds, not liking his appearance or his manner, said they had no cattle to sell, but if he cared to have it, they would give a year-old heifer for his bale. Though Elephant's bale was a most weighty one, and many times more valuable than Rabbit's, yet as he was so gruff and ugly, he was at last obliged to be satisfied with the little heifer.

Just as they had left the Watusi to begin their return journey, Elephant said to Rabbit, "Now mind, should we meet anyone on the road, and we are asked whose cattle these are, I wish you to oblige me by saying that they are mine, because I should not like people to believe that I am not as good a trader as yourself. They will also be afraid to touch them if they know they belong to me. Whereas, if they hear that they belong to you, every fellow will think he has as good a right to them as yourself, and you dare not defend your property."

"Very well," replied Rabbit, "I quite understand."

In a little while, as Rabbit and Elephant drove their cattle along, they met many people coming from market who stopped and admired them, and said, "Ah, what a fine cow is that! To whom does it belong?"

"It belongs to me," answered the thin voice of Rabbit. "The little one belongs to Elephant."

"Very fine indeed. A good cow that," replied the people, and passed on.

Vexed and annoyed, Elephant cried angrily to Rabbit, "Why did you not answer as I told you? Now mind, do as I tell you at the next meeting with strangers."

"Very well," answered Rabbit, "I will try and remember."

By-and-by they met another party going home with fowls and palm wine, who, when they came up, said, "Ah that is a fine beast, and in prime order. Whose is it?"

"It is mine," quickly replied Rabbit, "and the little scabby heifer belongs to Elephant."

This answer enraged Elephant, who said, "What an obstinate little fool you are. Did you not hear me ask you to say it was mine? Now, remember, you are to say so next time, or I'll leave you to find your own way home, because I know you are a horrible little coward."

"Very well, I'll do it next time," replied Rabbit in a meek voice.

In a short time they met another crowd, which stopped when opposite to them, and the people said, "Really, that is an exceedingly fine cow. To which of you does it belong?"

"It is mine. I bought it from the Watusi," replied Rabbit.

The Elephant was so angry this time, that he broke away from Rabbit, and drove his little heifer by another road, and to Lion, and Hyena, and Buffalo, and Leopard, whom he met, he said what a fine fat cow was being driven by cowardly little Rabbit along the other road. He did this out of mere spite, hoping that some one of them would be tempted to take it by force from Rabbit.

But Rabbit was wise, and had seen the spite in Elephant's face as he went off, and was sure that he would play him some unkind trick. And, as night was falling and his home was far, and he knew that there were many vagabonds lying in wait to rob poor travellers, he reflected that if his wit failed to save him he would be in great danger.

True enough, it was not long before a big blustering lion rose from the side of the road, and cried out, "Hello, you there. Where are you going with that cow? Come, speak out."

"Ah, is that you, Lion? I am taking it to Mugassa, the God, who is about to give a feast to all his friends, and he told me particularly to invite you to share it, if I should meet you."

"Eh? What? To Mugassa? Oh, well, I am proud to have met you, Rabbit. As I am not otherwise engaged I will accompany you, because everyone considers it an honour to wait upon Mugassa."

They proceeded a little further, and a bouncing buffalo came up and bellowed fiercely. "You, Rabbit, stop," said he. "Where are you taking that cow to?"

"I am taking it to Mugassa, don't you know. How would a little fellow like me have the courage to go so far from home if it were not that I am on service for Mugassa? I am charged also to tell you, Buffalo, that if you like to join in the feast Mugassa is about to give, he will be glad to have you as a guest."

"Oh, well, that is good news indeed. I will come along now, Rabbit, and am very glad to have met you. How do you do, Lion?"

A short distance off the party met a huge rogue elephant, who stood in the middle of the road, and demanded to know where the cow was being taken, in a tone which required a quick answer.

"Now, Elephant, get out of the way. This cow is being taken to Mugassa, who will be angry with you if I am delayed. Have you not heard of the feast he is about to give? By the bye, as you are one of the guests, you might as well help me to drive this cow, and let me get on your back, for I am dreadfully tired."

"Why, that's grand," said the Elephant, "I shall be delighted to feast with Mugassa, and, come get on my back. I will carry you with pleasure. And, Rabbit," whispered Elephant, as he lifted him by his trunk, "don't forget to speak a good word for me to Mugassa."

Soon a leopard and then a hyena were met, but seeing such a powerful crowd behind the cow, they affected great civility, and were invited to accompany Rabbit's party to Mugassa's feast.

It was quite dark by the time they arrived at Rabbit's village. At the gate stood two dogs, who were Rabbit's chums, and they barked furiously, but hearing their friend's voice, they came up and welcomed Rabbit.

The party halted, and Rabbit, after reaching the ground, whispered to the dogs how affairs stood, and the dogs wagged their tails approvingly, and yapped with fun as they heard of Rabbit's wit. It did not take long for the dogs to understand what was required of them, and one of them bounded off to the village, and after a short time returned with a pretended message from the great Mugassa.

"Well, my friends, do you hear what Mugassa says?" cried Rabbit, with a voice of importance.

"These dogs are to lay mats inside the village by the gate, and the cow is to be killed, and the meat prepared nicely and laid on the mats. And when that is done, Mugassa himself will come and give each his portion. He says that you are all very welcome.

"Now listen to me before I go in to Mugassa, and I will show you how you can all help to hurry the feast, for I am sure you are all anxious to begin.

"You, Hyena, you must kill the cow, and dress the meat, and Dogs will carry it in and lay it on the mats, but remember, if a bit is touched before Mugassa commands, we are all ruined.

"You, Elephant, you take this brass hatchet of Mugassa's, and split wood nicely for the hearth.

"Buffalo, you go and find a wood with a smooth bark and which burns well, and bring it to Elephant.

"Leopard, you go to the banana plantation, and watch for the falling leaf and catch it with your eyelids, in order that we may have proper plates.

"Lion, my friend, go and fill this pot from the spring, and bring water that Mugassa may wash his hands."

Having issued his instructions, Rabbit went strutting into the village, but after he had gone a little way he darted aside, and passing through a side door, went out and came creeping up towards an ant-hill. On the top was a tuft of grass, and from his hiding-place he commanded a view of the gate, and of all who might come near it.

Now Buffalo could only find one log with smooth bark, and the dogs shouted out to Buffalo that one log was not enough to roast or to boil the meat, and he returned to hunt up some more.

Elephant struck the log with his brass hatchet, which was broken at the first blow, and there was nothing else with which to cut the wood.

Leopard watched and watched for falling leaves, but failed to see any.

Lion's pot had a hole in the bottom, and he could never keep it full, though he tried ever so many times.

Meanwhile Hyena having killed the cow and dressed the meat beautifully, said to the dogs, "Now, my friends, the meat is ready. What shall I do?"

"You can help us carry the meat in, and lay it on the mats, if you like, for Mugassa must see it before anybody can touch it."

"Ah, but I feel extremely hungry, and my mouth waters so that I am sick with longing. May we not go shares and eat a little bit? It looks very nice and fat," whined the Hyena.

"Ah, no, we should not dare do such a thing. We have long ago left the woods, and its habits, and are unfit for anything but human society, but if you were allowed to eat any, you could fly into the woods, and we should have all the blame. No, no, come, help us carry it inside. You will not have to wait long."

The Hyena was obliged to obey, but contrived to hide in the grass some of the tripe. Rabbit, from behind his tuft of grass, saw it all, and winked in the dark.

When the meat was in, the dogs said, "It is all right now. Just stay outside until the other fellows arrive."

Hyena retired, and when he was outside of the gate he searched for his tripe, and lay down quietly to enjoy it, but as he was about to bite it, Rabbit screamed, "Ah, you thief, Hyena. You thief, I see you. Stop thief, Mugassa is coming."

These cries so alarmed Hyena that he dropped his tripe, and fled away as fast as his legs could carry him, and the others, Buffalo, Elephant, Lion, and Leopard, tired out with waiting, and hearing these alarming cries, also ran away, leaving Rabbit and his dog friends in quiet possession. They carried the tripe into the village, and closed the gate and barred it, after which they laughed loud and long, Rabbit rolling on the ground over and over with the fun of it all.

My friends, Rabbit was the smallest of all, but by his wisdom he was more than a match for two Elephants, Buffalo, Leopard, Lion, Hyena, and all. And even his friends, the dogs, had to confess that Rabbit's wit could not be matched. That is my tale.

What Employment Our Lord Gave To Insects

This tale has been edited and adapted from Kate Douglas Wiggin and Nora Archibald Smith's collection, The Talking Beasts, A Book of Fable and Wisdom, and illustrated by Harold Nelson. The book was published in 1922.

All the Insects assembled and went to our Lord to seek employment. On their arrival they said to our Lord, "You have given everyone his work. Now give us also a work to do, so that we may have something to eat."

Our Lord attended to the request of the Insects, and said to them, "Who will give notice that tomorrow all the Insects are to come?"

The Merchant-insect arose and said to our Lord, "The Cricket can give notice well."

So our Lord called the Cricket and said to him when he was come, "Go and give notice this evening, when the sun has set, that tomorrow morning all the Insects are to come to me, for I wish to see them."

The Cricket, obeying our Lord's command, went back to his house, waited until evening, until the sun set, and as soon as he had seen the setting of the sun, he prepared and arose to give notice. So when the Cricket had given notice until midnight, our Lord sent a man to him saying, "Go and tell the Cricket, that there has been much notice, and that it is now enough. Else he will have the headache."

But the Cricket would not hear of this and he said, "If I am out they will see me." So he went into his hole, stretched only his head out, and began to give notice. The Cricket went on giving notice until the day dawned. But when it was day he became silent and stopped giving notice. Then all the Insects arose and went to the prayer-place of our Lord, the Merchant alone being left behind. To all the Insects who came first, our Lord gave their employment, which they all took and went home.

Later the Merchant-insect went to our Lord, and our Lord said to him, "To all your people who came before, I have given their work, and they are gone. Now what kept you back that you came to me last?"

The Merchant-insect replied to our Lord, "My bags are many and on the day when I took my bags and bound them up in my large travelling sacks to load them upon my asses, then my people left me behind and came to you first."

Our Lord said to him, "All other employments are assigned. The people who came first took them and went away, but stop, I will also give one to you. Go, and having arrived at the entrance of the black ants, where there are a great many ant-heads, when you see these many heads of the black ants, take them, and fill your bags with them. Then load your bags upon your ass, carry them to market, spread mats there, and sell them."

So the Merchant-insect obtained his employment, drove his ass, and went from our Lord, picked up ant-heads at the entrance of the black ants, loaded his ass, and went his way to the market. As he went the ass threw off the large bag. Then, he alone not being able to lift the bag, he called people, saying, "Come, be so good as to help me. Let us take the sacks and load my ass."

Not one of the people would do so. Then the little red ants came after him, and when they were got to where he was, he said to them, "Please come and help me to load my ass".

The little red ants said to the Merchant-insect, "We will not help you for nothing."

The Merchant-insect said to the little red ants, "If you will not help me for nothing, then come and help me, and when I have come back from the market, I will pay you."

The little red ants helped him to load his ass, and the Merchant-insect drove his ass to the market, put down his sacks in the midst of the market-place, prepared the ground, spread his mat there, and having sold his ant-heads, he bought his things, and the market people began to disperse.

Then the Merchant-insect started on his way home, and as he went the little red ants saw him, and said to him, "Father-merchant, give us what you owe us."

The Merchant, however, refused them their due, and went on his way. Now, as he went he got fever so that he sat down under a tree, tied his ass fast, and took off the sacks from his ass's back. As he sat there the fever overpowered him, and he lay down. On seeing him lying there the little red ants assembled and came to him. Now the fever was consuming the Merchant-insect's strength, and when the little red ants saw this they assembled together and killed him.

There was one Insect who saw them kill him, and he ran to our Lord, and said to him, "All the little red ants assembled together and killed a man in the midst of the town, that I saw it."

When our Lord heard what the Insect said he called a man and sent him, saying, "Go and call the little red ants which kill people and bring them to me."

The messenger arose, went, called all the little red ants and brought them before our Lord. On seeing the little red ants, our Lord asked them, "Why did you kill the man?"

The little red ants answered, and said to our Lord, "The reason why we killed this man is this. When he went to market and his ass had thrown off the sacks. Those sacks were too heavy for him to take alone, so he called us, and when we came to him, he said to us, 'Please help me to take my large bag and load it upon my ass, that I may go to market. When I have sold my things and come back, I will pay you.' Accordingly we helped him to load his ass. But when he had gone to market and sold all his things there, we saw him on his return home, and went to him to ask him for what he owed us, but he refused it, drove his ass, and went homeward. However, he was only gone a little while, when he got fever, sat down under a tree, tied his ass fast, took off his sacks and laid them down, and on the same spot where he sat down, the fever overpowered him so that he lay down. Then on seeing him lying we went, assembled ourselves and killed him, because he had refused what he owed us."

Our Lord gave them right.

Our Lord said to the Merchant, "You go to market until your life stands still." Our Lord then said to the Cricket, "Do you give notice whenever it is time! This is your work."

Our Lord said to the little red ants, "Whenever you see any Insect unwell and lying down in a place, then go, assemble yourselves and finish it."

Now the Cricket begins to give notice as soon as it is evening and does not keep silence in his hole until the morning comes. This is its employment. The Merchant has no farm and does not do any work, but constantly goes to market. This is its employment, given to it by the Lord. Now the little red ants, whenever they see an Insect unwell and lying down they go and assemble themselves against that Insect, and, even if that Insect has not yet expired, they finish it. This our Lord gave to the little red ants for their employment.

I have now told you the fable of the Insects, which I have heard from Omar Pesami. This is finished.

The Adventures Of Saruti

This tale has been edited and adapted from Henry Morton Stanley's book, My Dark Companions, published in 1893 by Sampson, Lowe, Marston and Company, London.

Kabaka, I think my charms which my father suspended round my neck must be very powerful. I am always in luck. I hear good stories on my journey, I see strange things which no one else seems to have come across. Now on this last journey, by the time I reached Singo, I came to a little village, and as I was drinking banana wine with the chief, he told me that there were two lions near his village who had a band of hyenas to serve as soldiers under them. They used to send them out in pairs, sometimes to one district, and sometimes to another, to purvey food for them. If the peasants showed fight, they went back and reported to their masters, and the lions brought all their soldiers with them, who bothered them so that they were glad to leave a fat bullock tied to a tree as tribute. Then the lions would take the bullock and give orders that the peasant who paid his tribute should be left in peace. The chief declared this to be a fact, having had repeated proof of it.

At the next place, which is Mbagwe, the man Buvaiya, who is in charge, told me that when he went a short time before to pay his respects to the Muzimu, the oracle of the district, he met about thirty kokorwa on the road, hunting close together for snakes, and that as soon as they saw him, they charged at him, and would have killed him had he not run up a tree. He tells me that though they are not much bigger than rabbits, they are very savage, and make travelling alone very dangerous. I think they must be some kind of small dogs. Perhaps the old men of the court may be better able to tell you what they are.

At the next village of Ngondo a smart boy named Rutuana was brought to me, who was said to have been lately playing with a young friend of the same age at long stick and little stick. His friend hit the little stick, and sent it a great way, and Rutuana had to fetch it from the long grass. While searching for it, one of those big serpents which swallow goats and calves caught him, and coiled itself around him. Though he screamed out for help, Rutuana laid his stick across his chest, and clutching hold of each end with a hand, held fast to it until help came. His friend ran up a tree, and only helped him by screaming. As the serpent could not break the boy's hold of the stick, he was unable to crush his ribs, because his outstretched arms protected them, but when he was nearly exhausted the villagers came out with spears and shields. These fellows, however, were so stupid that they did not know how to kill the serpent until Rutuana shouted to them, "Quick! Draw your bows and shoot him through the neck." A man stepped forward then, and when close to him pierced his throat with the arrow, and as the serpent uncoiled himself to attack the men, Rutuana fell down. The serpent was soon speared, and the boy was carried home. I think that boy will become a great warrior.

At the next village the peasants were much disturbed by a multitude of snakes which had collected there for some reason. They had seen several long black snakes which had taken lodging in the anthills. These had already killed five cows, and lately had taken to attacking the travellers along the road that leads by the anthills, when an Arab, named Massoudi, hearing of their trouble, undertook to kill them. He had some slaves with him, and he clothed their legs with buffalo hide, and placed cooking-pots on their heads, and told them to go among the anthills. When the snakes came out of their holes he shot them one by one. Among the reptiles he killed were three kinds of serpents which possessed horns. The peasants skinned them, and made bags of them to preserve their charms. One kind of horned snake, very thick and short, is said to lay eggs as large as those of fowls. The mubarasassa, which is of a greyish colour, is also said to be able to kill elephants.

I then went to Kyengi, beyond Singo, and the peasants, on coming to gossip with me, rather upset me with terrible stories of the mischief done by a big black leopard. It seems that he had first killed a woman, and had carried the body into the bush, and another time had killed two men while they were setting their nets for some small ground game. Then a native hunter, under promise of reward from the chief, set out with two spears to kill him. He did not succeed, but he said that he saw a strange sight. As he was following the track of the leopard, he suddenly came to a little jungle, with an open space in the middle. A large wild sow, followed by her litter of little pigs, was rooting about, and grunting as pigs do, when he saw the monstrous black leopard crawl towards one of the pigs. Then there was a shrill squeal from a piggie, and the mother, looking up, discovered its danger, at which it furiously charged the leopard, clashing her tusks and foaming at the mouth. The leopard turned sharp round, and sprang up a tree. The sow tried to jump up after it, but being unable to reach her enemy in that way, she set about working hard at the roots.

While she was busy about it the peasant ran back to obtain a net and assistants, and to get his hunting-dog. When he returned, the sow was still digging away at the bottom of the tree, and had made a great hole all round it. The pigs, frightened at seeing so many men, trotted away into the bush, and the hunter and his friends prepared to catch the leopard. They pegged the net all about the tree, then let loose the dog, and urged him towards the net. As he touched the net, the hunters made a great noise, and shouted, at which the leopard bounded from the tree, and with one scratch of his paw ripped the dog open, sprang over the net, tapped one of the men on the shoulder, and was running away, when he received a wound in the shoulder, and stopped to bite the spear. The hunters continued to worry him, until at last, covered with blood, he lay down and died.

One day's journey beyond Kyengi, I came to the thorn-fenced village of some Watusi shepherds, who, it seems, had suffered much from a pair of lion cubs, which were very fierce. The headman's little boy was looking after some calves when the cubs came and quietly stalked him through the grass, and caught him. The headman took it so much to heart, that as soon as he heard the news he went straight back to his village and hanged himself to a rafter. The Watusi love their families very much, but it seems to be a custom with these herdsmen that if a man takes his own life, the body cannot be buried, and though he was a headman, they carried it to the jungle, and after leaving it for the vultures, they returned and set fire to his hut, and burnt it to the ground. When they had done that, the Watusi collected together and had a long hunt after the young lions, but as yet they have not been able to find them.

When the sun was half-way up the sky, I came from Kyengi to some peasants, who lived near a forest which is affected by the man-monkeys called nzike, or gorilla. I was told by them that the nzike know how to smoke and make fire just as we do. It is a custom among the natives, when they see smoke issuing through the trees, for them to say, "Behold, the nzike is cooking his food."

I asked them if it were true that the nzike carried off women to live with them, but they all told me that it was untrue, though the old men sometimes tell such stories to frighten the women, and keep them at home out of danger. Knowing that I was on the king's business, they did not dare tell me their fables.

By asking them all sorts of questions, I was shown to a very old man with a white beard, with whom I obtained much amusement. It appears he is a great man at riddles, and he asked me a great many.

One was, "What is it that always goes straight ahead, and never looks back?" I tried hard to answer him, but when finally he announced that it was a river, I felt very foolish.

He then asked me, "What is it that is bone outside and meat within?"

The people laughed, and mocked me. Then he said that it was an egg, which was very true.

Another question he gave me was, "What is it that looks both ways when you pass it?"

Some said one thing, and some said another, and at last he answered that it was grass.

Then he asked me, "What good thing was it which a man eats, and which he constantly fastens his eyes upon while he eats, and after eating, throws a half away?"

I thought and considered, but I never knew what it was until he told me that it was a roasted ear of Indian corn.

That old man was a very wise one, and among some of his sayings was that "When people dream much, the old moon must be dying."

He also said that "When the old moon is dying, the hunter need never leave home to seek game, because it is well known that he would meet nothing."

And he further added, that at that time the potter need not try to bake any pots, because the clay would be sure to be rotten.

Some other things which he said made me think a little of their meaning. He said, "When people have provisions in their huts, they do not say, Let us go into another man's house and rob him."

He also said, "When you see a crook-back, you do not ask him to stand straight, nor an old man to join the dance, nor the man who is in pain, to laugh."

And what he said about the traveller is very true. The man who clings to his own hearth does not tickle our ears, like him who sees many lands, and hears new stories.

The next day I stopped at a village near the little lake of Kitesa's called Mtukura. The chief in charge loved talking so much, that he soon made me as well acquainted with the affairs of his family as though he courted my sister. His people are accustomed to eat frogs and rats, and from the noise in the reeds, and the rustling and squealings in the roof of the hut I slept in, I think there is little fear of famine in that village. Nor are they averse, they tell me, to iguanas and those vile feeders, the hyenas.

It is a common belief in the country that it was Naraki, a wife of Uni, a sultan of Unyoro, who made that lake. While passing through, she was very thirsty, and cried out to her Muzimu spirit, the Muzimu which attends the kings of Unyoro, and which is most potent. And all at once there was a hissing flight of firestones in the air, and immediately after, there was a fall of a monstrously large one, which struck the ground close to her, and made a great hole, out of which the water spurted and continued leaping up until a lake was formed, and buried the fountain out of sight, and the rising waters formed a river, which has run north from the lake ever since into the Kafu.

Close by this lake is a dark grove, sacred to Muzingeh, the king of the birds. It is said that he has only one eye, but once a year he visits the grove, and after building his house, he commands all the birds from the Nyanzas and the groves, to come and see him and pay their homage. For half a moon the birds, great and small, may be seen following him about along the shores of the lake, like so many guards around a king, and before night they are seen returning in the same manner to the grove. The parrots' cries tell the natives when they come, and no one would care to miss the sight, and the glad excitement among the feathered tribe.

But there is one bird, called the Kirurumu, that refuses to acknowledge the sovereignty of the Muzingeh. The other birds have tried often to induce him to associate with the Muzingeh, but Kirurumu always answers that a beautiful creature like himself, with gold and blue feathers, and such a pretty crest, was never meant to be seen in the company of an ugly bird that possesses only one eye.

On the other side of Lake Mtukura is a forest where Dungu, the king of the animals, lives. It is to Dungu that all the hunters pray when they set out to seek for game. He builds first a small hut, and after propitiating him with a small piece of flesh, he asks Dungu that he may be successful. Then Dungu enters into the hunter's head, if he is pleased with the offering, and the cunning of the man becomes great. His nerves stiffen, and his bowels are strengthened, and the game is secured. When Dungu wishes a man to succeed in the hunt, it is useless for the buffalo to spurn the earth and moo, or for the leopard to cover himself with sand in his rage, for the spear of the hunter drinks his blood. But the hunter must not forget to pay the tribute to the deity, lest he be killed on the way home.

The friendly chief insisted that I should become his blood-fellow, and stay with him a couple of days. The witch-doctor, a man of great influence in the country, was asked to unite us. He took a sharp little knife, and made a gash in the skin of my right leg, just above the knee, and did the same to the chief, and then rubbed his blood over my wound, and my blood over his, and we became brothers. Among his gifts was this beautiful shield, which I beg Mtesa, my Kabaka, to accept, because I have seen none so beautiful, and it is too good for a colonel whose only hope and wish is to serve his king.

I am glad that I rested there because I saw a most wonderful sight towards evening. As we were seated under the bananas, we heard a big he-goat's bleat, and by the sound of it we knew that it was neither for fun nor for love. It was a tone of anger and fear. Almost at the same time, one of the boys rushed up to us, and his face had really turned grey from fear, and he cried, "There is a lion in the goat-pen, and the big he-goat is fighting with him."

They had forgotten to tell me about this famous goat, which was called Kasuju, after some great man who had been renowned in war, and he certainly was worth speaking about, and Kasuju was well known round about for his wonderful strength and fighting qualities. When we got near the pen with our spears and shields, the he-goat was butting the lion, who was young, for he had no mane, as he might have butted a pert young nanny-goat, and baaing with as full a note as that of a buffalo calf. It appears that Kasuju saw the destroyer creeping towards one of his wives, and dashing at his flank knocked him down.

As we looked on from the outside, we saw that Kasuju was holding his own very well, and we thought that we would not check the fight, but prepare ourselves to have a good cast at the lion as he attempted to leave. The lion was getting roused up, and we saw the spring he made, but Kasuju nimbly stepped aside and gave him such a stroke that it sounded like a drum. Then Kasuju trotted away in front of his trembling wives, and as the lion came up, we watched him draw his ears back as he raised himself on his hind feet like a warrior. The lion advanced to him, and he likewise rose as though he would wrestle with him, when Kasuju shot into his throat with so true and fair a stroke, that drove one of his horns deep into the throat. It was then the lion's claws began to work, and with every scratch poor Kasuju's hide was torn dreadfully, but he kept his horn in the wound, and pushed home, and made the wound large.

Then the lion sprang free, and the blood spurted all over Kasuju. Blinded with his torn and hanging scalp, and weakened with his wounds, he staggered about, pounding blindly at his enemy, until the lion gave him one mighty stroke with its paw, and sent him headlong, and then seized him by the neck and shook him, and we heard the cruel crunch as the fangs met. But it was the last effort of the lion, for just as Kasuju was lifeless, the lion rolled over him, dead also. We buried Kasuju honourably in a grave, as we would bury a brave man, but the lion we skinned, and I have got his fur with the ragged hole in the throat.

The singular fight we had witnessed, furnished us all with much matter for talk about lions, and it brought into the mind of one of them a story of a crocodile and lion fight which had happened some time before in the night. Lake Mtukura swarms with crocodiles, and situated as it is in a region of game they must be fat with prey. One night a full-grown lion with a fine mane came to cool his dry throat in the lake, and was quaffing water, when he felt his nose seized by something that rose up from below.

From the traces of the struggle by the water's edge, it must have been a terrible one. The crocodile's long claws had left deep marks, showing how he must have been lifted out of the water, and flung forcibly down, but in the morning both lion and crocodile were found dead, the crocodile's throat wide open with a broad gash, but his teeth still fastened in the lion's nose.

The wise old man whom I met, told me one thing I had nearly forgotten to say. He said, 'I know you are a servant of the king, and if ever you want the king's face to soften to you and his hand to open with gifts, compare yourself to the lid of a cooking-pot, which, though the pot may be full of fragrant stew, receives naught but the vapour, and the king who is wise will understand and will be pleased with his servant.'"

Man And Turtle

This tale has been edited and adapted from Kate Douglas Wiggin and Nora Archibald Smith's collection, The Talking Beasts, A Book of Fable and Wisdom, and illustrated by Harold Nelson. The book was published in 1922.

Let me tell you about Turtle of Koka.

A man from Lubi la Suku caught a Turtle in the bush. He came with it to the village. The people there said, "Let us kill it!"

Some of the people then asked, "How shall we kill it?"

The response was, "We shall cut it with hatchets."

Turtle replied, singing:

"Turtle of Koka,

And hatchet of Koka.

Hatchet not kill me a bit."

The people again asked, "What shall we kill him with?"

Some said, "We shall kill him with stones."

Fear grasped Turtle and he said, "I am going to die." Then he sang:

"Turtle of Koka,

And stone of Koka.

Stone will not kill me a bit."

The people said, "Let us cast him into the fire!"

Turtle sang:

"Turtle of Koka,

And fire of Koka.

Fire will not kill me a bit.

On my back,

It is like stone.

Not there can

Catch on fire."

The people said, "We will kill him with knives."

Turtle sang:

"Turtle of Koka,

And knife of Koka.

Knife will not kill me a bit."

The people said, "How shall we kill him?"

Others said, "Let us cast him into the depth of water."

Turtle then said, "Woe! I shall die there in the water! How shall I survive?"

The people said, "We have it! We have found the way that we can kill him!"

They carried him all the way to the river, where they cast him into the depths. Turtle dived down and after a while he emerged near the far bank. Turtle swam about freely and sang:

"In water, in my home!

In water, in my home!"

The people said, "Oh, Turtle has fooled us! We were going to kill him with hatchets. He said, 'Hatchet will not kill me a bit.' We spoke of casting him into the water. He said, 'I am going to die.' We came. We cast him into the water, but we saved him."

This is what caused the Turtle to live in the water. The people were going to kill him, but he was too shrewd and cunning.

The Boy Kinneneh And The Gorilla

This tale has been edited and adapted from Henry Morton Stanley's book, My Dark Companions, published in 1893 by Sampson, Lowe, Marston and Company, London.

In the early days of Uganda, there was a small village situated on the other side of the Katonga, in Buddu, and its people had planted bananas and plantains, which in time grew to be quite a large grove, and produced abundant and very fine fruit. From a grove of bananas when its fruit is ripe there comes a very pleasant odour, and when a puff of wind blows over it, and bears the fragrance towards you, I know of nothing so well calculated to excite the appetite, unless it be the smell of roasted meat. Anyhow, such must have been the feeling of a mighty big gorilla, who one day, while roaming about alone in the woods searching for nuts to eat, stopped suddenly and stood up and sniffed for some time, with his nose well out in the direction of the village. After a while he shook his head and fell on all fours again to resume his search for food. Again there came with a whiff of wind a strong smell of ripe bananas, and he stood on his feet once more, and with his nose shot out he drew in a greedy breath and then struck himself over the stomach, and said, "I thought it was so. There are bananas that way, and I must get some."

Down he fell on all fours, and put out his arms with long stretches, just as a fisherman draws in a heavy net, and is eager to prevent the escape of the fish.

In a little while he came to the edge of the grove, and stood and looked gloatingly on the beautiful fruit hanging in great bunches. Presently he saw something move. It was a woman bent double over a basket, and packing the fruit neatly in it, so that she could carry a large quantity at one journey.

The gorilla did not stay long in thinking, but crawled up secretly to her, and then with open arms rushed forward and seized her. Before the woman could utter her alarm he had lifted her and her basket and trotted away with them into the deepest bush. On reaching his den he flung the woman on the ground, as you would fling dead meat, and bringing the banana basket close to him, his two legs hugging it close to his round paunch, he began to gorge himself, muttering strange sounds while he peeled the fruit.

By-and-by the woman came to her senses, but instead of keeping quiet, she screamed and tried to run away. If it were not for that movement and noise, she perhaps might have been able to creep away unseen, but animals of all kinds never like to be disturbed while eating, so Gorilla gave one roar of rage, and gave her such a squeeze that the breath was clean driven out of her. When she was still he fell to again, and tore the peeling off the bananas, and tossed one after another down his wide throat, until there was not one of the fruit left in the basket, and the big paunch was swollen to twice its first size. Then, after laying his paw on the body to see if there was any life left in it, he climbed up to his nest above, and curled himself into a ball for a sleep.

When he woke he shook himself and yawned, and looking below he saw the body of the woman, and her empty basket, and he remembered what had happened. He descended the tree, lifted the body and let it fall, then took up the basket, looked inside and outside of it, raked over the peelings of the bananas, but could not find anything left to eat.

He began to think, scratching the fur on his head, on his sides, and his paunch, picking up one thing and then another in an absent-minded way. And then he appeared to have made up a plan.

Whatever it was, this is what he did. It was still early morning, and as there was no sign of a sun, it was cold, and human beings must have been finishing their last sleep. He got up and went straight for the plantation. On the edge of the banana-grove he heard a cock crow. He stopped and listened to it, and he became angry.

"Someone," he said to himself, "is stealing my bananas," and with that he marched in the direction where the cock was crowing.

He came to the open place in front of the village, and saw several tall houses much larger than his own nest, and while he was looking at them, the door of one of them was opened, and a man came out. He crept towards him, and before he could cry out the gorilla had squeezed him until his ribs had cracked, and he was dead. He flung him down, and entered into the hut. He saw a woman, who was blowing a fire on the hearth, and he took hold of her and squeezed her until there was no life left in her body. There were three children inside, and a bed on the floor. He treated them also in the same way, and they were all dead. Then he went into another house, and slew all the people in it, one with a squeeze, another with a squeeze and a bite with his great teeth, and there was no one left alive. In this way he entered into five houses and killed all the people in them, but in the sixth house lived the boy Kinneneh and his old mother.

Kinneneh had fancied that he heard an unusual sound, and he had stood inside with his eyes close to a chink in the reed door for some time when he saw something that resembled what might be said to be half animal and half man. He walked like a man, but had the fur of a beast. His arms were long, and his body was twice the breadth and thickness of a full-grown man. He did not know what it was, and when he saw it go into his neighbours' houses, and heard those strange sounds, he grew afraid, and turned and woke his mother, saying, "Mother, wake up! There is a strange big beast in our village killing our people. So wake up quickly and follow me."

"But where shall we fly, my son?" she whispered anxiously.

"Up to the loft, and lie low in the darkest place," replied Kinneneh, and he set her the example and assisted his mother.

Now those Uganda houses are not low-roofed like those of Congo-land, but are very high, as high as a tree, and they rise to a point, and near the top there is a loft where people stow their nets, and pots, and where spear-shafts and bows are kept to season, and where corn is kept to dry, and green bananas are stored to ripen. It was in this dark lofty place that Kinneneh hid himself and his mother, and waited in silence.

In a short time the gorilla put his head into their house and listened, and stepping inside he stood awhile, and looked searchingly around. He could see no one and heard nothing stir. He peered under the bed-grass, into the black pots and baskets, but there was no living being to be found.

"Ha, ha," he cried, thumping his chest like a man when he has got the big head. "I am the boss of this place now, and the tallest of these human nests shall be my own, and I shall feast every day on ripe bananas and plantains, and there is no one who can molest me, ha, ha!"

"Ha, ha!" echoed a shrill, piping voice after his great bass.

The gorilla looked around once more, among the pots, and the baskets, but finding nothing walked out. Kinneneh, after a while skipped down the ladder and watched between the open cane-work of the door, and saw him enter the banana-grove, and waited there until he returned with a mighty load of the fruit. He then saw him go out again into the grove, and bidding his mother lie still and patient, Kinneneh slipped out and ascended into the loft of the house chosen by the gorilla for his nest, where he hid himself and waited.

Presently the gorilla returned with another load of the fruit, and, squatting on his haunches, commenced to peel the fruit, and fill his throat and mouth with it, mumbling and chuckling, and saying, "Ha, ha! This is grand! Plenty of bananas to eat, and all, all my own. None to say, 'Give me some,' but all my very own. Ho, ho! I shall feast every day. Ha, ha!"

"Ha, ha," echoed the piping voice again.

The gorilla stopped eating and made an ugly frown as he listened. Then he said, "That is the second time I have heard a thin voice saying, 'Ha, ha!' If I only knew who it was that cried 'Ha, ha!' I would squeeze him, and squeeze him until he cried, 'Ugh, ugh!'"

"Ugh, ugh!" echoed the little voice again.

The gorilla leaped to his feet and rummaged around the pots and the baskets, took hold of the bodies one after another and dashed them against the floor, then went to every house and searched, but could not discover who it was that mocked him.

In a short time he returned and ate a pile of bananas that would have satisfied twenty men, and afterwards he went out, saying to himself that it would be a good thing to fill the nest with food, as it was a bore to leave the warm nest each time he felt a desire to eat.

No sooner had he departed than Kinneneh slipped down, and carried every bunch that had been left away to his own house, where they were stowed in the loft for his mother, and after enjoining his mother to remain still, he waited, peering through the chinks of the door.

He soon saw Gorilla bearing a pile of bunches that would have required ten men to carry, and after flinging them into the chief's house, return to the plantation for another supply. While Gorilla was tearing down the plants and plucking at the bunches, Kinneneh was actively engaged in transferring what he brought into the loft by his mother's side. Gorilla made many trips in this manner, and brought in great heaps, but somehow his stock appeared to be very small. At last his strength was exhausted, and feeling that he could do no more that day, he commenced to feed on what he had last brought, promising to himself that he would do better in the morning.

At dawn the gorilla hastened out to obtain a supply of fruit for his breakfast, and Kinneneh took advantage of his absence to hide himself overhead.

He was not long in his place before Gorilla came in with a huge lot of ripe fruit, and after making himself comfortable on his haunches with a great bunch before him he rocked himself to and fro, saying while he munched, "Ha, ha! Now I have plenty again, and I shall eat it all myself. Ha, ha!"

"Ha, ha," echoed a thin voice again, so close and clear it seemed to him, that leaping up he made sure to catch it. As there appeared to be no one in the house, he rushed out raging, champing his teeth, and searched the other houses, but meantime Kinneneh carried the bananas to the loft of the gorilla's house, and covered them with bark-cloth.

In a short time Gorilla returned furious and disappointed, and sat down to finish the breakfast he had only begun, but on putting out his hands he found only the withered peelings of yesterday's bananas. He looked and rummaged about, but there was positively nothing left to eat. He was now terribly hungry and angry, and he bounded out to obtain another supply, which he brought in and flung on the floor, saying, "Ha, ha! I will now eat the whole at once, all to myself, and that other thing which says, 'Ha, ha!' after me, I will hunt and mash him like this," and he seized a ripe banana and squeezed it with his paw with so much force that the pulp was squirted all over him. "Ha, ha!" he cried.

"Ha, ha!" mocked the shrill voice, so clear that it appeared to come from behind his ear.

This was too much to bear. Gorilla bounded up and vented a roar of rage. He tossed the pots, the baskets, the bodies, and bed-grass about, bellowing so loudly and funnily in his fury that Kinneneh, away up in the loft, could scarcely forbear imitating him. But the mocker could not be found, and Gorilla roared loudly in the open place before the village, and tore in and out of each house, looking for him.

Kinneneh descended swiftly from his hiding-place, and bore every banana into the loft as before.

Gorilla hastened to the plantation again, and so angry was he that he uprooted the banana-stalks by the root, and snapped off the clusters with one stroke of his great dog-teeth, and having got together a large stock, he bore it in his arms to the house.

"There," said he, "ha, ha! Now I shall eat in comfort and have a long sleep afterwards, and if that fellow who mocks me comes near, ah! I would", and he crushed a big bunch in his arms and cried, "ha, ha!"

"Ha, ha! Ha, ha!" cried the mocking voice, and again it seemed to be at the back of his head. Whereupon Gorilla flung his arms behind in the hope of catching him, but there was nothing but his own back, which sounded like a damp drum with the stroke.

"Ha, ha! Ha, ha!" repeated the voice, at which Gorilla shot out of the door, and raced round the house, thinking that the owner was flying before him, but he never could overtake the flyer. Then he went around outside of the other houses, and flew round and round the village, but he could discover naught. But meanwhile Kinneneh had borne all the stock of bananas up into the loft above, and when Gorilla returned there was not one banana of all the great pile he had brought left on the floor.

When, after he was certain that there was not a single bit of a banana left for him to eat, he scratched his sides and his legs, and putting his hand on the top of his head, he uttered a great cry just like a great, stupid child, but the crying did not fill his tummy. No, he must have bananas for that, and he rose up after a while and went to procure some more fruit.

But when he had brought a great pile of it and had sat down with his nice-smelling bunch before him, he would exclaim, "Ha, ha! Now, now I shall eat and be satisfied. I shall fill myself with the sweet fruit, and then lie down and sleep. Ha, ha!"

Then instantly the mocking voice would cry out after him, "Ha, ha!" and sometimes it sounded close to his ears, and then behind his head, sometimes it appeared to come from under the bananas and sometimes from the doorway Gorilla would roar in fury, and he would grind his teeth just like two grinding-stones, and chatter to himself, and race about the village, trying to discover where the voice came, but in his absence the fruit would be swept away by his invisible enemy, and when he would come in to finish his meal, there were only blackened and stained banana peelings, the refuse of his first feast.

Gorilla would then cry like a whipped child, and would go again into the plantation, to bring some more fruit into the house, but when he returned with it he would always boast of what he was going to do, and cry out "Ha, ha!" and instantly his unseen enemy would mock him and cry "Ha, ha!" and he would start up raving and screaming in rage, and search for him, and in his absence his bananas would be whisked away. And Gorilla's hunger grew on him, until his paunch became like an empty sack, and what with his hunger and grief and rage, and furious raving and racing about, his strength was at last quite exhausted, and the end of him was that on the fifth day he fell from weakness across the threshold of the chief's house, which he had chosen to make his nest, and there died.

When the people of the next village heard of how Kinneneh, a little boy, had conquered the man-killing gorilla, they brought him and his mother away, and they gave him a fine new house and a plantation, and male and female slaves to tend it, and when their old king died, and the period of mourning for him was over, they elected wise Kinneneh to be king over them.

Nianga Dia Ngenga And Leopard

This tale has been edited and adapted from Kate Douglas Wiggin and Nora Archibald Smith's collection, The Talking Beasts, A Book of Fable and Wisdom, and illustrated by Harold Nelson. The book was published in 1922.

Nianga Dia Ngenga took up his gun, saying, "I will go a-hunting." He reached the bush and he hunted, but he saw no game, so he said, "I will go home."

When he returned home, he found Mister Leopard stuck up in the fork of a tree.

When Leopard saw Nianga, he said, "Father Nianga, help me out!"

Nianga asked, "Why are stuck in a tree? Who has done this to you?"

Nianga said, "Help me down first. Then I shall tell you." Nianga took him down from tree and set him on the ground.

Leopard said, "Elephant has stuck me up in the fork of the tree. Sir, to whom one has given life, one gives more. I have been two days on the tree. Give me a little food."

Nianga said, "Where shall I find food?"

Leopard said, "Anywhere. Everywhere."

Nianga took up his dog. He gave it to Mister Leopard, and Mister Leopard ate it and said, "I am not satisfied."

Nianga took up another dog and gave it to Mister Leopard. On eating the second dog Mister Leopard said, "Still I have not eaten enough."

Nianga Dia Ngenga took up his cartridge-box. He gave that to Mister Leopard as well. Mister Leopard when he had eaten it, said, "Still I have not eaten enough."

Hare came along and found them talking. Hare asked, "Why are you quarrelling?"

Nianga said, "I found Mister Leopard in the fork of a tree. Says he, 'Take me out!' I took him out. Says he, 'Give me something to eat!' I gave him both my dogs and my cartridge-box. He says, 'Give me more to eat.' That is what we are quarrelling about."

Hare said, "Put Mister Leopard back on the tree where he was. Then I can see what all the fuss is about."

Mister Leopard was placed back in the tree and Hare moved off to a distance. He called Nianga and said, "You, Nianga, are unwise. Mister Leopard is a wild beast, and he catches people. You, who saved him, well, he wanted to devour you. Shoot him."

Nianga then shot Mister Leopard.

The City Of The Elephants

This tale has been edited and adapted from Henry Morton Stanley's book, My Dark Companions, published in 1893 by Sampson, Lowe, Marston and Company, London.

A Bungandu man named Dudu, and his wife Salimba, were one day searching in the forest a long way from the town for a proper redwood-tree, out of which they could make a wooden mortar wherein they could pound their manioc. They saw several trees of this kind as they proceeded, but after examining one, and then another, they would appear to be dissatisfied, and say, "Perhaps if we went a little further we might find a still better tree for our purpose."

And so Dudu and Salimba proceeded further and further into the tall and thick woods, and ever before them there appeared to be still finer trees which would after all be unsuited for their purpose, being too soft, or too hard, or hollow, or too old, or of another kind than the useful redwood. They strayed in this manner very far.

In the forest where there is no path or track, it is not easy to tell which direction one came from, and as they had walked round many trees, they were too confused to know which way they ought to turn homeward. When Dudu said he was sure that his course was the right one for home, Salimba was as sure that the opposite was the true way. They agreed to walk in the direction Dudu wished, and after a long time spent on it, they gave it up and tried another, but neither took them any nearer home.

The night overtook them and they slept at the foot of a tree. The next day they wandered still farther from their town, and they became anxious and hungry. As one cannot see many yards off on any side in the forest, an animal hears the coming step long before the hunter gets a chance to use his weapon. Therefore, though they heard the rustle of the flying antelope, or wild pig as it rushed away, it only served to make their anxiety greater. And the second day passed, and when night came upon them they were still hungrier.

Towards the middle of the third day, they came into an open place by a pool frequented by Kiboko, the hippo, and there was a margin of grass round about it, and as they came in view of it they saw there a grazing buffalo. Dudu bade his wife stand behind a tree while he chose two of his best and sharpest arrows, and after a careful look at his bow-string, he crept up to the buffalo, and drove an arrow home as far as the guiding leaf, which nearly buried it in the body.

While the beast looked around and started from the twinge within, Dudu shot his second arrow into his windpipe, and it fell to the ground quite choked. Now here was water to drink and food to eat, and after cutting a load of meat they chose a thick bush-clump a little distance from the pool, made a fire, and, after satisfying their hunger, slept in content. The fourth day they stopped and roasted a meat provision that would last many days, because they knew that luck is not constant in the woods.

On the fifth they travelled, and for three days more they wandered. They then met a young lion who, at the sight of them, boldly advanced, but Dudu sighted his bow, and sent an arrow into his chest which sickened him of the fight, and he turned and fled.

A few days afterwards, Dudu saw an elephant standing close to them behind a high bush, and whispered to his wife, "Ah, now, we have a chance to get meat enough for a month."

"But," said Salimba, "why should you wish to kill him, when we have enough meat still with us? Do not hurt him. Ah, what a fine back he has, and how strong he is. Perhaps he would carry us home."

"How could an elephant understand our wishes?" asked Dudu.

"Talk to him anyhow. Perhaps he will be clever enough to understand what we want."

Dudu laughed at his wife's simplicity, but to please her he said, "Elephant, we have lost our way. Will you carry us and take us home, and we shall be your friends for ever."

The Elephant ceased waving his trunk, and nodding to himself, and turning to them said, "If you come near to me and take hold of my ears, you may get on my back, and I will carry you safely."

When the Elephant spoke, Dudu fell back from surprise, and looked at him as though he had not heard aright, but Salimba advanced with all confidence, and laid hold of one of his ears, and pulled herself up on to his back. When she was seated, she cried out, "Come, Dudu, what are you looking at? Did you not hear him say he would carry you?"

Seeing his wife smiling and comfortable on the Elephant's back, Dudu became a little braver and moved forward slowly, when the Elephant spoke again, "Come, Dudu, be not afraid. Follow your wife, and do as she did, and then I will travel home with you quickly."

Dudu then put aside his fears, and his surprise, and seizing the Elephant's ear, he ascended and seated himself by his wife on the Elephant's back.

Without another word the Elephant moved on rapidly, and the motion seemed to Dudu and Salimba most delightful. Whenever any overhanging branch was in the way, the Elephant wrenched it off, or bent it and passed on. No creek, stream, gulley, or river, stopped him, and he seemed to know exactly the way he should go, as if the road he was travelling was well known to him.

When it was getting dark he stopped and asked his friends if they would not like to rest for the night, and finding that they so wished it, he stopped at a nice place by the side of the river, and they slid to the ground, Dudu first, and Salimba last. He then broke dead branches for them, out of which they made a fire, and the Elephant stayed by them, as though he was their slave.

Hearing their talk, he understood that they would like to have something better than dried meat to eat, and he said to them, "I am glad to know your wishes, for I think I can help you. Bide here a little, and I will go and search."

About the middle of the night he returned to them with something white in his trunk, and a young antelope in front of him. The white thing was a great manioc root, which he dropped into Salimba's lap.

"There, Salimba," he said, "there is food for you, eat your fill and sleep in peace, for I will watch over you."

Dudu and Salimba had seen many strange things that day, but they were both still more astonished at the kindly and intelligent care which their friend the Elephant took of them. While they roasted their fresh meat over the flame, and the manioc root was baking under the heap of hot embers, the Elephant dug with his tusks for the juicy roots of his favourite trees round about their camp, and munched away contentedly.

The next morning, all three, after a bathe in the river, set out on their journey more familiar with one another, and in a happier mood. About noon, while they were resting during the heat of the day, two lions came near to roar at them, but when Dudu was drawing his bow at one of them, the Elephant said, "You leave them to me. I will make them run pretty quick," saying which he tore off a great bough of a tree, and nourishing this with his trunk, he trotted on the double quick towards them, and used it so heartily that they both scurried away with their bellies to the ground, and their hides shrinking and quivering out of fear of the great rod.

In the afternoon the Elephant and his human friends set off again, and sometime after they came to a wide and deep river. He begged his friends to descend while he tried to find out the shallowest part. It took him some time to do this. But, having discovered a ford where the water was not quite over his back, he returned to them, and urged them to mount him as he wished to reach home before dark.

As the Elephant was about to enter the river, he said to Dudu, "I see some hunters of your own kind creeping up towards us. Perhaps they are your kinsmen. Talk to them, and let us see whether they be friends or foes."

Dudu hailed them, but they gave no answer, and, as they approached nearer, they prepared to cast their spears, so the Elephant said, "I see that they are not your friends. Therefore, as I cross the river, look out for them, and keep them at a distance. If they come to the other side of the river, I shall know how to deal with them."

They got to the opposite bank safely. But, as they were landing, Dudu and Salimba noticed that their pursuers had discovered a canoe, and that they were pulling hard after them. But the Elephant soon after landing came to a broad path smoothed by much travel, over which he took them at a quick pace, so fast, indeed, that the pursuers had to run to be able to keep up with them. Dudu, every now and then let fly an arrow at the hunters, which kept them at a safe distance.

Towards night they came to the City of the Elephants, which was very large and fit to shelter such a multitude as they now saw. Their elephant did not linger, however, but took his friends at the same quick pace until they came to a mighty elephant that was much larger than any other, and his ivories were gleaming white and curled up, and exceedingly long. Before him Dudu and Salimba were told by their friend to descend and salaam, and he told his lord how he had found them lost in the woods, and how for the sake of the kindly words of the woman he had befriended them, and assisted them to the city of his tribe. When the King Elephant heard all this he was much pleased, and said to Dudu and Salimba that they were welcome to his city, and how they should not want for anything, as long as they would be pleased to stay with them, but as for the hunters who had dared to chase them, he would give orders at once.

Accordingly he gave a signal, and ten active young elephants dashed out of the city, and in a short time not one of the hunters was left alive, though one of them had leaped into the river, thinking that he could escape in that manner. But then you know that an elephant is as much at home in a river, as a Kiboko, so that the last man was soon caught and was drowned.

Dudu and Salimba, however, on account of Salimba's kind heart in preventing her husband wounding the elephant, were made free of the place, and their friend took them with him to many families, and the big pa's and ma's told their little babies all about them and their habits, and said that, though most of the humankind were very stupid and wicked, Dudu and Salimba were very good, and putting their trunks into their ears they whispered that Salimba was the better of the two. Then the little elephants gathered about them and trotted by their side and around them and diverted them with their antics, their races, their wrestlings, and other trials of strength, but when they became familiar and somewhat rude in their rough play, their elephant friend would admonish them, and if that did not suffice, he would switch them soundly.

The City of the Elephants was a spacious and well-trodden glade in the midst of a thick forest, and as it was entered one saw how wisely the elephant families had arranged their manner of life. For without, the trees stood as thick as water-reeds, and the bush or underwood was like an old hedge of milkweed knitted together by thorny vines and snaky climbers into which the human hunter might not even poke his nose without hurt.

The burly elephants had, by much uprooting, created deep hollows, or recesses, wherein a family of two and more might snugly rest, and not even a dart of sunshine might reach them. Round about the great glade the dark leafy arches ran, and Dudu and his wife saw that the elephant families were numerous, for by one sweeping look they could tell that there were more elephants than there are human beings in a goodly village. In some of the recesses there was a row of six and more elephants. In another the parents stood head to head, and their children, big and little, clung close to their parents' sides. In another a family stood with heads turned towards the entrance, and so on all around, while under a big tree in the middle there was quite a gathering of big fellows, as though they were holding a serious palaver. Under another tree one seemed to be on the outlook. Another paced slowly from side to side. Another plucked at this branch or at that. Another appeared to be heaving a tree, or sharpening a blunted ivory. Others seemed appointed to uproot the sprouts, lest the glade might become choked with underwood. Near the entrance on both sides were a brave company of them, faces turned outward, swinging their trunks, napping their ears, rubbing against each other, or who with pate against pate seemed to be drowsily considering something. There was a continual coming in and a going out, singly, or in small companies. The roads that ran through the glade were like a network, clean and smooth, while that which went towards the king's place was so wide that twenty men might walk abreast. At the far end the king stood under his own tree, with his family under the arches behind him.

This was the City of the Elephants as Dudu and Salimba saw it. I ought to say that the outlets of it were many. One went straight through the woods in a line upriver, at the other end it ran in a line following the river downward. One went to a lakelet, where juicy plants and reeds throve like corn in a man's fields, and where the elephants rejoiced in its cool water, and washed themselves and infants. Another went to an ancient clearing where the plantain and manioc grew wild, and wherein more than two human tribes might find food for countless seasons.

Then said their friend to Dudu and Salimba, "Now that I have shown you our manner of life, it is for you to ease your longing for a while and rest with us. When you yearn for home, go tell our king, and he will send you with credit to your kindred."

Then Dudu and his wife resolved to stay, and eat, and they stayed a whole season, not only unhurt, but tenderly cared for, with never a hungry hour or uneasy night. But at last Salimba's heart remembered her children, and kinfolk, and her own warm house and village pleasures, and on hinting of these memories to her husband, he said that after all there was no place like Bungandu. He remembered his long pipe, and the talk-house, the stool-making, shaft-polishing, bow-fitting, and the little tinkering jobs, the wine-trough, and the merry drinking bouts, and he wept softly as he thought of them.

They thus agreed that it was time for them to travel homeward, and together they sought the elephant king, and frankly told him of their state.

"My friends," he replied, "be no longer sad, but haste to depart. With the morning's dawn guides shall take you to Bungandu with such gifts as shall make you welcome to your folk. And when you come to them, say to them that the elephant king desires lasting peace and friendship with them. On our side we shall not injure their plantations, neither a plantain, nor a manioc root belonging to them, and on your side dig no pits for our unwary youngsters, nor hang the barbed iron aloft, nor plant the poisoned stake in the path, so we shall escape hurt and be unprovoked." And Dudu put his hand on the king's trunk as the pledge of good faith.

In the morning, four elephants came up as bearers of the gifts from the king, carrying bales of bark-cloth, and showy mats, and soft hides and other things. Two fighting elephants stood beside the entrance to the city, and when the king elephant came up he lifted Salimba first on the back of her old companion, and then placed Dudu by her side, and at a parting wave the company moved on.

In ten days they reached the edge of the plantation of Bungandu, and the leader halted. The bales were set down on the ground, and then their friend asked Dudu and his wife, "Do you know where you are?"

"We do," they answered.

"Is this Bungandu?" he asked.

"This is Bungandu," they replied.

"Then here we part, that we may not alarm your friends. Go now on your way, and we go on our way. Go tell your folk how the elephants treat their friends, and let there be peace for ever between us."

The elephants turned away, and Dudu and Salimba, after hiding their wealth in the underwood, went arm in arm into the village of Bungandu. When their friends saw them, they greeted them as we would greet our friends whom we have long believed to be dead, but who come back smiling and rejoicing to us.

When the people heard their story they greatly wondered and doubted, but when Dudu and Salimba took them to the place of parting and showed them the hoof prints of seven elephants on the road, and the bales that they had hidden in the underwood, they believed their story. And they made it a rule from that day that no man of the tribe ever should lift a spear, or draw a bow, or dig a pit, or plant the poisoned stake in the path, or hang the barbed iron aloft, to do hurt to an elephant.

And as a proof that I have but told the truth go ask the Bungandu, and they will say why none of their race will ever seek to hurt the elephant, and it will be the same as I have told you.

Leopard And The Other Animals

This tale has been edited and adapted from Kate Douglas Wiggin and Nora Archibald Smith's collection, The Talking Beasts, A Book of Fable and Wisdom, and illustrated by Harold Nelson. The book was published in 1922.

Mister Leopard lived well, but one day hunger gripped him. He said to himself, "What shall I do? I will call all the animals in the world, saying, 'Come, let us have a medical consultation.' When the animals come then I may catch and eat them."

At once he called to Deer, Antelope, Soko, Hare, and Philantomba. They gathered, saying, "Why did you send for us?"

Leopard said, "Let us consult medicine, that we may be healthy."

The sun began to set and the animals began to beat the drums outside and sing the old songs. Mister Leopard himself was beating the drum as he sang:

"O Antelope! O Deer!

Your friend is sick.

Do not shun him!

O Antelope! O Deer!

Your friend is sick.

Do not shun him!

Deer then said, "Chief, the drum, how are you playing it? Bring it here so that I too can play it."

Mister Leopard gave him the drum, and Deer took the drum and sang:

"Not sickness,

Wiliness holds you

Not sickness,

Wiliness holds you!

Not sickness,

Wiliness holds you!"

Mister Leopard stood up and said, "You, Deer, do not know how to play the drum."

Then all of animals ran away, saying, "Mister Leopard has a scheme to catch us."

The Search For The Home Of The Sun

This tale has been edited and adapted from Henry Morton Stanley's book, My Dark Companions, published in 1893 by Sampson, Lowe, Marston and Company, London.

This tale is about King Masama and his tribe, the Balira, who dwelt far in the inmost regions, and who throng the banks of the great river. They were formerly very numerous, and many of them came to live among us, but one day King Masama and the rest of the tribe left their country and went eastward, and they have never been heard of since, but those who chose to stay with us explained their disappearance in this way.

A woman, one cold night, after making up her fire on the hearth, went to sleep. In the middle of the night the fire had spread, and spread, and began to lick up the litter on the floor, and from the litter it crept to her bed of dry banana-leaves, and in a little time shot up into flames. When the woman and her husband were at last awakened by the heat, the flames had already mounted into the roof, and were burning furiously. Soon they broke through the top and leaped up into the night, and a gust of wind came and carried the long flames like a stream of fire towards the neighbouring huts, and in a short time the fire had caught hold of every house, and the village was entirely burned. It was soon known that besides burning up their houses and much property, several old people and infants had been destroyed by the fire, and the people were horror-struck and angry.

Then one voice said, "We all know in whose house the fire began, and the owner of it must make our losses good to us." The woman's husband heard this, and was alarmed, and guiltily fled into the woods.

In the morning a council of the elders was held, and it was agreed that the man in whose house the fire commenced should be made to pay for his carelessness, and they forthwith searched for him. But when they sought for him he could not be found. Then all the young warriors who were cunning in wood-craft, girded and armed themselves, and searched for the trail, and when one of them had found it, he cried out, and the others gathered themselves about him and took it up, and when many eyes were set upon it, the trail could not be lost.

They soon came up to the man, for he was seated under a tree, bitterly weeping. Without a word they took hold of him by the arms and bore him along with them, and brought him before the village fathers. He was not a common man by any means. He was known as one of Masama's principal men, and one whose advice had been often followed.

"Oh," said everybody, "he is a rich man, and well able to pay. Yet, if he gives all he has got, it will not be equal to our loss."

The fathers talked a long time over the matter, and at last decided that to save his forfeited life he should freely turn over to them all his property. And he did so. His plantation of bananas and plantains, his plots of beans, yams, manioc, potatoes, ground-nuts, his slaves, spears, shields, knives, paddles and canoes. When he had given up all, the hearts of the people became softened towards him, and they forgave him the rest.

After the elder's property had been equally divided among the sufferers, the people gained new courage, and set about rebuilding their homes, and before long they had a new village, and they had made themselves as comfortable as ever.

Then King Masama made a law, a very severe law, to the effect that, in future, no fire should be lit in the houses during the day or night, and the people, who were now much alarmed about fire, with one heart agreed to keep the law. But it was soon felt that the cure for the evil was as cruel as the fire had been. For the houses had been thatched with green banana-leaves, the timbers were green and wet with their sap, the floor was damp and cold, the air was deadly, and the people began to suffer from joint aches, and their knees were stiff, and the pains travelled from one place to another through their bodies. The village was filled with groaning.

Masama suffered more than all, for he was old. He shivered night and day, and his teeth chattered sometimes so that he could not talk, and after that his head would burn, and the hot sweat would pour from him, so that he knew no rest.

Then the king gathered his chiefs and principal men together, and said, "Oh, my people, this is unendurable, for life is with me now but one continuous ague. Let us leave this country, for it is bewitched, and if I stay longer there will be nothing left of me. My joints are stiffened with my disease, and my muscles are withering. The only time I feel a little ease is when I lie on the hot ashes outside the house, but when the rains fall I must needs withdraw indoors, and there I find no comfort, for the mould spreads everywhere. Let us at once to seek a warmer clime. Behold where the sun issues daily in the morning, hot and glowing. There, where his home is, must be warmth, and we shall need no fire. What say you?"

Masama's words revived their drooping spirits. They looked towards the sun as they saw him mount the sky, and felt his cheering glow on their naked breasts and shoulders, and they cried with one accord, "Let us go and seek the place where he comes."

And the people got ready and piled their belongings in the canoes, and on a certain day they left their village and ascended their broad river, the Lira. Day after day they paddled up the stream, and we heard of them from the Bafanya as they passed by their country, and the Bafanya heard of them for a long distance up, from the next tribe, the Bamoru, and the Bamoru heard about them arriving near the Mountain Land beyond.

Not until a long time afterwards did we hear what became of Masama and his people. It was said that the Balira, when the river had become shallow and small, left their canoes and travelled by land among little hills, and after winding in and out amongst them they came to the foot of the tall mountain which stands like a grandsire amongst the smaller mountains. Up the sides of the big mountain they straggled, the stronger and more active of them ahead, and as the days passed, they saw that the world was cold and dark until the sun showed himself over the edge of the big mountain, when the day became more agreeable, for the heat pierced into their very marrows, and made their hearts rejoice.

The greater the heat became, the more certain were they that they were drawing near the home of the sun. And so they pressed on and on, day after day, winding along one side of the mountain, and then turning to wind again still higher. Each day, as they advanced towards the top, the heat became greater and greater. Between them and the sun there was now not the smallest shrub or leaf, and it became so fiercely hot that finally not a drop of sweat was left in their bodies.

One day, when not a cloud was in the sky, and the world was all below them, far down like a great buffalo hide, the sun came out over the rim of the mountain like a ball of fire, and the nearest of them to the top were dried like a leaf over a flame, and those who were behind were amazed at its burning force, and felt, as he sailed over their heads, that it was too late for them to escape. Their skins began to shrivel up and crackle, and fall off, and none of those who were high up on the mountain side were left alive. But a few of those who were nearest the bottom, and the forest belts, managed to take shelter, and remaining there until night, they took advantage of the darkness, when the sun sleeps, to fly from the home of the sun. Except a few poor old people and toddling children, there was none left of the once populous tribe of the Balira.

We who live by the great river have taken the lesson, which the end of this tribe has been to us, close to our hearts, and it is this. Kings who insist that their wills should be followed, and never care to take counsel with their people, are as little to be heeded as children who babble of what they cannot know, and therefore in our villages we have many elders who take all matters from the chief and turn them over in their minds, and when they are agreed, they give the doing of them to the chief, who can act only as the elders decree.

Elephant And Frog

This tale has been edited and adapted from Kate Douglas Wiggin and Nora Archibald Smith's collection, The Talking Beasts, A Book of Fable and Wisdom, and illustrated by Harold Nelson. The book was published in 1922.

I often tell of Mister Elephant and Mister Frog, who were both courting folk at one and the same house.

One day Mister Frog spoke to the sweetheart of Mister Elephant, saying, "Mister Elephant is my horse."

The girls told Mister Elephant, when he came at night, saying, "You are the horse of Mister Frog!"

Mister Elephant went to Mister Frog's, saying, "Did you tell my sweetheart that I am your horse?"

Mister Frog said, "No. I did not say so."

After this they went together to find the sweetheart of Mister Elephant.

On the way, Mister Frog told Mister Elephant, "Grandfather, I have not strength to walk. Let me get up on your back!"

Mister Elephant said, "Get up, my grandson."

Mister Frog jumped straight up onto Mister Elephant's back. When a while had passed, he told Mister Elephant, "Grandfather, I am going to fall. Let me seek small cords to bind you in the mouth so that I can stay safe."

Mister Elephant consented. When a little more time had passed, he spoke again to Mister Elephant, saying, "Let me seek a green twig to fan the mosquitoes off you."

Mister Elephant said, "Go," and Mister Frog fetched a twig.

Then, when they walked up to the place where they were to meet the sweethearts, the girls saw them, and they went to meet them, shouting, "You, Mister Elephant, are the horse indeed of Mister Frog!"

A Hospitable Gorilla

This tale has been edited and adapted from Henry Morton Stanley's book, My Dark Companions, published in 1893 by Sampson, Lowe, Marston and Company, London.

A tribe dwelt on the banks of the Black River just above Basoko town, and at that time the thick forest round about them was haunted by many monstrous animals. Big apes, chimpanzees, gorillas and such creatures, which are not often seen nowadays. Not far from the village, in a darksome spot where the branches met overhead and formed a thick screen, and the lower wood hedged it closely round about so that a tortoise could scarcely penetrate it, there lived the Father of the Gorillas. He had housed himself in the fork of one of the tallest trees, and many men had seen the nest as they passed by, but none as yet had seen the owner.

But one day a fisherman in search of rattans to make his nets, wandered far into the woods, and in trying to recover the direction home struck the Black River high up. As he stood wondering whether this was the black stream that flowed past his village, he saw, a little to the right of him, an immense gorilla, who on account of the long dark fur on his chest appeared to be bigger than he really was. A cold sweat caused by his great fear began to come out of the man, and his knees trembled so that he could hardly stand, but when he perceived that the gorilla did not move, but continued eating his bananas, he became comforted a little, and his senses came back. He turned his head around, in order to see the clearest way for a run, but as he was about to start, he saw that the gorilla's eyes were fixed on him.

Then the gorilla broke out into speech and said, "Come to me, and let me look at you."

The fisherman's fear came back to him, but he did as he was told, and when he thought he was near enough, he stood still.

Then the gorilla said, "If you are kin to me, you are safe from harm. If not, you cannot pass. How many fingers have you?" he asked.

"Four," the fisherman answered, and he held a hand up with its back towards the gorilla, and his thumb was folded in on the palm so that it could not be seen by the beast.

"Aye, true indeed. Why, you must be a kinsman of ours, though your fur is somewhat scanty. Sit down and take your share of this food, and eat."

The fisherman sat down, and broke off bananas from the stalk and ate heartily.

"Now mind," said the gorilla, "you have eaten food with me. Should you ever meet in your wanderings any of my brothers, you must be kind to them in memory of this day. Our tribe has no quarrel with any of yours, and your tribe must have none against any of mine. I live alone far down this river, and your tribe lives further still. Mind our password, *Tu-wheli, Tu-wheli*. By that we know who is friendly and who is against us."

The fisherman departed, and speeding on his way reached his village safely, but he kept secret what he had seen and met that day.

Some little time after, the tribe resolved to have a grand hunt around their village, to scare the beasts of the forest away. For in some things they resemble us. If we leave a district undisturbed for a moon or so, the animals think that we have either departed the country or are afraid of them. The apes and the elephants are the worst in that respect, and always lead the way, pressing on our heels, and often sending their scouts ahead to report, or as a hint to us that we are lingering too long.

The people loaded themselves with their great nets, and first chose the district where the Gorilla Father lived. They set their nets around a wide space, and then the beaters were directed to make a large sweep and drive all the game towards the nets, and here and there where the netting was weak, the hunters stood behind a thick bush, their heavy spears ready for the fling.

Well, it just happened that at that very time the Father of the Gorillas was holding forth to his kinsmen, and the first they knew of the hunt, and that a multitude of men were in the woods, was when they heard the horrid yells of the beaters, the sound of horns, the jingle of iron, and the all-round swish of bushes.

The fisherman, like the rest of his friends, was well armed, and he was as keen as the others for the hunt, but soon after he heard the cries of the beaters, he saw a large gorilla rushing out of the bushes, and knew him instantly for his friend, and he cried out "Tu-wheli! Tu-wheli!" At the sound of it the gorilla led his kinsmen towards him, and passed the word to those behind, saying, "Ah, this is our friend. Do not hurt him."

The gorillas passed in a long line of mighty fellows, close by the fisherman, and as they heard the voice of their father, they only whispered to him, "Tu-wheli, Tu-wheli," but the last of all was a big, sour-faced gorilla, who, when he saw that the pass was only guarded by one man, made a rush at him. His roar of rage was heard by the father, and turning back he knew that his human brother was in danger, and he cried out to those nearest to part them. "The man is our brother," he cried, but as the fierce gorilla was deaf to words, the father loped back to them, and slew him, and then hastened away as the hunters were pressing up.

These, when they came up and observed that the fisherman's spear was still in his hand, and not painted with blood, were furious, and they agreed together that he should not have a share of the meat, "For," said they, "he must have been in a league against us." Neither did he obtain any share of the spoil.

A few days after this the fisherman was proceeding through a part of the forest, and a gorilla met him in the path, and said, "Stay, I seem to know you. Are you not our brother?"

"Tu-wheli, Tu-wheli!" he cried.

"Ah, it is true, follow me," and they went together to the gorilla's nesting-tree, where the fisherman was feasted on ripe bananas, berries, and nuts, and juicy roots, and he was shown which roots and berries were sweet, and which were bitter, and so great was the variety of food he saw, that he came to know that though lost in the forest a wise man need not starve.

When the fisherman returned to his village he called the elders together, and he laid the whole story of his adventures before his people, and when the elders heard that the berries and roots, nuts, and mushrooms in the forest, of which they had hereto been afraid, were sweet and wholesome, they exclaimed with one voice, that the gorillas had proved themselves true friends, and had given them much useful knowledge, and it was agreed among them that in future the gorillas should be reckoned among those, against whom it would not be lawful to raise their spears.

Ever since then the tribes on the Black River avoid harming the gorilla, and all his kind big and little. Neither will any of the gorilla trespass on their plantations, or molest any of the people.

Historical Notes

This section contains some brief biographical notes about the original collectors and their books featured in this collection. These notes have been adapted from those primarily on Wikipedia along with other supporting sources and notes.

Henry Morton Stanley

Henry Morton Stanley was born in 1841 as John Rowlands in Denbigh, Denbighshire, Wales. His mother Elizabeth Parry was 18 years old at the time of his birth. She abandoned him as a very young baby and cut off all communication. Stanley never knew his father, who died within a few weeks of his birth. As his parents were unmarried, his birth certificate describes him as a bastard; he was baptised in the parish of Denbigh on 19 February 1841, the register recording that he had been born on 28 January of that year. The entry states that he was the bastard son of John Rowland of Llys Llanrhaidr and Elizabeth Parry of Castle. The stigma of illegitimacy weighed heavily upon him all his life.

The boy John was given his father's surname of Rowlands and brought up by his grandfather Moses Parry, a once-prosperous butcher who was living in reduced circumstances. He cared for the boy until he died when John was five. Rowlands stayed with families of cousins and nieces for a short time, but he was eventually sent to the St. Asaph Union Workhouse for the Poor. The overcrowding and lack of supervision resulted in his being frequently abused by older boys. Historian Robert Aldrich has alleged that the headmaster of the workhouse raped or sexually assaulted Rowlands, and that the older Rowlands was "incontrovertibly bisexual".

Rowlands emigrated to the United States in 1859 at age 18. He disembarked at New Orleans and, according to his own declarations, became friends by accident with Henry Hope Stanley, a wealthy trader. He saw Stanley sitting on a chair outside his store and asked him if he had any job openings. He did so in the British style, "Do you need a boy, sir?" The childless man had indeed been wishing he had a son, and the inquiry led to a job and a close relationship between them. Out of admiration, John took Stanley's name. Later, he wrote that his adoptive parent died two years after their meeting, but in fact the elder Stanley did not die until 1878. This and other discrepancies led John Bierman to argue that no adoption took place. Tim Jeal goes further, and, in Chapter Two of his biography, subjects Stanley's account in his posthumously published Autobiography to detailed analysis. Because Stanley got so many basic facts wrong about his purported adoptive family, Jeal concludes that it is very unlikely that he ever met rich Henry Hope Stanley, and that an ordinary grocer, James Speake, was Rowlands' true benefactor until Speake's sudden death in October 1859.

Stanley reluctantly joined in the American Civil War, first enrolling in the Confederate States Army's 6th Arkansas Infantry Regiment and fighting in the Battle of Shiloh in 1862. After being taken prisoner at Shiloh, he was recruited at Camp Douglas, Illinois, by its commander Colonel James A. Mulligan as a "Galvanized Yankee." He joined the Union Army on 4 June 1862 but was discharged 18 days later because of severe illness. After recovering, he served on several merchant ships before joining the US Navy in July 1864. He became a record keeper on board the USS Minnesota, and participated in the First Battle of Fort Fisher and the Second Battle of Fort Fisher, which led him into freelance journalism. Stanley and a junior colleague jumped ship on 10 February 1865 in Portsmouth, New Hampshire, in search of greater adventures. Stanley was possibly the only man to serve in all three of the Confederate Army, the Union Army, and the Union Navy.

Following the Civil War, Stanley became a journalist in the days of frontier expansion in the American West. He then organised an expedition to the Ottoman Empire that ended catastrophically when he was imprisoned. He eventually talked his way out of jail and received restitution for damaged expedition equipment.

In 1867, the emperor of Ethiopia, Tewodros II, held a British envoy and others hostage, and a force was sent to achieve the release of the hostages. Stanley accompanied that force as a special correspondent of the *New York Herald*. Stanley's report on the Battle of Magdala in 1868 was the first to be published. Subsequently, he was assigned to report on Spain's Glorious Revolution in 1868. In 1870, Stanley undertook several assignments for the *Herald* in the Middle East and the Black Sea region, during which time he apparently carved his name into the stones of the ancient palace at Persepolis in Persia.

Stanley travelled to Zanzibar in March 1871, later claiming that he outfitted an expedition with 192 porters. In his first dispatch to the *New York Herald*, however, he stated that his expedition numbered only 111. This was in line with figures in his diaries. During the 700-

mile (1,100 km) expedition through the tropical forest, his thoroughbred stallion died within a few days after a bite from a tsetse fly, many of his porters deserted, and the rest were decimated by tropical diseases.

Stanley found David Livingstone on 10 November 1871 in Ujiji, near Lake Tanganyika in present-day Tanzania. He later claimed to have greeted him with the now-famous line, "Dr. Livingstone, I presume?" However, this line does not appear in his journal from the time — the two pages directly following the recording of his initial spotting of Livingstone were torn out of the journal at some point—and it is likely that Stanley simply embellished the pithy line sometime afterwards. Neither man mentioned it in any of the letters they wrote at this time, and Livingstone tended to instead recount the reaction of his servant, Susi, who cried out, "An Englishman coming! I see him!" The phrase is first quoted in a summary of Stanley's letters published by *The New York Times* on 2 July 1872. Stanley biographer Tim Jeal argued that the explorer invented it afterwards to help raise his standing because of "insecurity about his background", though ironically the phrase was mocked in the press for being absurdly formal for the situation. Stanley joined Livingstone in exploring the region, finding that there was no connection between Lake Tanganyika and the Nile. On his return, he wrote a book about his experiences: How I Found Livingstone; travels, adventures, and discoveries in Central Africa.

In 1874, the New York Herald and the *Daily Telegraph* financed Stanley on another expedition to Africa. His ambitious objective was to complete the exploration and mapping of the Central African Great Lakes and rivers, in the process circumnavigating Lakes Victoria and Tanganyika and locating the source of the Nile. Between 1875 and 1876 Stanley succeeded in the first part of his objective, establishing that Lake Victoria had only a single outlet – the one discovered by John Hanning Speke on 21 July 1862 and named Ripon Falls. If this was not the Nile's source, then the separate massive northward flowing river called by Livingstone, the Lualaba, and mapped by him in its upper reaches, might flow on north to connect with the Nile via Lake Albert and thus be the primary source.

It was therefore essential that Stanley should trace the course of the Lualaba downstream (northward) from Nyangwe, the point where Livingstone had left it in July 1871. Between November 1876 and August 1877, Stanley and his men navigated the Lualaba up to and beyond the point where it turned sharply westward, away from the Nile, identifying itself as the Congo River. Having succeeded with this second objective, they then traced the river to the sea. During this expedition, Stanley used sectional boats and dug-out canoes to pass the large cataracts that separated the Congo into distinct tracts. These boats were transported around the rapids before being rebuilt to travel on the next section of river. In passing the rapids many of his men were drowned, including his last white colleague, Frank Pocock. Stanley and his men reached the Portuguese outpost of Boma, around 100 kilometres (62 mi) from the mouth of the Congo River on the Atlantic Ocean, after 999 days on 9 August 1877. Muster lists and Stanley's diary (12 November 1874) show that he started with 228 people and reached Boma with 114 survivors, with he being the only European left alive out of four. In Stanley's *Through the Dark Continent* (1878) Stanley said that his expedition had numbered 356, the exaggeration detracting from his achievement.

Stanley was then approached by King Leopold II of the Belgians, the ambitious Belgian monarch who had organized a private holding company in 1876 disguised as an international scientific and philanthropic association, which he called the International African Association. Soon after Stanley returned from the Congo, Leopold II tried to recruit him. Stanley, still hopeful for British backing, brushed him off. However, Leopold persisted and eventually, Stanley gave in when British backing never came.

Stanley, much more familiar with the rigors of the African climate and the complexities of local politics than Leopold (who never in his whole life set foot in the Congo), persuaded his patron that the first step should be the construction of a wagon trail around the Congo rapids and a chain of trading stations on the river. Leopold agreed, and in deepest secrecy, Stanley signed a five-year contract at a salary of £1,000 a year and set off to Zanzibar under an assumed name. To avoid discovery, materials and workers were shipped in by various roundabout routes, and communications between Stanley and Leopold were entrusted to Colonel Maximilien Strauch.

In time Stanley gained glimmerings of the magnitude of Leopold's ambition. Before Stanley arrived in the Congo, he had been told that the purpose of his mission was to construct a series of trading stations to open the Congo to international trade, but, in fact, Leopold secretly meant to carve out an entire nation. When Leopold admitted what he really had in mind, he was explicit, "It is a question of creating a new State, as big as possible, and of running it. It is clearly understood that there is no question of granting the slightest political power to the negros in this project. That would be absurd." When Colonel Strauch put the king's plan to Stanley, he was shocked and replied that creating a state in this way would be "madness" and told the king, "On the contrary, they [the Congolese] will retain their own tribal chiefs and be as jealous as ever of every tribal right."

In October 1882, Leopold wrote angrily to Strauch: "The terms of the treaties Stanley has made with native chiefs do not satisfy me. There must at least be an added article to the effect that they delegate to us their sovereign rights ... the treaties must be as brief as possible and in a couple of articles must grant us everything."

Tim Jeal has described how a dissatisfied Leopold destroyed as many of Stanley's early treaties as he could get his hands on, side-lined him as a negotiator, and substituted forgeries produced by new negotiators appointed by himself. Jeal found one previously unknown original Stanley treaty in Brussels and quoted from this and the only other surviving original treaty, showing that Stanley had not claimed the land from the chiefs, but had made rental agreements with them, paid for with goods, giving him the right to trade in certain areas, build trading stations and a road, but nothing else.

Because Leopold never trusted Stanley to deliver to him his own private state on the Congo, he would not send him back there as governor, which Stanley had expected to happen on leaving in 1885. Before that, Stanley had written to the king that no Belgian officer was entitled to treat the Congolese "as though they were conquered subjects ... This is all wrong. They are subjects – but it is we who are simply tenants."

Tippu Tip, the most powerful of Zanzibar's slave traders of the 19th century, was well known to Stanley, as was the social chaos and devastation brought by slave-hunting. It had only been through Tippu Tip's help that Stanley had found Livingstone, who had survived years on the Lualaba under Tippu Tip's friendship. Four years earlier, the Zanzibaris had thought the Congo deadly and impassable and warned Stanley not to attempt to go there, but when Tippu Tip learned in Zanzibar that Stanley had survived, he was quick to act. Villages throughout the region had been burned and depopulated. Tippu Tip had raided 118 villages, killed 4,000 Africans, and, when Stanley reached his camp, had 2,300 slaves, mostly young women and children, in chains ready to transport halfway across the continent to the markets of Zanzibar.

Having found the new ruler of the Upper Congo, Stanley had no choice but to negotiate an agreement with him, to stop Tip coming further downstream and attacking Leopoldville, Kinshasa and other stations. To achieve this, he had to allow Tip to build his final river station just below Stanley Falls, which prevented vessels from sailing further upstream. At the end of his physical resources, Stanley returned home, to be replaced by Lieutenant Colonel Francis de Winton, a former British Army officer.

In 1886, Stanley led the Emin Pasha Relief Expedition to "rescue" Emin Pasha, the governor of Equatoria in the southern Sudan. King Leopold II demanded that Stanley take the longer route via the Congo River, hoping to acquire more territory and perhaps even Equatoria After immense hardships and great loss of life, Stanley met Emin in 1888, charted the Ruwenzori Range and Lake Edward, and emerged from the interior with Emin and his surviving followers at the end of 1890.

But this expedition tarnished Stanley's name because of the conduct of the other Europeans on the expedition. Army Major Edmund Musgrave Barttelot was killed by an African porter after behaving with extreme cruelty. James Sligo Jameson, heir to Irish whiskey manufacturer Jameson's, bought an 11-year-old girl and offered her to cannibals to document and sketch how she was cooked and eaten. Stanley found out only when Jameson had died of fever. In a number of publications made after the expedition, Stanley asserts that the purpose of the effort was singular; to offer relief to Emin Pasha.

On his return to Europe, Stanley married Welsh artist Dorothy Tennant. They adopted a child named Denzil, who was the son of one of Stanley's first cousins, though Stanley concealed this fact from the public and possibly even from Dorothy. Denzil later donated around 300 items to the Stanley archives at the Royal Museum of Central Africa in Tervuren, Belgium in 1954.

Mainly at his wife's behest, Stanley entered Parliament as a Liberal Unionist member for Lambeth North, serving from 1895 to 1900. He disliked politics and made little impression on Parliament. He became Sir Henry Morton Stanley when he was made a Knight Grand Cross of the Order of the Bath in the 1899 Birthday Honours, in recognition of his service to the British Empire in Africa. In 1890, he was given the Grand Cordon of the Order of Leopold by King Leopold II.

Stanley died at his home at 2 Richmond Terrace, Whitehall, London on 10 May 1904. At his funeral, he was eulogised by Daniel P. Virmar. His grave is in the churchyard of St Michael and All Angels' Church in Pirbright, Surrey, marked by a large piece of granite inscribed with the words "Henry Morton Stanley, Bula Matari, 1841–1904, Africa". Bula Matari translates as "Breaker of Rocks" or "Breakstones" in Kongo and was Stanley's name among locals in Congo. It can be translated as a term of endearment for, as the leader of Leopold's expedition, he commonly worked with the labourers breaking rocks with which they built the first modern road along the Congo River.

Mary H Kingsley

Mary Henrietta Kingsley was born in London on 13 October 1862, the daughter and oldest child of physician, traveller and writer George Kingsley and Mary Bailey. She came from a family of writers, as she was also the niece of novelists Charles Kingsley and Henry Kingsley.

Mary had little formal schooling, other than German lessons at a young age. She did, however, have access to her father's large library and loved to hear her father's stories. She did not enjoy novels that were deemed more appropriate for young ladies of the time, such as those by Jane Austen or Charlotte Brontë, but preferred books on the sciences and memoirs of explorers. In 1886, her brother Charley entered Christ's College, Cambridge, to read law, which allowed Mary to make several academic connections and a few friends.

After a preliminary visit to the Canary Islands, Kingsley decided to travel to the west coast of Africa. Generally, the only non-African women who embarked on often dangerous journeys to Africa were the wives of missionaries, government officials, or explorers. Exploration and adventure had not been seen as fitting roles for English women, though this was changing under the influence of figures such as Isabella Bird and Marianne North.

Kingsley landed in Sierra Leone on 17 August 1893 and from there travelled further to Luanda in Angola. She lived with local people, who taught her necessary survival skills for living in the wilderness, and gave her advice. She often went into dangerous areas alone. Her training as a nurse at the de:Kaiserswerther Diakonie had prepared her for slight injuries and jungle maladies that she would later encounter. Kingsley returned to England in December 1893.

Upon her return, Kingsley secured support and aid from Dr. Albert Günther, a prominent zoologist at the British Museum, as well as a writing agreement with publisher George Macmillan, for she wished to publish her travel accounts.

She returned to Africa yet again on 23 December 1894 with more support and supplies from England, as well as increased self-assurance in her work. She longed to study "cannibal" people and their traditional religious practices, commonly referred to as "fetish" during the Victorian Era. In April, she became acquainted with Scottish missionary Mary Slessor, another European woman living among native African populations with little company and no husband. It was during her meeting with Slessor that Kingsley first became aware of the custom of twin killing, a custom which Slessor was determined to stop. The native people believed that one of the twins was the offspring of the devil who had secretly mated with the mother and since the innocent child was impossible to distinguish, both were killed and the mother was often killed as well for attracting the devil to impregnate her. Kingsley arrived at Slessor's residence shortly after she had taken in a recent mother of twins and her surviving child.

Later in Gabon, Kingsley canoed up the Ogooué River, where she collected specimens of fish previously unknown to western science, three of which were later named after her. After meeting the Fang people and travelling through uncharted Fang territory, she daringly climbed the 4,040 metres (13,250 ft) Mount Cameroon by a route not previously attempted by any other European.

When she returned home in November 1895, Kingsley was greeted by journalists eager to interview her. The reports that were drummed up about her voyage, however, were most upsetting, as the papers portrayed her as a "New Woman", an image which she did not embrace. Kingsley distanced herself from any feminist movement claims, arguing that women's suffrage was "a minor question; while there was a most vital section of men disenfranchised women could wait".

Over the next three years, she toured England, giving lectures about life in Africa to a wide array of audiences. She was the first woman to address the Liverpool and Manchester chambers of commerce.

Kingsley upset the Church of England when she criticised missionaries for attempting to convert the people of Africa and corrupt their religions. In this regard, she discussed many aspects of African life that were shocking to English people, including polygamy, which, she argued was practiced out of necessity. After living with the African people, Kingsley became directly aware how their societies functioned and how prohibiting customs such as polygamy would be detrimental to their way of life. She knew that the typical African wives had too many tasks to manage alone. Missionaries in Africa often required converted men to abandon all but one of their wives, leaving the other women and children without the support of a husband – thus creating immense social and economic problems.

Kingsley's beliefs about cultural and economic imperialism are complex and widely debated by scholars today. Though, on the one hand, she regarded African people and cultures as those who needed protection and preservation, she also believed in the necessity of British economic and technological influence and in indirect rule, insisting that there was some work in West Africa that had to be completed by white men. Yet in *Studies in West Africa* she writes: "Although a Darwinian to the core, I doubt if evolution in a neat and tidy perpendicular line, with Fetish at the bottom and Christianity at the top, represents the true state of affairs."

Kingsley wrote two books about her experiences: *Travels in West Africa* (1897), which was an immediate best-seller, and *West African Studies* (1899), both of which gained her respect and prestige within the scholarly community. Some newspapers, however, such as *The Times* under pro-imperialist editor Flora Shaw, refused to publish reviews of her works. Though some have argued that such refusals were grounded in the anti-imperialist and pro-African arguments presented in Kingsley's works, this is unlikely to explain her sometimes unfavourable reception, because she was both a supporter of the activities of European traders in West Africa and the concept of indirect colonial rule.

After the outbreak of the Second Boer War, Kingsley travelled to Cape Town on the SS Moor in March 1900, and volunteered as a nurse. She was stationed at Simon's Town hospital, where she treated Boer prisoners of war. After contributing her services for about two months, she developed symptoms of typhoid and died on 3 June 1900. An eyewitness reported that, "She rallied for a short time but realised she was going. She asked to be left to die alone, saying she did not wish anyone to see her in her weakness. Animals," she said, "went away to die alone." In accordance with her wishes, she was buried at sea.

Kingsley's tales and opinions of life in Africa helped draw attention to British imperial agendas abroad and the native customs of African people that were previously little discussed and misunderstood by people in Europe. The Fair Commerce Party formed soon after her death, pressuring for improved conditions for the natives of British colonies. Various reform associations were formed in her honour and helped facilitate governmental change. The Liverpool School of Tropical Medicine founded an honorary medal in her name. In Sierra Leone, the Mary Kingsley Auditorium at the Institute of African Studies, Fourah Bay College (University of Sierra Leone), was named after her.

Kate Douglas Wiggin

Kate Douglas Smith Wiggin was born in Philadelphia, the daughter of lawyer Robert N. Smith, and of Welsh descent. Kate experienced a happy childhood, even though it was coloured by the American Civil War and her father's death. Kate and her sister Nora were still quite young when their widowed mother moved her little family from Philadelphia to Portland, Maine, then, three years later, upon her remarriage, to the little village of Hollis. There Kate matured in rural surroundings, with her sister and her new baby brother Philip.

Notably, she once met the novelist Charles Dickens. Her mother and another relative had gone to hear Dickens read in Portland, but Wiggin, aged 11, was thought to be too young to warrant an expensive ticket. The following day, she found herself on the same train as Dickens and engaged him in a lively conversation for the course of the journey, an experience which she later detailed in a short memoir titled *A Child's Journey with Dickens* (1912).

Her education was spotty, consisting of a short stint at a dame school, some home schooling under the "capable, slightly impatient, somewhat sporadic" instruction of Albion Bradbury (her stepfather), a brief spell at the district school, a year as a boarder at the Gorham Female Seminary, a winter term at Morison Academy in Baltimore, Maryland, and a few months' stay at Abbot Academy in Andover, Massachusetts, where she graduated with the class of 1873. Although rather casual, this was more education than most women received at the time.

Wiggin met dry goods (specifically, linen) importer George Christopher Riggs on her way to England in 1894. The pair are said to have hit it off and had agreed to marry even before the ship docked in England. In the Ellis Island logs from Wiggin's 1894 trip back to New York City from Liverpool, the two sign their names next to each other, indicating their closeness. The pair married in New York City on March 30, 1895, at All Souls Church. George Riggs soon became one of Wiggin's biggest advocates as she became more successful.

After the marriage she continued to write under the name of Wiggin. Her literary output included popular books for adults, and with her sister, Nora A. Smith, she published scholarly work on the educational principles of Friedrich Fröbel: *Froebel's Gifts* (1895), *Froebel's Occupations* (1896), and *Kindergarten Principles and Practice* (1896), and she wrote the classic children's novel *Rebecca of Sunnybrook Farm* (1903), as well as the 1905 best-seller *Rose o' the River*. *Rebecca of Sunnybrook Farm* became an immediate bestseller, both it and *Mother Carey's Chickens* (1911) were adapted to the stage. Houghton Mifflin collected her writings in 10 volumes in 1917.

For a time, she lived at Quillcote, her summer home in Hollis, Maine. Quillcote is around the corner from the town's library, the Salmon Falls Library, which Wiggin founded in 1911. Wiggin founded the Dorcas Society of Hollis & Buxton, Maine in 1897. The Tory Hill Meeting House in the adjacent town of Buxton, Maine inspired her book, and later play, *The Old Peabody Pew* (1907).

Wiggin was an active and popular hostess in New York and in the community of Upper Largo, Scotland, where she had a summer home and where she organized plays for many years, as detailed in her memoir *My Garden of Memory*.

In 1921, Wiggin and her sister Nora Archibald Smith edited an edition of Jane Porter's *The Scottish Chiefs*, an 1809 novel of William Wallace, for the Scribner's Illustrated Classics series, illustrated by N.C. Wyeth. During the spring of 1923, Kate Wiggin travelled to England as a New York delegate to the Dickens Fellowship. There she became ill and died, at age 66, of bronchial pneumonia. At her request, her ashes were brought home to Maine and scattered over the Saco River. Her autobiography *My Garden of Memory* was published after her death. In sorting through material for her autobiography, she put many items in a box she and her sister labelled "Posthumous." Her sister Nora A. Smith later published her own reminiscences, titled *Kate Douglas Wiggin as her Sister Knew Her*, from these materials.

Wiggin was also a songwriter and composer. For *Kindergarten Chimes* (1885) and other collections for children, she wrote some of the lyrics, music, and arrangements. For *Nine Love Songs and a Carol* (1896), she composed all of the music.

Many of Kate Douglas Wiggin's novels were made into movies. Perhaps the most famous film adaptation of her books is the *Rebecca of Sunnybrook Farm* (1938 film), which stars Shirley Temple.

Nora Archibald Smith

Nora Archibald Smith was the sister of Kate Douglas Wiggin, known best for her novel *Rebecca of Sunnybrook Farm*. Both girls were born in Philadelphia to Robert Noah Smith and Helen Elizabeth (Dyer) Smith. Their father died shortly after Nora's birth and their mother then moved the family to Portland, Maine. She soon remarried and the family moved into Nora and Kate's stepfather's (Dr. Albion Bradbury) house in Hollis, Maine. It was in the farmhouse called "Quillcote" that both Nora and Kate grew up and to which they would later retire.

In 1873, while Kate attended finishing school in Andover, Massachusetts, Dr. Bradbury moved the family to California. Kate opened the first free kindergarten west of the Rocky Mountains on Silver Street in San Francisco, California while Nora was teaching in the public schools of Tucson, Arizona. In 1877 Nora was awarded an A.B. From Santa Barbara College. In 1880 Nora and Kate founded the California Kindergarten Training School together and Nora received a certificate from the school in 1881.

Nora then went on to become the superintendent of the free kindergarten on Silver Street and later to take over the running of the California Kindergarten Training School in 1889. Ms. Smith was president of the California Froebel Society, an executive member of the committee of the International Kindergarten Association, and the vice-president (1891-1892) of the kindergarten department of the National Education Association.

Nora Archibald Smith collaborated with her sister to write or edit fifteen books. Nora, a writer in her own right, also published many serial stories and academic journal articles on early childhood education. Two of Nora's poems *Doll's Calendar* and *Feast of the Doll* were set to music by composer Grace Chadbourne.

About The Editor

I was born in 1962 into a predominantly sporting household – Dad being a good footballer, playing senior amateur and lower league professional football in England, as well as running a series of private businesses in partnership with mum, herself an accomplished and medal winning dancer.

I obtained a degree in History from Leeds University before wandering rather haphazardly into the emerging world of business computing in the late nineteen-eighties.

I followed a succession of amateur writing paths alongside my career in technology, including working as a freelance journalist and book reviewer, my one claim to fame being a by-line in a national newspaper in the UK, The Sunday people.

I also spent 10 years treading the boards, appearing all over the south of the UK in pantos and plays, in village halls and occasionally on the stage of a professional theatre or two.

Following the sporting theme I worked on live TV broadcasts for the BBC, ITV, TVNZ, EuroSport and others as a rugby "Stato", covering Heineken Cups, Six Nations, IRB World Sevens and IRB World Cups in the late '90's and early '00's.

You can find out more at: www.clivegilson.com

www.ingramcontent.com/pod-product-compliance
Lightning Source LLC
Chambersburg PA
CBHW060810190726
48285CB00002B/612